Reckless Vow

Reckless Billionaires

Maxine Henri

Copyright © 2024 by Maxine Henri

All rights reserved.

www.maxinehenri.com

Cover designed by Sweet 'N Spicy Designs

Edited by Jessica Snyder at HEA Author Services

This book is a work of fiction. The characters, incidents and dialogue are drawn from the author's imagination and are not to be construed as real. Any resemblance to actual events or persons, living or dead is fictionalized or coincidental.

No part of this book may be reproduced in any form or by any electronic or mechanical means, including information storage and retrieval systems, without written permission from the author, except for the use of brief quotations in a book review.

 Created with Vellum

"Each time you happen to me all over again."
The Age of Innocence, Edith Wharton

Chapter 1

Brook

"It's not like we need her money."

I cross my arms and glare at the man who has just read Roberta Montgomery's will to me and my sisters.

He looks down his nose at me from behind his mahogany desk, his expression pleasant but stern. Like he's summoning all the patience he can to let me—us—voice our opinions but he doesn't consider them pertinent.

Rupert Montgomery, Grandmother's younger brother and her will executor, seems like an asshole. Not the obvious kind, but one who hides behind a carefully maintained smile—a creepy smile.

"It can do a lot of good," London points out.

Of course, my older sister who runs a gazillion charitable endeavors would see the silver lining in all of this. Besides, her happily-in-a-relationship status doesn't make it hard to comply with Roberta's conditions.

Not the same case for me. But as I pointed out, I don't need her money. None of us do, so what was Granny Dearest thinking?

"She didn't even know us." London's twin, my other sister Paris, rubs her very pregnant belly.

"She did follow your life closely." Rupert takes off his glasses and puts them down on the thick binder with my grandmother's will.

The reading of the will took about forty minutes. Whatever can be in all those appendices is beyond me. Thank God we're not expected to sit through every single detail.

Or are we? Shit.

I fidget in my chair and reach into my jeans pocket to pull my phone out. It's an impulse to distract myself from the bizarre situation happening here. Or from life in general.

I stop myself and wipe my palms on the sides of my thighs as if they were sweaty. Maybe they are.

In the absence of my phone, my right thumb comes to my lips and I graze my teeth over my raw cuticle.

Sydney, my oldest sister, gives me an admonishing look like I'm one of her pupils in school. My sister is a teacher.

While I know my habit of manicure by tooth isn't healthy, I don't appreciate being scolded for it—or anything—by my siblings.

But that has always been the dynamic. I'm their baby sister. Never mature enough. Never organized enough. Failing the whole adulting gig at the age of almost twenty-seven.

That's why I stayed away for so long. To gain my independence.

Okay, I stayed away primarily for another reason, but being off the hook from my sisters' well-meant but unsolicited support had been an appreciated side-benefit.

I glare at Syd but drop my hand and almost sit on it. I don't. I'm not going to behave like a fidgeting child to give her the satisfaction.

She smiles at me with her teacher's patience and turns to Rupert. "What do you mean she followed our lives? We've never met her."

Our mommy chose our dad. An heiress fell for a blue-collar worker. Her mother severed any contact with her in return. End of story.

Mommy kept her sizable trust fund and after she passed, Dad invested it smartly and got us all a healthy start in life. A blue-collar worker wasn't such a poor match, after all. Not that Roberta Montgomery ever acknowledged that. Or us.

All four of us, perched on heavy brocade-clad chairs, turn to Rupert, who clears his throat and puts his glasses back on.

"Look, girls, I told her on many occasions she should reach out and get to know you, but Roberta was a stubborn woman. She lost her daughter—that's how she perceived it—when your mother married your father. And shortly after, she lost her husband. The grief left her somewhat bitter. And after your mother died, well... the grief overcame her."

He pauses, looking at his hands. Sadness and a ghost of some other emotion linger on his face. If I'm not mistaken, a memory passed through his mind.

The situation is quite surreal. Out of the five people in this opulent office in my great grandmother's mansion, he is the only one grieving.

Yet here we are, trying to comprehend why our estranged grandmother left us a fortune. With the weirdest condition ever.

It must be some kind of a joke. I look around his office and spy the red light blinking in the corner.

We're being recorded. It's not unusual for a wealthy man to have surveillance, but the current conversation feels like a sketch from a hidden camera show.

"So she was bitter and refused to actually meet us,

but you said she followed our lives? How?" Sydney returns to her original question.

He startles and blinks a few times, as if while lost in his memories he forgot we were here.

Clearing his throat, he straightens the paperwork on his desk. "She had an agency monitoring your activities, so she could use her influence to help you out."

A sharp letter opener lies on his desk. It could be used as a weapon. Would it pierce skin? The jugular would be the place to aim for. There would be a lot of blood.

"She spied on us?" London snorts, and I snap out of my morbid fantasy.

This is my problem—my mind keeps escaping to these gruesome made-up scenarios, distracting me from the task at hand, stealing my attention.

"I wouldn't call it that." Rupert makes a face like we offended him.

"That's fucked up." I lean back and look at my sisters, who seem equally shocked by the revelation.

He glares at me, as if my cussing was the thing to frown upon here. "You went to Oxford," he practically accuses me.

"Are you suggesting Roberta had something to do with that?" Sydney sounds indignant on my behalf.

I'm speechless, but I can see the blood spraying

from his neck where the letter opener would land. I shake my head to refocus.

It would make for a great scene, but that is for later. I need to stop picturing it now. *Right now, Brook Lowe.*

"Obviously, Brooklyn was qualified to study there, but I'm sure Roberta's influence didn't hurt her chances. And I'm sure you enjoyed the premium housing you were awarded on the campus."

He smiles at me with the fake grin he's been wearing like a pro, then turns to Paris. "As you did winning the prestigious designer award in your first year at the Pratt Institute."

Then it's Sydney's turn. "Or your continuous well-paid substitute teacher contracts when you were aimless."

He dares to judge Sydney for those years after her ex-husband's betrayal?

But he's not done yet. "You didn't mind cashing the yearly anonymous donations," he accuses London, and then, as if realizing what an asshole he's being, he adds, "to use it for a worthy cause."

London folds her arms across her chest. "So you're claiming the woman we've never met has been a secret benefactor in our lives. Not that we needed or wanted her help. And now she's decided to meddle in our lives from her grave?"

"No need for your tone." Rupert looks genuinely

affronted. "Roberta was a very traditional woman, and at the end of her life she was heartbroken all of her granddaughters live without being properly wed."

Half of my brain is listening to his nonsense while the other side is still trying to reconcile that the essay I wrote nine years ago—where I channeled the darkest experience of my then eighteen years of life—may not have been enough to get me a spot in the creative writing program at Oxford.

When I woke up today, I didn't imagine I'd end up questioning all my life's accomplishments.

And I can't fathom that a grandmother who I've entirely forgotten exists—her doing completely—would demand I get married.

"As I said, I don't need Roberta's money." Yes, I use her given name because I don't feel in any way related to the deranged woman.

I flinch at the thought, because she was my mother's mother and that should count for something. Especially since I don't remember Mommy at all. I was barely three when she passed.

"What will happen with the money if we all refuse the inheritance? Or rather, its archaic conditions?" Lo asks.

Of course, London cares about the money. She already sees the number of people she could help with it. And I get it, but at this point I need to get out of here and write that letter-opener scene.

And question all I've ever achieved.

Or thought I achieved.

Thank you, *Granny*.

"Oh, yes, that's a wonderful question." Rupert curves his lips, but on his stern face it's unclear if that's an attempt to smile. Still just a creepy grin. "In such case, and I really hope it doesn't get to that, the money will be donated to various organizations."

He pulls a sheet of paper from the thick binder and hands it to London, who takes it with hope on her face.

I guess we all could get on board with donating shitloads of money. We're rich, but Roberta Montgomery and her brother are next level. Their wealth is several degrees above ours.

London gasps and hands the list to Paris. Paris swallows and clutches her chest, visibly paling. I jump up from my seat, cross to her and snatch the paper away.

Sydney joins me and peers over my shoulder while I blink at the alphabetical roster of organizations, institutions and some private groups.

"Fuck." Sydney sums up what we've all just discovered.

"That's right. Granny Dearest challenges our

morals till her last breath." London stands up. "Rupert, I'd like a copy of the will."

"Of course." He opens a drawer and hands her a binder. "I was expecting it."

She takes it from him. "We'll be in touch." She turns on her heel. "Let's go."

We scramble to pick up our purses and exit the office without looking back at our great uncle.

But I stop and turn. Glancing at the letter opener one last time, I memorize its shape and texture.

When I look up, Rupert is studying me, his expression blank. I shrug, and before I can stop myself I whisper, "Sorry for your loss."

I give him a smile that I hope shows I'm sincere. If he ever imagined a family reunion, I'm sure it wasn't this.

He jerks his head as if affronted, or shocked. I'm not sure if I can just turn and leave. I don't know why I extended my condolences exactly, but perhaps he should acknowledge them?

We stare at each other. Do I have his pale green eyes? I've always looked different from my sisters who took after our father. Maybe I have more in common with this stranger than I thought.

I've been an outsider in my own family for so long that this odd connection—and I recognize it's only in my head—spreads warmth through my body.

"Your sisters are waiting for you," Rupert's housekeeper says, interrupting the moment, and I dash out without looking back.

"Let's go see Dad," Sydney suggests as we climb into Paris's town car that has been waiting for the past hour.

"Good idea. He must be curious and anxious about this bullshit." Paris keeps rubbing her belly.

As the car moves, my sisters pull out their phones and call their significant others, while I stare out the window at the passing city.

I have no one to call.

I turn to the rear window. In my mind the house we've just visited shrinks slowly on the horizon as we move away, leaving me strangely empty.

In reality, we've already turned into the city traffic, and all I can see is a sea of cars.

But the odd connection lingers, and so does the emptiness.

I have been living aimlessly for several months. After almost nine years in England, I returned to help Paris when she was going through a tough time with her baby and the baby's daddy.

To be honest, that was just an excuse to escape a toxic relationship with my ex. Or maybe Paris saved me from spiraling into a pattern that has been woven through my life—getting attached to the wrong people.

Syd, Lo and Paris are telling the gist of the afternoon to their partners.

Any of them could easily marry tomorrow. Their men adore them, and they live together, anyway. A marriage certificate is a formality for them.

I remember the list of recipients of Granny's fortune if I fail to comply with her condition and shiver.

One thing is clear—Roberta Montgomery got things done her way regardless of other people's feelings. And I don't have much say in the matter.

I need to find myself a husband. Fast.

Chapter 2

Brook

"I'm really sorry," Dad repeats for the thousandth time, as if this crisis was his fault.

Yes, I'm calling it a crisis and going with the dramatics, because I'm on the verge of crying at this point.

Even surrounded by my family, I've never felt this alone.

I'm single.

The status has never bothered me. It's been a one hundred percent improvement from the fucked-up dynamics I had with Dylan Sinclair, my ex.

Over the past few months I've spent in New York, I've started appreciating my single status.

Maybe it was reconnecting with my roots, with my family, or just a change of scenery, but I finally, for the first time in my life, feel like the ground under me is not shifting violently.

Like I can remain still for a moment, or ten, and enjoy the serenity. Without running. Without escaping. Without avoiding.

And now I fucking have to get married?

Damn you, Roberta.

I haven't begun to unpack the whole issue of her meddling with my life prior to today. Today's ultimatum is enough to deal with at the moment.

"Daddy, don't worry about it. We'll figure it out." Paris kisses his forehead and he squeezes her hand.

He looks so defeated in the wheelchair. The last round of radiation damaged his vertebrae, decreasing his mobility.

Every time I see him, I regret the years I stayed away. I'll never get them back, but at least now I can cherish every moment with him.

It's been over a year since he was diagnosed with cancer and he's still here with us, so that's what I try to focus on.

My currently aimless existence has provided one benefit—after Paris got settled with Finn, her partner, I moved in with Dad and Mom. Well, my stepmom, Bianca.

Under any other circumstances, this would be

pathetic at my age, but spending time with my dad is priceless.

Though they are planning to move to their house in Florida, so Dad can fully focus on his recovery in some state-of-the-art facility.

I'll be their house sitter, and I'm glad I can help in some way. I had planned to spend the time working on my current manuscript, and figuring out if I'm returning to England or staying here.

I guess now I'll have to look for a husband. Fuck.

"You have to give it to her—she was smart." Dad chuckles humorlessly.

"Dominic is coming over to review the will." London paces by the floor-to-ceiling windows in the sitting room.

"All of you have partners. It's not such a big deal for you," I point out.

"I won't be blackmailed into getting married by an old lady I've never met," London snaps, ignoring the real issue here.

I have no one to marry.

"Okay, all of these are the worst of the worst humanity has ever created." Sydney throws the list of beneficiaries to the coffee table along with her phone. "I might be on the FBI's watch list because of my search history now. On paper, they're legal, but tied to environmental atrocities, support of extremist groups, and political groups accused of arms trafficking." She shudders visibly.

"An evil grandmother if I ever met one," I say.

"And we haven't even met her." Paris sighs.

"We should check where her money came from." The idea gives me a boost and I perk up. Maybe there is a way out. "I mean, how was that list compiled? Did she support those groups while she was alive? Is her fortune in any way connected? Can we use that to contest the will? Expose her?"

"You and your imagination." London snorts and I flinch. "Roberta Montgomery was a pillar of society, American royalty."

Of course my sister would dismiss my idea. That has always been the case. I'm the dreamer of the family. The baby they never saw as equal.

And maybe my suggestion is less than ideal, but I'm desperate here. A fact nobody seems to acknowledge.

"And clearly a bit unhinged if she showed us her affection by spying on us and blackmailing us into the traditional institution of marriage." I raise my thumb to my mouth and immediately put it back in my lap.

"Let's wait for Dominic to review the will to see if there is a way out." Sydney smiles at me. Perhaps she wants to smooth London's words, but more likely she's just patronizing me.

I don't know anymore. Everyone has been supportive since I returned, but their attention only makes me feel like I'm failing.

Like they just feel sorry for me because I left so young, and God knows what I've been up to, and now they need to reintegrate me into the real world.

They don't know what I do. When my agent came up with the secret identity, I liked the idea. It's helped my success.

I've never shared that with my family because the girl that left here years ago wanted them to accept me for who I am. Not for the accolades I achieve.

As if Sydney manifested the man, Dominic Cressard, a high-profile lawyer and London's boyfriend, walks in and greets everyone.

London drops the binder into his hands after a kiss. He unbuttons his suit jacket and sits down, opening the binder without a word. London briefed him on the phone.

"I'm going to lie down," Dad announces, and I jump to his side.

"Let me help you."

I grab the handles of his wheelchair and push him to the bottom of the stairs in the foyer. Snaking my arm under his, I help him stand up. Using me as a crutch, he starts his ascent.

The house isn't fitted for his needs, and the

required renovations and adjustments are a point of tension between him and Mom.

Dad is proud, and he doesn't want any changes until they are necessary.

The lift is obviously necessary, but I'm not going to push the point.

"Are you okay, darling?" the man who can barely stand asks me, and I blink a few times.

"Of course, I'm fine. It's been an interesting day, though."

We reach the landing and turn toward his bedroom where I help him sit on his bed. He leans sideways and I lift his legs.

"Do you want to get changed?"

"I'm fine." He waves away the idea, clearly tired. "I'm just going to rest for a moment and Bianca will come to help me later. With the tea and all her opinions." He rolls his eyes, but there is adoration behind his comment.

I kiss his forehead.

"Sit with me for a moment, Brook."

I perch by his side and he squeezes my hand. "I hope Dom finds a way out of this mess. Roberta Montgomery hurt your mother a lot, but I never forgave myself for being the reason for their feud. I'm sorry the old witch reached out to hurt you now."

"She's not hurting me, Daddy."

"Your mommy wanted to reconcile with her so badly. She valued family and was too kind, overlooking their betrayal. She always wished they could have a relationship."

His words hit me with a wave of regret. Is he telling me I should have made more effort over the years? That my mommy valued family and I didn't?

"Don't worry, Daddy, I can find a fake husband and flip her off." It's easier to crack a joke than to face the truth.

We both laugh, but Dad gets serious. "I'm sorry I drew you away. It's one of the biggest regrets of my life."

So he isn't blaming me, but himself. God, why do I always project blame on myself?

No blinking can save me anymore and a tear escapes, rolling warmly down my cheek. "You didn't—"

"I had my hand in the way things turned out back then and I'm sorry about it. I hope to stick around for many more years, but this illness has made me realize what's what. Time with people who matter is up there as the most important thing. And I robbed us both of that. And I'm afraid I might have robbed you of more than father/daughter time."

I can't stand facing him, so I scoot closer and lie beside him. He wraps his arm around me and I rest my cheek on his chest.

This way, I can let the stupid tears fall.

Is he right? I've never assigned much responsibility to him for what happened before I left New York.

That one night when he caught us kissing, he was trying to protect me. It was just normal parental behavior. Protecting his baby girl.

At seventeen, I didn't recognize it as such, but in retrospect even if he hadn't caught us, things would have turned out the same regardless.

There is another man to blame for what happened. Not that I care anymore. It's been too long.

But now I'm thinking about that kiss and my body gets all warm, and I want to sit up and step away because being aroused—am I aroused?—while I'm hugging my dad is the last thing I want to feel.

"I'm here now, Daddy. My decision to stay in England after my graduation had nothing to do with you. I only wish I would have come home more often."

But I was scared. Too scared to spend any time in this house filled with memories I fought long and hard to bury as deep as possible.

I'm still avoiding *his* room and it's been almost ten years. Some things can't be fixed with any amount of therapy.

Dad doesn't respond, and after a moment, wrapped in the memories I wished I could erase, I realize his breathing has evened out.

I lift my head and sure enough he's dozed off. Standing up carefully, I kiss his cheek and leave the room.

"How are you feeling, kitten?" I hear Finn ask Paris as I come downstairs.

"I discovered I have an evil grandmother, but otherwise we're good. Hunter and Dom are pouring through the will if you want to join them." She sighs.

While I was gone, Syd's fiancé must have also arrived. I head to the kitchen to join my sisters and Mom.

They are gathered around the large square kitchen island, drinking Mom's lemonade. I guess the men are in the sitting room with the damn binder.

"Dad fell asleep." I open a cabinet to get a wine glass. Fuck the lemonade.

"Here, darling." Mom hands me a bottle of Chardonnay. "Anyone else?"

The three other women refuse. I'm not sure what Syd's reason is, but Lo doesn't drink because Dom abstains, and Paris obviously doesn't drink because she's pregnant.

I raise the bottle toward Mom, but she shakes her head.

Once again the outsider, I pour myself a generous portion and gulp it down, trying to make a point.

Not sure what point, but here we are. They expect me to act out, so I do.

I lift the bottle for a refill when the doorbell sounds. Mom frowns and leaves to get the door. She normally has a housekeeper to do it, but when family is home, she always sends the housekeeper away early.

London scoffs at me and opens her mouth, but then thinks better of it. Like for a moment, she actually recognized that I might need some liquid reinforcement.

"How long do we have to stay married?" I ask.

"For a year, and Rupert decides if the marriage is legit. I guess divorcing within a year might be considered a scam? I don't know. We need to talk to him after Dominic decides what the next move is." London shrugs and turns to the kitchen's arched entrance.

"It's the day of ghosts," she exclaims. "Hey, little bro."

I set my glass down so I don't drop it and draw attention to myself. I need to disappear to deal with my heart pulsing in my temple.

The kitchen gets incredibly hot suddenly, and somehow dimmer and brighter at the same time.

The universe certainly decided to fuck with me today. Big time.

It's like thinking about that kiss conjured *him* in real life. Seeing the man—because he is no longer the boy I've tried to forget—many other memories rush to consume me.

To eat away at all my defenses. To destroy my barely maintained composure.

Because on a shitty day like today I can't catch a break, and the boy I used to love has shown up out of nowhere.

I shake my head, but no... Of all the fucked-up images my mind devises, this particular vision is a cruel reality.

Baldo fucking Cassinetti is truly standing in our childhood home's kitchen.

My first love.

The boy who broke my heart.

My stepbrother.

Chapter 3

Brook

His eyes land on me after my sisters fawn over him and gush about his sudden appearance. What the fuck is that about?

As far as I know, he hasn't come home since the night he abandoned me. But all thoughts of the past blur under his present gaze.

I was a girl when his smile spread goosebumps on my skin.

Nine years later, I have the same reaction. And for a brief—the briefest—moment, I allow myself to admire the fine specimen he has become.

Somehow the last nearly ten years have filled him out in all the right places. His tailored suit hugs his muscles beautifully.

The scruff on his face lines the perfect square of his jaw, and he has a man bun. I'm not a fan, but damn does it add a sexy roughness to his polished appearance.

And those eyes. I couldn't resist the dark irises then, and being under their scrutiny now is doing things to me I don't want to feel.

He's your stepbrother, the devil on my shoulder reminds me. I never subscribed to that obstacle in the past because we're not related by blood, but I go with it this time. I need the boundary.

Because, again, why the fuck is he here?

The worst thing is... a part of me wants to run into his arms.

He lost that right the night he left me behind.

I have imagined this moment so many times in my head. I rehearsed it, planned what I'd say, scripted the words.

They all still float somewhere in my conscience, but they don't form fully. In all my fantasies, vengeance and the need for closure drove my actions.

Never did I consider the influx of emotions surging through me currently. It's like my entire system goes into survival mode.

And in the eternal beats of time—that I'm pretty sure amount to mere minutes in reality—I have to relearn how to breathe, how to think, how to walk, how to human.

And since I can't find my sass, or the English language, and all my paralyzed efforts are consumed by the last remnants of common sense that are stopping me from the primal need to flee, I decide to channel my hatred for him.

The most uncool of my feelings, but desperate times and all that...

Sufficiently equipped with that sentiment, I jump down from the counter and saunter toward him. Yes, I saunter, and based on his darkened expression and set jaw, he's affected.

It feels like a win. Not that there's a competition.

"Tokyo," he rasps.

I swallow a whimper, most of my confidence deserting me. Showing up here after nine years is dreadful, but how dare he use that name with me?

For the benefit of the others, I mirror my sister's welcome and I half hug him.

My body betrays me.

Even that excuse of an embrace sends my cells into high alert, immediately recognizing what they want. What they need. What they crave.

His touch. His caress. His attention.

Him.

Goddammit.

To stop myself from kicking him in the crotch—because yes, that's where my survival instincts go—I immediately turn and dash to the glass door that opens to the backyard.

I stare into the darkness.

Ignore him.

Ignore your body.

Ignore the pain in your chest.

My breathing almost finds a rhythm. It's chaotic, but it's something. I can do this. He must be here for a brief visit.

I mean, he came unannounced, I'm sure of that. Mom would have mentioned something. She looked surprised, so that means it's perhaps an unplanned visit.

He was in the neighborhood. Okay, not reasonable, but I'm adjusting.

And then my gaze collides with his in the glass's reflection, and for the love of every murder, why is he still here?

I whip around, but don't look at him. "When are you leaving?"

A part of me is marginally aware that it's a fucked-up question.

But that part is shut up by all the other parts that don't care about being a well-adjusted human, but rather focusing on the next minute. A minute that is so fucking hard in his presence.

"Brook!" Paris warns.

Her tone suggests everything she—and probably everyone else—is thinking. *What's wrong with you? That's not polite! How could you?*

"I'll take the tea upstairs," Mom says. "You'll be here?" She looks at her long-lost son and I feel like the worst person ever.

Go figure—there's still room to sink lower after all the surprises of the day.

That's it. It's not so much him as the will and marriage looming over me. No wonder I'm out of my element. I'm not normally a bitch.

And now I'm lying to myself.

For fuck's sake. I go back to my wine glass and refill it. Only now I end up standing beside him and that isn't helping me find composure. How and when did he even move to this corner?

Hoping to seem casual, I round the large counter—thank God for this humongous kitchen—and position myself at the opposite corner, hiding my face in the large glass.

Not that I'm looking at him. It's just that he's right across from me and all.

God, that suit fits him well. It gives him an air of dominance, like he's in charge here.

Has he always been like this? Owning the room with his mere presence?

We were the youngest of the bunch, so I guess we kind of remained in the shadows.

The confidence he oozes is a turn-on. It pleases me to learn this new tidbit about him.

What? I don't care. I don't care.

Still, I can't *not* observe him.

My sisters update Baldo on Dad's health. Something passes through his face, messing up his composure. It's a fleeting tick of the jaw that is gone immediately.

What was that about? Was it only my imagination, which usually serves up gruesome, bloody images?

I look at the floor and run an outline of a dead body with my eyes. If someone—none of the people here, I'm not that crazy—a fictional character hit his head on the corner of the counter, how would they fold as they fell?

"It's iron clad."

I jump at Dominic's voice and file the image for... well, I file it away.

He joins us, with Hunter and Finn on his heels. He drops the will on the middle of the counter.

The bang reminds me that Baldo's presence is not my only problem at the moment. Fucking roller coaster of a day.

I need to get married.

And why is it so hot in here?

I'm only half-listening to everyone around me.

Introductions are made, explanations are given. My sisters whine about their unplanned, fast weddings.

As if that was the issue.

I'm the one who doesn't have a partner.

I'm the one who has to go through this farce while Baldo is watching.

Out of everyone witnessing my humiliation, he's the one person I can't do this in front of. I can't have him finding out how alone I am. How lonely I am. How desperate I am.

How I'll have to look for a fake husband.

I groan, and when a hand comes to my back I almost yelp.

At some point during this cheerful conversation, Mom came back down. And while Bianca isn't my birth mother, her instincts are dead on because she caresses my back.

And just like when I was a little girl, the soothing circles provide me with strength. Or at least a measure of comfort.

It's not lost on me that she's chosen to stand by me while I'm sure she wants every waking minute with her son. How pathetic must I be in her eyes, if she picked me at this moment?

Okay, Brook, grow up. He is here and you can't make him leave, so you'd better focus on what matters.

If only the conversation in the room would finally move to the most pressing issue.

While they continue to yap away, I consider my options.

Is there a place online where I can find a husband? Like mail-order brides? There might be some sort of a modern alternative. Or I can order a bride. That would upset Granny's need for tradition.

The thought almost cheers me up. It would if the man I pretend is not here wasn't staring at me.

Or I think he is. While he converses with the others, I can feel the burn of his attention.

"I'd suggest that you"—Dominic looks at Paris and Sydney—"since you're living together anyway, get hitched at the city clerk's office now to comply with the paperwork and then have the weddings you planned later." He looks at London. "I got us an appointment at city hall already."

She grins at him. "I love you."

Finally, my turn.

"Great, and now that we've resolved the issues that weren't pressing since you were going to get married anyway, can we focus on me?" My tongue trips a bit.

Just how much of that wine did I have? And shouldn't alcohol cheer me up?

Nobody rushes to offer suggestions. It doesn't feel

like my family is looking for a solution. The silence screams of their pity and my desperation.

But someone is thinking of a solution, and his words floor me.

"I'll marry you."

Chapter 4

Baldo

What the fuck is wrong with me? Did I just offer to marry my stepsister?

Everyone seems to be stunned to silence. Well, I think Brook gasped. Or maybe it was my mother.

I can't look at them.

It's the worst idea ever.

Someone should protest. Immediately. It's not like I can squeal "just kidding." That would be cruel.

But someone needs to point out how stupid this is.

What was I thinking?

I wasn't.

Visiting home, seeing everyone, meeting the new members of my family... It's all overwhelmed me way more than I expected.

What *was* I expecting?

An emotional reunion with my mother. That's what.

I was hoping to hug my mom, and if I got lucky avoid my stepdad, Micah.

I didn't expect a happy reunion. I didn't count on all the memories rushing in the minute I stepped foot on the property.

I was so unsure about actually ringing the bell that I climbed the fence. Really mature. In my thousand-dollar suit, no less.

Just like the old times. The climb. Not the suit.

What I didn't anticipate was the sense of loss and longing that this visit has stirred in me. And that was all before I even lay eyes on *her*.

She was the last person I wanted to face.

The one who got away. The one who stood me up.

With her blonde hair up in a messy bun, wearing a tank top and a cardigan, comfortable and not sexy at all, she still looks like a vision.

I don't allow myself to dwell on what isn't, what would have or could have been, but Brook Lowe has been my obsession for way too long.

And while I've toned down the obsessive behavior lately, I still think of her more than I should.

I've never let her go completely. But I also never planned on seeing her again. That's why I've stayed away for years.

What are the odds she'd be here the night I decide to pay my mother an unannounced visit? I haven't even been to New York since I left that night.

And she has been in the UK for the past nine years. So what the fuck is she doing here now?

And what am I doing proposing? She stood me up and chose her dad over me, and I come back almost ten years later and offer her marriage?

I'm certifiable.

"That's actually not the worst solution," London offers.

What the fuck? No, it is the worst solution. One that should have never been on the table. *You put it there, asshole.*

Brooklyn looked so desperate and lonely. So lost. The fire that burned in her all those years ago is missing. I wonder what or who doused it.

A perverted part of me wishes it was because of the way we parted.

So beautiful and fucking sexy with her defiant glower, practically shooting daggers at me. So maybe some fire is left. Full of hatred, as if I wronged her somehow.

And yet, even filled with venom, she'd be the poison I'd want to take. Or the woman I'd want to marry, apparently. Fuck.

She barely touched me when she greeted me, and yet I swear my cock twitched.

I can't stop watching her. Her nails are battered, looking so sad on her slender fingers.

When she held her glass to her face, practically hiding, something snapped in me, activating an outlandish need to protect her, to make the situation—her life—better for her.

"Wouldn't that be incestuous?" Paris scrunches her face.

I finally glance at Brook. She's standing there, pale and paralyzed, tapping her fingers on the counter, staring at the tiny lines in the marble's pattern. Fuck.

"It's not like they're actually related." Sydney shrugs.

Why are we not putting breaks on this? I should just take it back.

"And it would be a nice fuck you to our *beloved* grandmother." Does London sound excited about the idea?

"Don't you live abroad?" Hunter asks.

That's right. My way out. My mind offers that thought, but my mouth asks, "Where do you live?" As if that matters. As if I don't know.

Brook looks up and our eyes meet. "I live here."

Does she? Last I heard she was in London.

I can live in London. What? What the fuck?

"You've decided to stay," Paris says cheerfully.

Brook blinks a few times. "Yes, yes, I'm staying."

It feels like she's just made that decision on the spot. To avoid marrying me. Smart girl. Certainly smarter than me.

"I'm opening a club in Manhattan," I announce, "so I guess I'll be here more often." What the fuck is coming out of my mouth?

"A club?" Sydney asks. "There is so much we need to catch up on, but I'm so glad we'll see more of you."

I curve up my lips, hoping I seem as excited as she is. I would be. I didn't expect this reunion to happen, let alone for it to affect me this much.

But there are more pressing issues to tackle right now.

My eyes find Brook again and then continue scanning the room. Mom is gone. Sometime after my proposal she left.

What's up with that? I'd expect her to be the first one to protest.

What does her retreating mean?

"So does the will allow for a long-distance marriage?" London asks. "Or are you planning to stay around more?" She looks at me.

I have no plan. But my no-plan certainly didn't include staying in New York.

"I think that's something that can be arranged, but my business is in Europe and Asia. I'll need to travel."

"Brook can travel with you." Paris slides off the tall chair, holding her belly.

A glance at Brook confirms she's less than thrilled about all the meddling. Why is everyone talking about her like she isn't here? Has it always been like that?

London stands up as well and rubs her hands together. "It makes perfect sense. You were always close, so you'll get along, and you're family, so we don't have to let a stranger in for this fucked-up situation. It's make-believe, anyway."

I guess this is happening. I'm fucking getting married.

My mind immediately starts planning how I'll make a year of marriage in the US work with all my other responsibilities across the world.

And for a brief moment, I get excited. I'm a restless bastard. A nomad of a sort, and this new challenge excites me.

There is only one problem. Brook would be a part of that life.

And then I stop myself. I'm being the same asshole as the rest of the family, ignoring her opinion on the matter.

Turning my head, I catch her biting her cuticle. She looks even more desperate and lost than before, and I grab the edge of the counter to keep from wrapping my arms around her.

Why is everyone getting ready to leave as if the matter is settled? Fuck.

"It was just an idea, Brook," I say, and she snaps her eyes to me. "We don't have to do it. I'm sure there is another solution."

"This one would be an easy one," Dom offers.

Shut up, fucker. Let her decide.

Her eyes dart around, meeting the expectant looks of her sisters, who seem to want to be done with this. Who, despite all odds, believe this is the perfect solution.

How many times has she stood under this metaphorical firing squad? Crushed under our family's expectations. She only ever wanted to fit in. To be one of them.

From her non-cosmopolitan name to being always the baby of the family, she never felt like she had a voice.

And yet, in the end, when it came to us, she chose them. That's how strong her need for acceptance used to be. And still is, I guess.

She squares her shoulders and grins—her very best fake grin that I still recognize—and shrugs. "But I want a huge rock."

Chapter 5

Baldo

London snorts. "Then it's settled. Figure out the details and let's all get married." She rolls her eyes but cozies up to Dominic.

The three couples say good bye and leave.

"I'll go find Mom," I say, before the complications of being alone with Brook dig their claws into me.

Fuck, how are we going to be married if I can't stand the idea of being alone with her?

Though in the hour since I arrived, my mind has been exploring all the ways I'd like to spend alone time with her, including bending her over the counter.

Not helpful, dear brain. Staying mad at her and away from her was the best move ever, but I guess we can't all get smarter with age.

One look at her and I'm a certifiable idiot, thrown back into my ridiculous obsession.

"That's a good idea. I'll be in my room." She dashes out of the kitchen.

I'll be in my room? That sounded almost like an invitation. We need to discuss where we go from here, but does she want me to come upstairs?

Can I cope with all that *the upstairs* holds in the form of memories, broken dreams, flattened fantasies and unfulfilled passions?

Perhaps I don't need to discover my limits today. *Coward.*

I cross the foyer, hoping Mom is in the library. The light under the door confirms that some things have not changed.

The surprise is that she isn't in her reading corner.

The room is dim and the three floor-to-ceiling bookshelves with any and all literature available to man make the room even darker.

Especially at night when the only source of natural light, the picture window overlooking our backyard, isn't available.

That's where I find her. Standing by the window, Mom stares into the darkness.

For a moment, my mind transports me back to my childhood. I used to sit on the floor here and play while she read. And I was summoned here anytime I was in trouble.

And let's face it, out of all eight of us, I was here

the most. Mom let Micah discipline his daughters, and my older brothers were smarter in their mischief.

Or perhaps I was crying for more attention.

God, the shit I used to stir.

"It's nice to have you here. I worried the day would never come." Mom turns to face me. "What brought you back?"

She walks to the corner and takes a seat in her reading chair, gesturing to the love seat at her side.

"Business." I take the seat, hating how strained the air is with unasked questions and unanswered ones.

"You should have come sooner." The words reek of admonition, but her tone is filled with sadness.

Like she understands I couldn't. Like she knows that in some ways she chose Micah over me. And while that didn't push me away, it still kept us apart. I don't know anymore. It's been too long.

"I'm sorry about Micah."

I'm talking about his illness, but once it's out, it feels like more than that. Am I sorry for all that other shit? Another thing I don't know anymore.

After I left, my hurt over losing Brook was enough to deal with, and I didn't assign further blame to anyone else.

Maybe I should have.

Or maybe I should have reached out sooner.

"Me too." She nods, and it's unclear what she is

referring to. Maybe we both just needed to acknowledge something that doesn't matter anymore.

She smiles at me and continues. "He's tenacious and he hasn't given up yet, so that's good."

Or perhaps we're only talking about the illness and I'm trying to read too much between the lines. Seeking something that isn't there.

I'm perfectly happy not to dissect the past. Nothing good would come of it.

"Are you sure you know what you're doing?" Mom asks, and this time it's clear she's talking about the present, but I fear the past is a part of it.

"It's a reasonable solution. Why not?"

It's the least reasonable solution. Perhaps if we were just stepsiblings and nothing else. Not that we are anything else anymore.

"You both call me Mom." She sums up her reservations.

Brook was little when they moved in with us, and Mom is the only mother she's ever known. The other Lowe sisters have always called her Bianca, but for Brook she's been nothing but Mom.

"You didn't stay in the kitchen to voice your opinion." I shift in my seat.

She nods, as if acknowledging something, but I'm not sure what. "I interfered once before, and it cost me my son."

Fuck. That's about as close to admitting her part in Brook's decision to stay behind nearly a decade ago as I'll ever get.

I thought this was already water under the bridge, but Mom's words open new wounds on top of the old, festering ones.

Fuck. Fuck. Fuck.

My jaw is so tense I might crack it. But I won't fuss over something that no longer matters.

How I'm going to avoid it all while married to Brook is another can of worms, and I'm set on ignoring that one as well.

It's only a year.

I survived nine years not addressing my hurt—I can plow through twelve more months.

"If you and Brook go through with it, I don't want Micah to know," Mom says finally, and it pisses me off all over because again she's choosing him.

"I don't see how we can hide that we live together," I say, instead of all the words I want to hurl at her.

Where did this resentment come from? I guess there isn't a place deep enough in my soul to bury it without it flooding out the minute I fucking step into this house.

"The doctor cleared him for travel today. We're leaving for Florida. It's better for him. To gain strength.

Brook is house-sitting for us, so I guess the two of you can live here for the time being."

I better get used to stepping into the fucking house then.

"If I understand correctly, we need to stay married for a year."

"We'll only be gone for a month. We want to return to spend time with Paris's baby. We can deal with the rest later." She picks up her book and puts on her glasses.

Am I being dismissed? Is the conversation finished for her?

"That doesn't seem like the best plan. A month will pass quickly and—"

"Micah's disease has taught me to live for each day." She snaps the book closed. "Right now he lives for meeting his grandchild, and that's what we're focusing on." She digs her fingers between the pages and pulls the book open again.

"Whatever you say, Mom." I stand up, kiss her forehead and turn to leave.

"I'm just sorry I won't be here to spend more time with you. Promise me we will have time to catch up," she says to my back.

"We will."

"I'm sorry."

Fuck this conversation with all its double meanings. I stay rooted, the door handle in my hand, but I don't push the door open.

I want to pretend I didn't hear her, because that would mean accepting that she really, truly knew what happened back then.

But I don't have it in me to unearth that further, so I don't acknowledge her. But neither do I move.

"For not fighting for you all those years ago," she confirms. "Now I'm staying out of it."

I leave without responding. I came tonight to see my mother, to hug her, to tell her I love her and leave.

Instead, all sorts of shit has been stirred up in my head about the past.

And I fucking got engaged.

Chapter 6

Brook

My legs.

They move instinctively, feet tapping and twirling on the soft carpet, my arms weaving through the air, shaking off the frustration of the day.

What a fucking day.

The music pulses through my earbuds into every crevice of my exhausted body. The fast, rhythmic beat echoes the frantic pace of my heart.

I close my eyes, letting the music sweep through me as I seek a sweet escape. Usually, each beat is a drum roll, banishing my troubles, freeing me from the tight grip of stress.

Music has always been my therapist, my confidant. Today, it doesn't seem to understand my need to let go.

My body moves in sync with the pulsating rhythm, but I'm not finding relief.

My worries tend to fade away to the beat, swaying and shimmying, but none of today's occurrences can fade away.

Baldo Cassinetti proposed to me.

The girl in me rejoiced, because that was something I used to dream about.

There's probably still a diary in my desk drawer in the corner of my room where I practiced the Cassinetti signature.

Not that anything that ensued after I fell for the boy would ever allow for a wedding or any future together.

Yet here we are.

Baldo Cassinetti proposed to me.

The heartbroken woman doesn't understand what's happening. He took me by surprise, to say the least. What was he thinking?

I twirl in place a few times, bobbing my head, hoping some other way of thinking triggers understanding, but nothing happens.

I stumble, but catch myself before falling, and I may have even saved the move gracefully.

Not that this is a performance.

What am I going to do? I just got out of a toxic relationship. I can't spend a year of my life with a man who took so much from me. Who left me behind without looking back.

So much went wrong that night when we were planning to run away.

A lot of it cost me years in therapy. Most of it left me empty and sheltered, building walls I don't even know how to climb anymore.

I couldn't protest his ridiculous proposal because, as London pointed out, it's an easy solution to the stupid conundrum.

They all remember Baldo and I being close growing up. None of them know just how close we had become.

Or how suddenly we weren't close. Rather as far from each other as possible.

Not that I could have explained any of that to my sisters earlier, thus me refusing the proposal would have only rendered me "difficult," as they've always perceived me.

Perhaps if he wasn't standing there, I'd have found my brain and come up with a rational explanation.

I want a huge rock? Really?

A new, slower song starts, and I sway to the rhythm, hoping to erase the images of him from my head.

God, did he grow up into a fine man. So fucking

sexy, I had to clench my pussy every time I chanced a look at him.

The sultry song isn't helpful in erasing the thought. I trace my palms up my thighs, around my hips, along my ribcage and back, while my ass rocks. The contact is soothing and caressing, grounding me in my own body.

Maybe there still is a way out. It would take putting on my big girl panties and talking to the man, convincing him it's not a good idea.

With his business, he can't be locked in New York.

Fuck. I completely forgot about my spontaneous decision to stay in New York. It was out of desperation, hoping he'd reconsider.

The stubborn bastard shook it off, but I'm sure he's regretting it now.

Yes, we should just discuss it and announce it was a stupid idea. Then I'll call my friends and brainstorm some solutions, without my family's interference.

The beat changes again and, boosted by my solution, I spring and lean back and forth, enjoying the movement.

Fully immersed in my own little world, I let the melodies weave through my soul, stitching up the frayed edges of my day. I spin, fully diving into the fluid movement.

In my whirl of blissful ignorance, my eyes meet his dark irises.

"What the fuck?" I stumble to a halt and rip my earbuds out so violently that one of them flies across the room. "Ever heard of knocking?"

"I knocked. A few times." Amusement tugs at Baldo's lips.

How long has he been perched against the door frame? And why does he look so smug? And so fucking hot?

The boy I used to know was attractive, but this man should come with a warning: dangerous to your ovaries and panties.

Can he smell the pheromones? My core clenches. Who knew my pussy could weep.

His arms crossed in front of him, his biceps bulge. So casual and sure of himself. Now I know why it's been so hard for me to find sexual satisfaction. This man ruined me. Without even truly having me.

Sweat glistens on my skin from what I thought was a private dance session, and I hold my head high as his gaze roams up and down my body hungrily.

Yeah, mister, you missed out. The desire in his expression gives me an unwarranted jolt of vindication.

It's satisfying to see I'm not the only one affected. It's also really, really bad. Dangerous. Not that my body cares.

In fact, my body flips me off with all its reactions: shallow breath, pounding heart, drenched pussy, goosebumps, and I'm pretty sure sometime between leaving the kitchen and now I started running a fever.

His eyes darken with something. If I was naïve, I'd call it lust. We stare at each other for I don't know how long before he cocks his head as if in question.

Oh, right, yes, we need to talk. We need to put a stop to this stupid scheme. Don't we?

I clear my throat. "I like to dance the stress off."

Yes, explain yourself to him. Because he invaded your privacy, spied on you during a private moment, and you owe him an explanation. *Go, Brook.*

"I can see that."

That's all he says, but my body rejoices at hearing his voice like he's just complimented me. What's wrong with me?

Everything. Everything is wrong with me when it comes to him.

I fold my arms across my chest, mirroring him. Only I'm not, because his stance is casual while I'm gearing up for a fight. To protect myself.

"What are you doing here?" I ask.

"I have business in New York, and I came to visit Mom."

I was referring to my room, but okay, let's broaden it up.

"You couldn't have picked a better time." I meant it as a question, I think. My tone is laced with sarcasm, so it came out as a statement. Or an accusation.

"There has never been a good time to return." He pushes off the frame and steps closer, shutting the door.

My childhood room is still very much like I left it, with all the signs of my teenage personality. A poster of One Direction, pink and white throw pillows, a collection of mugs and my murder mystery paperbacks.

I didn't bother to redecorate it since I came back, because what for? With Baldo stepping inside, I regret that neglect. The room—and me by extension—just feels more pathetic.

Like he went into the big world and made something of himself, carrying his experience with swagger, while I stayed in my old pink, girlie room, with nothing to show for the past nine years.

The rational me knows it's not true, but his presence is overwhelming and all-consuming, not leaving much space for logic.

He came to this room before—many times in secret—and in some sense it feels the same. My body trembles, my mouth goes dry.

Only years ago, I'd have jumped up to lock the door and wrap my arms around his neck. Today, I want to yank the door open to get more oxygen and wrap my hands around his throat.

And squeeze.

Okay, I don't want that. I want him to squeeze his hands around my neck. Pleasant shivers shudder through me and I barely stifle a moan. What the hell?

He narrows his eyes. "Are you okay?"

Unsuccessful stifle then. "Sure. Do you want to go downstairs and talk?" That sounded reasonable, I think. An exit strategy.

"In a hurry to see me out?" He smirks and takes another step in.

It takes all my willpower not to step back. No way in hell am I going to show him that he affects me.

I snort. "Ah, look, and I thought you lost all common sense."

He takes another step, and his scent hits my nose. For fuck's sake, no break with this man. And why is my room so small? Has it always been like this?

We're so close now, he has to look down at me. I will my eyes to meet his, anxiety causing my tongue to dart out to lick my lips.

A fucking mistake.

Baldo's eyes flicker with hunger. He raises his hand and my heart takes off, galloping around my poor chest.

He tucks a strand of hair behind my ear. Only he doesn't remove his hand after, just lets it linger there. Electricity courses between us while I try to remember why I hate him.

A lock of hair falls across his face, and I almost copy his move but stop myself. "What's up with the man bun?"

He shrugs. "You don't like it?"

"I hate it."

In the absence of any sensible need to remove myself from the current closeness, I can at least hate his hair. God, where the fuck did I leave my wits?

"Duly noted."

His fingers trace the skin of my neck, along my shoulder, down my arm.

A very elegant retrieval of his hand from my ear. What his touch does to me isn't healthy.

I swallow because my mouth is so dry and, of course, it prompts my tongue to dart out again. Only this time, I catch myself and retract. Unlike his move, mine lacks grace completely.

It seems to amuse him and encourage him as well, because the same hand he's just removed from me—and thank God for that—returns.

Only this time, his thumb touches my bottom lip. Right where it is still damp from my tongue.

A woman with my life experience, especially when it comes to toxic men, should bite his finger off. I know that beyond any shadow of a doubt.

But as if someone kidnapped my body and my

sanity without my knowledge, my lips part. Not only that, they close around the tip of his finger.

He hums. The sound strips me of any propriety or inhibition, and I suck. He tastes like salt and sin. I want his fingers elsewhere. Jesus.

He groans and grabs my throat with his other hand, squeezing gently.

What the fuck am I doing?

What the fuck are we doing?

What the fuck is he doing?

Jumping away from me. That's what. Out of the two of us, he regains his senses first, drops his hand and steps back.

Leaving me completely vulnerable, exposed and embarrassed.

"We should talk about the next steps. Other than the big rock you demanded."

He puts his hands in his pockets, but removes them quickly because the action prompts me to look down. And lo and behold, he's sporting a semi.

We're so fucked.

"Do you think it's a good idea?" I try to move gracefully to my desk and sit on the chair.

"Do you want to call it off? We can, of course."

The way he throws it out there hurts. It shouldn't, but it does, and that pisses me off.

"But you would be the one announcing it, because I'm for sure not backing out. It would only confirm what they all think about me."

"What do they think of you?" He frowns.

What, now he's my therapist? "Never mind. What were you thinking, anyway? Proposing?"

"Are you blaming me for wanting to help you out?"

And here is his true reason. He rode to the rescue. Poor Brook needed saving. Fuck him.

"I'm not backing out either," he continues. "I'll marry you."

"Why?"

He shrugs. "To stop the funding of questionable organizations."

That stings a bit. Not the reason I wish for. I *wished* for. A long time ago. "Great. Let's get married then. It's make-believe, after all."

I guess we'll go with being stubborn rather than reasonable.

He pulls out his phone, unlocks it with his thumb print and hands it to me. "Save your number."

I do that and return the phone, practically dropping it in the effort to avoid even the slightest touch.

"I'll call you."

He ambles away, shutting the door behind him, leaving my heart in pieces at my feet.

Not for the first time.

I need to get a grip. And I will. Today was just a big surprise. Tomorrow I'll be better prepared to face him.

Baldo Cassinetti proposed to me.

And I'll marry him. Make-believe. Nothing else.

Chapter 7

Brook

LO

I'm married.

PARIS

Congrats. We're getting hitched tomorrow. If I can still walk.

SYD

What's wrong with your legs?

PARIS

Swollen. Brook?

My legs are not swollen.

PARIS

(Eye-roll emoji)

LO

Syd, Brook, stay on topic here. Married yet?

> **SYD**
> Hunter is whisking me away to Vegas this weekend (multiple heart emojis)
>
> **PARIS**
> Oh, that's so romantic.
>
> **LO**
> And unnecessary. Brook?
>
> In ten minutes.
>
> **PARIS**
> Still a bit weird you're marrying your brother.
>
> **LO**
> Stepbrother.
>
> **SYD**
> I'm going to Vegas.

Of course he's late.

I pace in front of the Bronx supreme court building, sweat trickling down my spine.

I opted for a simple black T-shirt and jeans, but the late April day decided to grace us with unreasonably high temperatures.

I should have worn shorts. Or maybe I'm uncomfortable because I'm about to marry the man who broke my heart. One who doesn't even care enough to show up on time.

Maybe he changed his mind.

In which case, I can't be mad at him. Because not going through with this would be the right thing to do.

But in some ways, it feels like déjà vu. Though I guess from his perspective, it was me who didn't show up last time.

I stop and consider that angle of events. I've been so wrapped in my disillusion of him not coming back for me that night, I never thought... I'm not going there.

The thought already sends a shock wave of regret down my body. And I worked hard to not feel regret.

I'm quite certain my therapist bought several cars and properties from the hours we worked on resolving the regret and self-loathing I harbored after that night.

All the memories rushing at me speeds up my pulse. I put my hands over my frantic heart and start counting my breaths.

I haven't had a panic attack in years. What was it I learned about overcoming them? How does box breathing work? Fuck if I know.

So instead I chant in my head. *It wasn't my fault. It wasn't my fault. It wasn't my fault.*

"Are you okay?" The raspy baritone snaps me back to reality.

For a beat, I'm pretty sure it calmed me. It's like his voice has the ability to reach into my soul and caress it.

Bullshit.

I take him in, sorting through the fog of memories,

pulling my head back to the present. And fuck. My. Life.

The man is wearing a bespoke—no way an off-the-rack would fit this well—suit. Okay, not even the whole suit. Due to the current weather, he shed the jacket.

It's hot after all.

Like really, really hot.

Like a heatwave just changed my trickle of sweat into a river pouring down my spine. And my face... I hope it doesn't look as red as it feels.

So now all six feet five inches of muscles and planes of his perfect body stand in front of me in a crisp white shirt, chocolate vest and pants.

To add to his overwhelming presence, he's wearing sunglasses. Along with the five o'clock shadow on his square jaw, it gives him the air of a bad guy.

What does that song say? Good boys go to heaven, but bad boys bring heaven to you?

With the sun shining from behind him, he might be just some heavenly creature. Or a well-disguised devil, probably.

And for the love of God, his hair is cut. It's buzzed on the sides and longer, perfectly mussed on top.

What the whole image does to my ovaries is concerning. I swallow, remind myself of the need to breathe and open my mouth. Not to say anything—I'm speechless—just to salivate.

"Brook?" He cocks his head.

"You cut your hair," I croak. My voice doesn't sound healthy.

"Of course I did." He shrugs.

Because of course he did? Because I told him I didn't like it? Or he'd grown his hair all this time and then just this morning decided to change his image?

He should have kept the man bun. It was easier to dislike him.

Electricity zaps through me when he extends his hand, rubbing my arm like I need consoling. I do, I guess. Jesus.

"You're crying."

Oh shit. I wipe my cheeks quickly. My little moment of panic before he showed up. I forgot about that in the influx of physical sensations his arrival incited.

"You're late," I snap to cover my meltdown.

"Oh, you worried I stood you up?" He puts his hands into his pockets and, fuck, I hate how gorgeous he looks.

"It wouldn't be the first time."

He flinches. "That's rich coming from you."

How dare he? Memories try to take over, but I can't go there. Not now. And hopefully not ever.

This will be a long year as it stands already.

I wish I could see his eyes. Stupid shades.

"You could have come earlier. We better go."

"I'm not late. We still have ten minutes. Were you so anxious to marry me you got the time wrong, sweetheart?"

Asshole.

I check my watch and swallow. I truly was early. Maybe for the first time in my life.

I showed up early for my fake wedding. I don't even want to think about the wicked ways of my subconscious.

I turn, but he doesn't follow.

"Is this what you're wearing?" He assesses me like I'm dressed in a trash bag.

I march back to him and make the mistake of underestimating the distance. Now I'm almost pressed against him. Not good.

But at least I maintain a level voice. "I don't see why I would dress up for a farce of a wedding."

"To keep up appearances." He smiles at me with patience. Fuck him. "For all we know, your great uncle might require wedding photos."

When I called Rupert to inform him about my upcoming nuptials, he raised his concerns about the validity of it. Especially since I'm marrying my stepbrother.

I fabricated a story about how we've been dating for a while and we're just tying the knot like Roberta wanted. Since we've both been living in Europe, we might get away with the dating lie.

Just barely though. Because unlike London who is legitimately living with Dom and running several charitable endeavors with him, or Paris who is very pregnant with Finn's baby, and Sydney who has been co-parenting Hunter's little girl for almost two years, Baldo and I don't have one picture together to corroborate the ruse.

And then there is the issue of Roberta supposedly keeping tabs on us.

He's right. We need to pretend harder.

I sigh.

"Wait here," he orders.

"Yes sir," I mock him, but I realize my mistake.

Because he raises his glasses, and if I've ever seen hunger in a man's eyes... Oh my. He licks his lips, but then he shakes his head and enters the building.

I remain rooted and let out a long breath, trying to calm my nerves. Why am I nervous? And so fucking turned on?

In the minutes I stand there waiting for him—and where the hell did he go?—I find my breathing, level up my mindset and remember why I'm doing this.

Baldo returns and I try not to look at him to maintain that tenuous mindset.

"Let's go." He grabs my hand and leads me toward a car that's just pulled to the curb.

I want to ask where we are going but I'm dealing with the contact of my hand in his. It feels so effortless, so natural, so us. And there goes my freshly adjusted mindset.

We're already seated in the car when I recover. "Where are we going? We'll miss our appointment."

I turn to glare at him, but he raises his finger to silence me. He's on the phone. How much did I miss while I was recovering from... well, from him?

A long year ahead of me, for sure.

"Thank you. We'll be there in half an hour." He hangs up and gives directions to the driver.

Turning to me, he flashes me a smile. "You were saying?"

"Where the hell are you taking me?"

He narrows his eyes, like he really doesn't understand my question. "To get changed."

I blink and look outside as if that could explain his behavior better. But at least it gives me a comeback. "This is not the way to the house."

"No, it's not."

"Where. Are. We. Going?"

How I wish I could claw his eyes out. There would be blood and it would be messy. Smothering would be the way to go, but he's much bigger than me.

His response reaches the fantasy playing in my distracted mind, but I miss the meaning. What was his answer? No way I'm asking again.

He watches the traffic, his head turned slightly. So composed. So well put together. So arrogant.

And then I notice his index finger fluttering, tapping against his thigh. That slight fidgeting makes my lips curl up. It makes him more human.

Or it makes me feel more human. It brings the distracted me peace to realize there is a bit of chaos in him as well.

"So we're missing the ceremony because of a dress?"

"We're not missing anything."

I check my watch. "Our appointment was five minutes ago."

"I rescheduled it."

"Why?"

"Jesus, Brook, keep up. To get you a dress. We have two hours to get back." The exasperation in his voice feels like a slap.

"I'm sorry I'm not a mind reader. You manhandled me into your car. Maybe next time explain yourself first." I fold my arms and turn to watch the traffic.

We continue in silence until the car stops on a swanky street with designer boutiques.

Baldo gets out of the car and comes round behind it

to open my door. I ignore the hand he offers and push myself out.

Now he's a gentleman? Screw him.

"This way." He puts his hand on the small of my back and an unwarranted, involuntary shudder rakes through me.

If I continue having these shivering reactions to his every touch, I might go mad by the time this marriage is over. And it hasn't even started.

He steers me toward a luxurious store. There are no clothes displayed in the windows. In fact, there are no windows at all.

The front is all glossy black with golden accents. It's over the top and yet tasteful.

"It looks closed."

"They are waiting for us."

"What? We didn't know we were coming half an hour ago." I snort.

"It only took me five minutes to have it organized."

My heartbeat spikes again. I might need to see a cardiologist after this. As we approach the entrance, the door opens and a tall woman greets us.

Before I move, I look at Baldo. "This wasn't necessary."

He leans in, his breath like a touch of silk on my skin, his scent an aphrodisiac. "Anything for my bride."

Chapter 8

Baldo

Why was she crying? The thought has been driving me crazy since I arrived at the courthouse.

It has been in the back of my mind as I bribed the clerk to move our appointment and called my concierge services to arrange a branch of my favorite appointment-only store booked for us.

It has been gnawing at me while I sparred with her—because why would she make anything easy?

When I led her to my car, holding her hand. When I put my hand at the base of her spine.

All the while I fought a hard-on that threatened to tent in my pants. The woman smells like I remember—vanilla and peaches—and all new—sin and temptation.

She'd always had a personality that drew me to her. Tenacious. Stubborn. Mad at the world. But aren't all teenagers? And that's what we were back then.

During the few interactions we've had since my baffling proposal, I've glimpsed the same strength in her, but laced with vulnerability, and fuck if that isn't attractive.

For a moment, I even considered this one-year marriage might be fun. Like we could really go for it and enjoy each other.

But there are too many unresolved issues between us. Too many burning memories. Too many regrets.

She made her choice all those years ago and I accepted it. It's not like she is the only woman in the world. Though sometimes it feels that way.

"Oh, these were made for you," the shop clerk gushes.

I abandon the shelves of ties I've been perusing mindlessly and turn to see for myself. I turn too fast because blood rushes to my temples—and my groin—suddenly.

Brook wears a dress that hugs her torso and flares out at her waist into a skirt ending just above her knees.

It's simple but elegant. Classic. It's cream rather than white, and I wonder if that's a coincidence or a choice.

She twirls in front of the mirror and smooths the skirt. The fucking dress is backless.

I'm standing there like an idiot, staring and trying to recall this quarter's projection for my night clubs to keep my dick from giving opinions about the vision of the woman in front of me.

Brook chats with the clerk, not paying attention to my gawking, and then she leans forward, reaches under the fabric through the openings at her arms and adjusts her tits.

No financial projections can save me. "I have to take this call." I practically run outside.

I pace the sidewalk to deal with the situation in my pants. I never knew shopping could be this stressful. Why did I want her in a dress, anyway?

She was just fine in those jeans. And now I'm thinking about how amazing her ass looked in them.

Spectacular. That's how.

And that's how screwed I am.

I should have never come to the States again. Or gone to visit my mom. Or proposed. So yeah, back to I should have never come to the States.

I take a long breath and, the asshole that I am, I pull the door open and growl, "Are we done here?"

The young clerk and Brook whip around, but Brook recovers first. "It wasn't my idea to come to begin with. I didn't want a new dress."

I didn't want—or rather—shouldn't have done a lot of things, but here we are. And since she's still in the dress that will be the death of me, I turn to the clerk. "She needs shoes with that."

"Isn't he charming?" Brook glares at me, and then smiles at the clerk.

The poor woman, who was probably informed I'm a VIP customer, darts her eyes between us and then finds her professionalism and smiles at Brook. "What size are you?"

Another fifteen minutes and the women emerge. She paired the cream dress with bright red stilettos, and there goes my sanity and decency.

Just like that, I don't care about the dress anymore, because I'm busy picturing her bent over a counter in nothing but those heels.

"Could you just wrap the clothes I came in and ring it up for me," Brook says, and the clerk moves behind the glass stand with a touch screen while my *fiancée* pulls out her credit card.

"Over my dead body." I step to the counter. "Add it to my tab." I place my loyalty card on the smooth surface.

Brook puts her hands on her hips, her nostrils flaring. "It's my dress and shoes. I'll pay for them."

I glare at her for a few beats, not even sure what point I want to make.

"Yours are the clothes you chose to wear this morning."

For some outlandish reason, I have to win the argument. Slowly, I move my eyes to the clerk, commanding her action without words.

She snatches my card and runs it through the reader. "Thank you for your visit, Mr. Cassinetti."

Brook purses her lips, moving them to the side. I forgot she used to do that when she was annoyed—instead of biting her tongue or grinding her molars—or thinking.

And for once, I'm glad she's silent. This day has been taxing enough.

She grabs the bag with her old clothes and marches outside. Practically ripping the car door off its hinges—quite an achievement on an Escalade—she gets in.

I slide to the other side, beside her. She's pouting, wrinkling the bag in her hands. God, she is adorable.

Almost the entire ride back we are silent while she refuses to look at me, bouncing her leg and chewing on her cuticle.

"You should replace that nasty habit with some other stress reliever." I grab her wrist and pull it away from her face.

The feel of her pulse on my fingertips shouldn't make me want her this badly. Like that first night in her room when I held her throat while she almost sucked my finger, her heartbeat messes with me more than I care to admit.

Her cheeks heat up while she attempts to kill me with her eyes. "I wouldn't be this stressed if you weren't around to piss me off."

God, her fury makes her hot. I want to rile her up further, just to enjoy the passion in her reactions.

But that's probably a terrible idea. By the way I've been reacting to her, the less contact we have, the better.

I drop her hand and turn to the other side. "You bring the best out of me, sweetheart."

The car pulls to the curb and she yanks her door open. "You know what? You used to be my favorite person to talk to." It's an accusation more than a regret.

"You want to go down memory lane right now?"

If she loved talking to me so much, why did she stand me up?

Her eyes flare with something that I'm not sure is fury anymore. "You're right, *darling*, let's focus on our bright future." The words are laced with poisoned honey.

She slams the door and strides to the building, not waiting to see if I'm following. Fuck.

"Brook," I call after her, almost running over a couple leaving the building. "Wait."

She stops in the middle of the bright foyer, not necessarily waiting for me, more likely not sure where to go.

The dome-shaped hall has a glass ceiling and she stands in the middle of the sun cone, looking both pissed and lost. So fucking hot.

"We need to take the elevator to the fifth floor. But before we go, I've got something for you."

She eyes me suspiciously. I deserve that, probably.

I reach into my pants pocket and pull out a velvet box, my gaze on her face. Her eyes widen and she swallows.

"You demanded a huge rock." I slide the ring from the box and take her hand.

Set in a delicate, intricately designed band of white gold, a halo of smaller, sparkling diamonds surrounds a vivid ruby.

Brook gasps, her free hand flying to her chest.

"Will you do me the honor..." I push the ring only to her first tiny knuckle and stop.

Am I really doing this? Are we really doing this? Haven't we hurt each other enough already?

In a rush of memories, regrets and unresolved feelings for this woman, I hesitate. Unable to push the ring all the way down, but even less willing to take it back.

For almost ten years I've been suspended in limbo, never truly understanding why she didn't come. Why she decided to never see me again.

So many unanswered questions. Even more regrets and resentment.

In many ways, this feels like forever. Or maybe a part of me wishes it was. I better bury that part deep.

Perhaps a year with her will give me some answers, help me accept, find forgiveness or understanding.

All things I never realized I wanted. Needed. Or maybe we can find out what if...

Brook's hand trembles slightly in mine and, fully aware I might be making the biggest fucking mistake... or the best decision of my life, I slide the ring on her finger.

Chapter 9

Brook

"I swear he had second thoughts, and what's worse—it scared me. Like there's a part of me that really wanted to go through with it."

I almost whimper and my friend Saar squeezes my hand.

"Of course you did. You needed to get married and stop your horrible grandmother from distributing her wealth to spread evil."

The small bistro down the street from the dance school is almost empty at this time of day, the lunch hour finished and the dinner crowd not yet pushing in.

"I made you a plate of tapas to enjoy with your wine." Cora, the owner, puts a tray in front of us. "Are you going to dance?"

"Yes, I'm taking my friend." I introduce Saar to Cora.

"I wish I could join you." Cora sighs.

Ever since I started coming here I enjoyed the food, but mostly the company of the feisty owner. Today, the spark is dimmed in her eyes.

"You'll join us one day. You work too hard." I try to give her an encouraging smile.

She put her life on hold to run this place, founded by her grandfather, after her father got sick.

"Yes, one day I'll have people working for me and I'll dance every day." She utters a humorless chuckle.

"That sounds like a brilliant plan." Saar raises her glass.

"Enjoy, ladies, I better go catch up on paperwork before the evening rush starts." Cora smiles at us and trudges behind the small bar counter.

"She seems nice," Saar comments.

"Yeah. She's wonderful. But so busy, she has no time to enjoy her life. Hopefully she can join us for the class soon."

I smooth my dress. My fucking wedding dress.

After the ceremony, Baldo tipped the clerk to take a few pictures of us. We posed, pretending to be a genuine couple, and then we left.

Baldo announced he had business to take care of and got me a cab. I went home, picked up my dance bag and messaged Saar. She has been wanting to try my burlesque class for a while, and I could use the company.

I didn't change clothes. I was going to but... Fuck me if I know why I didn't.

I'm grateful Saar is here because I needed someone who's not family to listen to me, to accept the situation and help me sort through my feelings.

Without judgment. Without reservations. Without well-meant opinions.

I wish she could be here more often, but she's a model and her life is mostly in Europe. The irony is, we lived on the same side of the pond, at times in the same city, but our paths never crossed before.

I met Saar through Paris because she's Finn's sister. We bonded quickly in more ways than one—the youngest siblings, a love of dancing and clubbing, and our less than stellar track record with men.

"When he hesitated, the girl who didn't end up with Baldo Cassinetti reappeared from somewhere and wanted it to be real. I worried I'm going to lose him again. Not that I have him. Or even want him. It was just a moment of..." I groan. "I don't know."

Saar bites into her carrot stick. "You were overwhelmed. From what you've told me..." She counts on her fingers. "He got a haircut. He had a store opened to get you a dress, and then he got you a ring because you made an off-hand comment about wanting one.

My panties are melting and I haven't even met the man."

"Not just any ring." I sigh, extending my fingers to admire the jewel.

"Not just any ring. It's breathtaking."

"That's not what I mean. Way back when, I told him that I never wanted a diamond like everyone else. That I wanted a ruby. And he promised me—when we were seventeen—that one day he'd propose with a ruby." I swallow the memory. "Is this some cruel joke he is playing? Like getting me a ruby for a fake wedding to rub it in my face that *we* never really happened?"

"Oh, Brook, sweetie, you're overthinking it." She may want to calm me, but she worries her bottom lip.

"Saar?"

"It's nothing." She takes a sip of her wine. "Well... I doubt this is a ring that he bought on a whim. It looks custom made."

I wish she didn't voice my concern. A ruby by itself would send a message. But it would be practically impossible for him to get it in the few days since his proposal.

Then again, he had a boutique opened for us on a few minutes' notice, so perhaps he could command a jeweler the same way.

What does it mean? And why can't I ask him?

Baldo used to be the easiest person to talk to, and now... I feel completely out of my element when around him.

"Yeah, either it's an elaborate *fuck you* message he put a lot of thought and money into, or... I don't want to contemplate the alternative."

I pop a cheese cube with an olive into my mouth.

The creamy texture of the cheese perfectly mixes with the briny, slightly tangy bite of the olive, and I try to focus on the rich taste instead of the turmoil in my head.

Jesus, I don't even like olives.

And I don't get anywhere early.

Or tongue-tied.

What the hell have you done to me, Baldo Cassinetti?

"Or he's doing all those things because he wants a second chance." Saar shrugs.

"That's not happening." I'm not even sure why I'm so determined to keep it that way. "Our parents would never approve. Mom asked us to keep the marriage a secret from Dad."

"I can see how it's weird for them, but at the end of the day, they would want you to be happy."

Happiness is the last thing I feel when around Baldo.

Lust? Maybe.

Resentment? For sure.

Hope? Unfortunately.

"Half of the time he looks at me like I'm his arch-nemesis, anyway."

"You just said a part of you wanted—"

"I'm trying to tell you I need saving because the situation has made me insane. The man is hot, but also infuriating. And there is so much history, we wouldn't even finish discussing it by the time the year is over and he'll return to his normal life. Besides, he's my brother."

"Whatever you say." Saar raises her hands, but she sounds as sure about my determination as I am. Which isn't much.

"Let's go clubbing tonight." I huff and take another olive.

Because apparently I now love olives.

* * *

"Celeste Delacroix?" Saar squeals the minute we enter the studio.

"Merde, that's an unexpected surprise." Celeste, the dance teacher, claps her hands. "Saar. How long has it been?"

"Too long." My two friends hug each other, giggling.

"Apparently, no introductions are needed." I grin.

"Years ago, Celeste choreographed a fashion show I

was in. She gave me a Snickers bar and we became friends."

"And I almost lost the job. It's frowned upon to feed a model." Celeste's eyes gleam with mischief. "But we fell out of touch after this one—" she bumps her hip against Saar's, winking, "...became famous and moved to Europe."

"Or because you opened your own dance school and got a gazillion gigs in clubs across Manhattan," Saar teases.

The years of being overbooked came to an abrupt end because of Finn's—and Saar's—father. Shit, I don't think the two of them made the connection yet.

Celeste's face falls, but she recovers quickly. The truth will come out, eventually. I only hope it won't impact this little circle of friends I forged unexpectedly.

"We better start the class." Celeste looks over her shoulder at the full room of eager dancers.

"Before we do—" Saar gives me a devilish smile. "Brook got married today," she announces.

"Mon Dieu!" Celeste looks at me wide-eyed. "Tell us everything. And what are you doing here on such a special day?"

I glare at Saar, who shrugs and whispers, "What? You need to practice faking it." She grins, having way too much fun with this.

Before I can wipe that grin from her face, Celeste grabs my hand. "Look at that ring. How original. Truly special."

The other women gather around and gush over my ruby.

"Who is the man?" Celeste asks in that soft, lyrical intonation of her French accent. "Why did you never say anything?"

Oh god, lying to Rupert Montgomery was easy because he's been kind of an asshole in all of this, but selling the story to my friends, people I like and respect, that's a different ball game.

"His name is Baldo."

I swallow, but then I lean into the story. I'm a decent storyteller, after all. "We've known each other for years and we've been dating back in Europe. He came here to be with me and we just..." I smile and it's not even that fake, which should concern me. "We eloped."

A communal "oh" echoes through the room when all the ladies swoon over the romance.

Celeste narrows her eyes. "Okay, let's start the class." Her accent is slightly more pronounced than usual.

Everyone scatters to their spots, and I find Saar's eyes. She shrugs, but we both know that Celeste didn't buy my story.

Not such a good storyteller after all.

The music starts, and while usually I love this class I can't get into it, lost in my thoughts.

For one, Celeste's reaction is worrisome. How will Rupert believe me if I gave my best performance here and failed to sell it?

I stumble through the class distracted, turning the wrong way, almost bumping into another dancer while forgetting the steps of the choreography.

When the class is finally over, I rush Saar toward the changing rooms, hoping we can squeeze out of there before coming under more scrutiny.

"What are you doing?" Saar protests. "I haven't seen Celeste for years. I want to catch up with her."

Ever since Paris introduced me to burlesque, Celeste has become a friend. And under any other circumstances, I'd want to hang out with the two women I love and admire.

"Okay, let's wait for her." I groan.

As soon as I say it, Celeste comes out of her office, beautiful as ever in her curves-hugging dress with a low neckline. Any other woman might look like she is trying too hard to look sexy. Celeste wears it effortlessly and with grace.

Today, a frown distorts her glamorous appearance. Shit. I told Saar the truth. I'm sure there is no harm in sharing it with Celeste.

We walk out of the studio together and I'm hoping we can just avoid the topic of my unexpected nuptials.

"Are you okay? Has he forced you?" Celeste stops and rubs her hand up and down my arm, her eyes filled with concern.

I frown, my mind running a mile a minute, but I come up empty-handed. What is she talking about? Why would she think Baldo forced me?

"You told me how toxic that relationship was, so I'm just surprised you would jump into marriage with him."

I let out a stranded chuckle of relief. "Oh, Celeste, I didn't marry Dylan."

I shake my head, grinning like an idiot. Because here I was worried she saw through my lie, while Celeste assumed I married my ex.

"I didn't remember his name, but you dated the guy and then you came here, so..." She eyes me with suspicion.

"You thought she married Dylan." Saar snorts. "I would drag her to my lawyer to file an annulment if that was the case."

Neither of them has ever met Dylan, but after I told each of them about his tantrums and scenes, about his need to instigate fights all the time and his overbearing, unhealthy jealousy, neither of my friends is a fan of him.

"So, who is your husband?" Celeste puts her hands on her hips, her voice laced with exasperation.

The word husband hits like a punch to my gut. It wouldn't have any significance if my groom was anyone but Baldo.

"Don't do that," Saar reprimands, and I realize my cuticle is at my mouth.

I force a smile and face Celeste. "Do you have a gig tonight or can you come out with us? I'll fill you in."

Chapter 10

Brook

"You need to fuck him," Celeste yells.

We're in a VIP box at some club Saar recommended because she knows the owner, but there is hardly any privacy and conversation is mostly screamed over the loud music.

I laugh and raise my glass, "To fucking my husband!"

We drain our cocktails and dissolve in a fit of giggles.

Two men approach our table and Saar flips them off. "She's a married woman," my friend slurs, and another round of laughter grips us.

The night has been a success, if I may say so. I needed this. Dance, drink and laughter. Forget about the man I married earlier today.

About his haircut, my wedding dress, and the ring.

About all the feelings he stirs in me like the years have never passed.

But they did pass, and we're not who we used to be. Not anymore. I wish my body would get on board with that idea.

"I can't fuck him. It will complicate things." I gesture for another round of cocktails.

"Bullshit. It would be a release, not a complication. The two of you should totally bang. You're newlyweds, after all." Saar points at me and the motion propels her forward. She almost slides down the sofa.

We burst out laughing again.

"Let's dance." Celeste stands up. "You need to sober up before you go home to your husband." She thrusts her hips forward, still pushing her initial suggestion of banging.

And God, I do want to. As pathetic as it is, nobody has ever made my body tingle in the way Baldo used to, and still does, and he hasn't really touched me yet either.

Definitely a long year ahead of me. Jesus. Or perhaps it could be a fun year. If we have to play house for twelve long months, we might as well make the best of it.

"I'll join you in a minute." Saar waves us off.

"Are you okay?" I unfold myself from the sofa and

Celeste grabs my hand, pulling me with her, swaying her hips.

Saar shows me two thumbs up, but before I turn to follow Celeste, her face turns serious as her eyes dart around.

"Is she looking for someone?" I lean to whisper-yell into Celeste's ear.

"I've been wondering just how well she knows the owner since she insisted this is where we should come tonight." Celeste winks.

"Ha... you're right."

I'm so absorbed with my own problems, I almost missed that. Saar didn't mention who the owner was, but she is probably hoping to run into him tonight.

"Life is too short to delve into problems. Resolve them. In the bedroom. Believe me, if you have to live with him for a year, you better release all that tension." Celeste laughs and drags me to the middle of the dance floor.

I dive into the rhythm, and with the help of all the alcohol I've consumed, I finally let loose and forget about my fake husband, our living situation, and his romantic gestures that he immediately contradicts with his behavior.

Hours later, Saar insists we're leaving. As we shove through the dancing crowd, I follow her gaze to the upper level where a well-dressed man—Jesus, he's gorgeous—stands with two women cozying up to him. His glare sends shivers down my spine.

"Who is that?" I ask.

"Nobody," Saar snaps, making two things crystal clear. He isn't nobody, and she doesn't want to talk about him right now. What's up with that?

I forget all about it in the cab, immersed in my own conundrum. Baldo turns me on. That's not something that happens often.

When it comes to physical connection with men, I stay in my head and can't let go completely.

Would it be different with him? Could I get past my own baggage and unravel with the man who was supposed to be my first?

That night...

"Ma'am, we're here." The driver's voice startles me, interrupting my memory. Thank God for that.

I straighten up and pay the fare. Stumbling to the entrance, I try and fail to find my keys. Groaning, I reach for the bell, but the door opens.

My eyes meet Baldo's and I freeze. The man is breathtaking. And clearly pissed.

"Honey, I'm home." I hiccup.

I'm vaguely aware my sarcasm isn't the right weapon at the moment, but my drunken mind offers it anyway.

I step forward and lose my footing. Baldo snakes

his arm around my waist and keeps me upright. Unfortunately, I'm now flush against the planes of his impressive body.

He's still wearing his perfect white shirt and his suit pants, but the fabric doesn't prevent my body from heating up at the feel of every dip and bulge of this perfect man.

I meet his eyes and my breath hitches, or perhaps the oxygen dissolves around us because my lungs struggle to get their fill.

Kiss me.

As soon as the thought flickers through the fog in my head, my lips part. His gaze bores into me, warring, but he doesn't move.

Kiss me.

I beg with my eyes, my lips, my inner thoughts.

The entry hall is dim, the only light coming from the kitchen down the corridor and from the porch outside.

We're both lost in the shadow of the house that witnessed the tragic end of our story.

Or was it only the first act?

We remain in the strange embrace, not moving, the cool evening air spreading goosebumps down my spine.

His closeness feels like everything I ever missed in my life. Which is a stupid, sappy thought, but the longing in me is real.

Kiss me.

His Adam's apple bobs up and down a few times and then he kicks the door closed, steadies me and steps back.

"Shame." I pout, and oops, I didn't mean to mourn the loss of him out loud. It makes me giggle. Another wrong move if his glower is any indication.

"Jesus, Brook, you're drunk. Where the fuck have you been?" He stomps through the hall leading to the kitchen.

Either he expects me to follow or he doesn't care about my answer.

I follow.

But the scene in the kitchen sobers me up. In one corner of the large island, two plate settings wait along with wine glasses and Mom's special-occasion candle stand.

The whole visual is even more romantic because it's not in the formal dining room. It's at the corner where we used to eat our breakfast cereal.

Together. Secretly holding hands.

My heart hammers in my temples as I try to blink away tears forming behind my eyes. When I land my gaze on the enormous bouquet of purple orchids—my favorite—I stop breathing.

This is too much.

"You cooked for me?" I want to sound indifferent, but my voice comes out broken.

Baldo stands by the door to the yard, his back to me. Scrolling on his phone. How does a man do all of this for me and then check his social media? Asshole.

He turns to me, and I'm reminded he was pissed when he opened the door. That hasn't changed if I'm to guess by the glare. "I have been calling you, worried, all night."

"What? I can't go out?" Apparently, *I'm* the asshole tonight. The man inspires the worst in me.

He shakes his head. "You can go out. But why the fuck didn't you answer your phone?"

Well, Baldo Cassinetti has just joined the rest of the family in patronizing me. Though I may deserve it at the moment. I rummage through my bag. "Oh shit, I lost it again."

"You lost your phone?" He doesn't believe me.

I nod.

"Just how much have you drunk? And what do you mean *again*?"

This might cheer him up. "Me and my phones..." His glower intensifies. Like he's had enough of me. I swallow. "It's a long story." I don't think he'd consider my chronic inability to keep a phone amusing. I smile at him. "You cooked."

He snorts. "I ordered a meal, so we... Never mind." He pockets his phone and crosses the floor.

Don't leave. Don't leave.

"Did you want to celebrate our nuptials?" I try to sound cheerful, but I don't think this night is salvageable anymore.

Also, I'm too drunk to analyze what the fuck is going on in his head. Or be mature enough to simply ask.

He stops on the threshold and turns slowly. "Our *fake* wedding, you mean?" The way he stresses the word squeezes at my stomach. "I thought we could talk about how this marriage would work, so we can respect each other's boundaries. And perhaps celebrate that you duped your granny."

Oh, so it wasn't a romantic gesture, just plain business. He could have fooled me.

"Sorry, I didn't know we had plans," I snap. "You forgot to mention it."

He rakes his hand through his hair. It remains sticking out in every direction, and for some reason I love it. It makes him a bit less perfect, which is a relief.

Like his perfect was too different from my chaotic, but now we're somehow closer. Just like when he tapped his finger in the car.

"We can still eat." I step to him and place my hand on his chest.

He sucks in a breath, and I take it as a win. And it stupidly encourages me, and my drunken mind, filled with my friends' stupid advice, acts before I can stop myself. "Or maybe we should consummate..."

Raw hunger flickers through his eyes. We stare at each other for the longest moment, all our baggage filling up every molecule of air between us.

And in that moment, I wish I could take my suggestion back. Not because I don't want to sleep with him. I do. Maybe even more than I wanted to nine years ago.

But in his eyes I see a mixture of things, warring with a sentiment I really wish wasn't there. Baldo wants me as much as I want him, as evidenced by his ragged breath, his hand gripping my hip and, if I'm not mistaken, a bulge in his pants.

But there is so much hurt between us and so much resentment. If we went through with it, we would only make things worse.

Without talking or moving, at a standstill in the middle of the house that haunts us with our story, we pant as our eyes lock in a battle between want and should.

I'm paralyzed by the avalanche of memories and all the questions I want to ask. But also by my body's all-consuming desire for this man.

Such an unknown sensation for me. I've never trembled for a man like this.

Baldo reaches up to tuck a strand of hair behind my ear. Unlike that first night in my room, he removes it quickly like I burned him.

Heat spreads up my neck and cheeks, and my heart hammers as I try to figure out how we can gracefully remove ourselves from this stalemate. How not to feel rejected.

Trapped between our need for each other and the reality that the time for that passed long ago.

And then Baldo resolves the situation for us. "You're drunk. Go to bed."

For some reason, it feels like he's broken my heart all over again.

He turns and his footsteps echo long after he leaves me there, standing in the air infused with my favorite flowers.

Chapter 11

Baldo

Fucking woman.

I don't know why I cared where she went last night. And what was I thinking, setting up a celebratory meal? What is there to celebrate? My insanity apparently.

I step into the shower.

I plan my life carefully so I'm always in control. That was the only thing that helped me heal after Brook left me behind.

And now, having her in my life, my control is slipping. I need to resolve that quickly.

It's like where she's concerned, my entire mind goes into this protective mode. Like she needs a knight in shining armor. Fuck that. I've never been that man. So why am I trying to be that for her?

It's not like she is a damsel in distress… though she

looked pretty lost the first night I arrived. Somewhere along the line, someone killed her resilience.

All that strength I used to admire about her. It's been tamed. Replaced by these loud cries for attention. What happened to her?

And how does an adult lose their phone? Why is she living with her parents? There are so many questions I want to ask her.

But somehow we don't seem to find words when we are together. Or rather, the past is clouding our judgment. We need to fuck.

I mean, *talk*. We need to talk.

Fuuuuck.

And when she suggested consummating our farce marriage...

I fist my cock and pump the irritation away. The water beats down on my tight shoulders. I've been too tense ever since I set foot in the US.

She looks at me like I wronged her somehow, and then she suggests we fuck. And I considered it for a moment there. Not that I'd take advantage of an inebriated woman.

Our coexistence is charged without the additional sexual tension, and the last thing we need is the awkwardness of the morning after.

The way she stumbled into my arms.

The way she propositioned me.

And then immediately hesitated, despite the loaded energy coursing between us as we stood in the kitchen for God knows how long.

I wanted to bend her over the counter and punish her for taunting me.

For all her sarcasm and scowling. For clubbing and getting drunk. For not telling me where she went, and with whom. Fuck.

I need to kill the thoughts I have about her, or by the time this fake marriage is over I'll need carpal tunnel surgery.

I grip myself harder and fuck the thoughts of Brook out of my head with my hand. Or that's what I keep telling myself, but as I paint the glass shower wall with white ribbons, it's her name that dies on my lips.

While I get dressed, I listen for any signs of her being awake, but it's only eight o'clock and she'll probably sleep in after last night.

I choose my tie and pocket square, opting for a light green color. Like her eyes. What the fuck?

I throw the garments back into the drawer and pull out a dark blue tie. That's better.

There are so many things I still need to adjust for my new life here.

I need to have my things packed and shipped, or go shopping. I came prepared for a week, not a year.

The only way to survive this will be to avoid each

other. That's what we need to do. I can rent an office in the city. It's not just Brook that tilts my world on its axis. It's this house as well.

I'm staying in a guest room because I can't set foot in my old room. But the ghost of the past is still present everywhere.

Yes, I need to find an office space somewhere near the new club location, and then I can spend my time buried in work.

As I walk down to the kitchen, my phone rings.

"Talk to me, Chloe."

"Have you found the place yet, and when are you coming back?" My business manager dives right into it.

"I should finalize the venue today. I'm about to meet with Cormac Quinn." I drop the phone on the counter in the kitchen and hit the speaker icon, so I can make my coffee.

Thank God Mom has a top end espresso machine, because my taste in coffee couldn't be satisfied on this side of the pond. I make a mental note to have my premier coffee beans shipped from Italy.

"I asked two questions." Chloe has always been very efficient. One of the things I like about her. Not right now, though.

"As we discussed already, I'll be working from here for the time being."

"We didn't discuss. You announced."

Reckless Vow

"I'm your boss."

"So, for years you resolutely declined all ideas of moving the business across the Atlantic, and now you not only decide to expand there, but you're moving there? I thought you were going to scout the location and come back."

I almost want to tell her I got married, just to enjoy her reaction.

"You were the one pestering me about expanding to the US. You bailed out of taking this trip last minute, forcing me to come. You're the reason I'm here. You should be happy."

We've had this conversation several times since I announced my decision to stay and oversee the project here, and she still hopes to fish something more out of me.

"I'm happy, but it's just sudden and weird, and I think you're not telling me something."

Her heels echo through the line, and I can almost see her pacing her office in her smart business suit and stilettos.

Chloe mostly works from our office in Paris where she designed her space to her liking, including the extravagant marble floors. Completely unsuitable for an office, but Chloe loves to surround herself with luxury.

She started working for me as a waitress and

worked her way up fair and square. We may have mixed work and pleasure on an occasion years ago, but we quickly realized our working relationship is too valuable to fuck up with sex.

"Chloe," I warn.

"It's just weird. There are people to schmooze and officials to wine and dine, and I can't get it all done by myself. Find an American manager and come back."

"If I remember correctly, I'm your boss, not the other way around. I got to go now, unless there is a relevant reason you called."

She sighs and gives me an update on a few things she's achieved, a few problems at some of our clubs and the top line business projections.

"You see, you're doing great without me."

"At least you're still an asshole."

I chuckle. "Have a lovely day, Chloe."

I disconnect the call, glad she didn't push further. Because I'm not going to explain myself to her.

I don't understand how I got in this situation myself, so how do I tell someone who knows me well that I got married? On a whim?

Fucking idea of opening the club in New York. My entertainment enterprise has been thriving without me setting foot in America.

My mood is worse than it was when I woke up after tossing and turning for most of the night. The asshole in me whined that I turned Brook down. The noble me just didn't want to argue the point anymore.

Before I leave the house, I call my concierge to start a search for an office in SoHo.

* * *

"So, what do you say?" Cormac Quinn leans against a dark counter in the cavernous space he's trying to sell me on.

"I don't know, Corm, you were talking about a premium waterfront property when we spoke last year. What happened to that?"

I walk around, looking for any signs of problems with the structure, already calculating how fast we can have this place up and running.

It helps that it used to be a nightclub. At least the remodeling won't be that substantial.

This place is perfect for what we need, but I'm not going to show him my enthusiasm. The man is cocky enough.

"I sold it."

"A premium waterfront property? You sold it fast." There is something fishy about that. I don't like not understanding the business moves of my associates.

I don't mind some grayness in my dealings, but when things are inexplicable, it raises red flags.

He grinds his molars while wearing his typical smirk, but my question has caused tension.

I've known Corm Quinn for a few years now. He invested in some of my clubs as a silent partner.

When we finally decided New York needed one of my clubs, I asked Corm to find us a venue. He has properties all over the world, but this is his home turf.

"It wouldn't suit your needs. I sold it to your brother-in-law, Finn van den Linden."

I don't really know Finn, but Corm spits his name with so much venom, I make a mental note to look into Paris's husband.

I look around the space, my mind already seeing the VIP section and the bar on this level. "Why are you not using it for yourself? You have a club in the city. Why would you invite competition?"

"I have another endeavor that is taking up all my time and effort. I don't have time for another club."

"What endeavor?"

"I can't talk about it yet, but soon you'll find out."

"Entertainment industry?"

"No, financial sector."

I raise my eyebrow, but I guess while I know Corm through my clubs, he has other interests.

"Okay. This place should work well, but it will require a lot of renos. The rent is too steep. This is our entry to the US and the club needs to be the best, the most luxurious we can offer, but I want to be careful with my investment."

"What if the price went down by twenty percent?" He crosses his arms over his chest.

Now that would be just plain unbelievable, and raises more red flags. "What's the catch, Corm? And don't waste my time here."

"I thought you were staying around. What's the rush?"

What does he know about me extending my visit? Or the reasons behind it. The fucker rubs me the wrong way today. Or maybe I'm just impatient after not sleeping last night.

"What's the catch?" I rein in my irritation.

"I'd go in with twenty percent."

Now I understand why he offered his help. He's smart. Since he can't develop this space himself, he wants to ensure friendly competition.

"A silent partnership, like in Milan and Prague?" I don't mind sharing the risk. Twenty percent is a good cash infusion for me and little to no influence for him, with a guaranteed income from his investment.

"Maybe I'd like to have some say—"

"No. I don't need your investment. I'm not going to say no to getting your cash, but I'm running the show and making all the decisions."

"You're a control freak, Cassinetti."

"And it's made me billions, Quinn. If you're in with twenty percent, I'm taking this place. Otherwise, I'll go look elsewhere. I'm not in a hurry." I shrug.

"So you're staying longer." He smirks.

Fucker.

I glare.

He shakes his head, chuckling. "There is someone I'd like to be an official spokesperson for this club. Make it happen and you got yourself a deal."

Business-wise, I'd be in a hurry to lock down a building like this one, but then I'm stuck here for a year, so I don't need to rush.

But what the fuck is his angle here? "A spokesperson? Is this your way of getting into someone's pants? A bit desperate, isn't it?"

"Fuck you."

"Okay, indulge me."

"Saar van den Linden. She's practically related to you."

"The model?" I frown.

It only occurs to me now the woman shares the last name with my brother-in-law. In Europe she goes by Saar only, and her face is plastered on billboards everywhere.

Corm nods. But his face is unreadable, and I'm not sure if he wants to punish the woman or reward her with this collaboration.

I refrain from rolling my eyes. "Okay, get her on board."

"I was hoping since you have family connections to the van den Lindens—"

"I'm not in a match-making business," I growl, but I want this location locked, so I offer him my hand. "I can see if she is available and interested, but that's as much as I'm willing to do."

"Well, then, you got yourself a deal."

This deal is connecting me to New York in many ways, and with my newly married status, I'm just not sure that's a good thing.

Chapter 12

Brook

"You must admit that his refusal was kind of gallant," Celeste says dreamily.

"I can't believe you still believe in romance." Saar laughs and stuffs her mouth with a handful of popcorn.

"I can't believe someone scarred you so badly that you don't. Who was that club owner, anyway?"

I felt so shitty, and not only due to my hangover, that I invited my friends over to help me sort through the bitter aftertaste of Baldo's rejection.

"Just someone I used to know, but it turns out he isn't worth the trouble."

"No second chance for you?" I tease with sarcasm.

"Oh, because it's going so well for you. You're a glowing endorsement for second chances."

"And fake marriages." I sigh.

"Sorry, baby, I didn't mean to be a bitch." She sends me an air kiss from her seat.

We are lounging on the back patio, with iced teas and snacks on the table. The weather is gracing us with lovely temperatures, so we're taking advantage of it.

"Yes, you did." I pout.

"Stop whining, both of you," Celeste says. "You're gorgeous, smart women. You don't need second chances, you just need one right chance at true love."

Saar makes a gagging sound and I giggle. Once upon a time, I thought Baldo was my true love. I know better now.

The door swooshes open as if I summoned the man with my thoughts. For some reason my face heats, and I quickly snatch my glass from the table.

This is what things have come to. I need to reset myself to find my groove around the man. Okay, I haven't seen him since my theatrics last night, so perhaps the embarrassment is well grounded.

He's wearing a suit with a navy tie and pocket square, an arresting confidence and a grin that doesn't reach his eyes.

Celeste jumps up from her chair. "Oh my, is this your husband?" She smiles and extends her hand. "I'm Celeste Delacroix."

He kisses her hand instead of shaking it. "Baldo Cassinetti. Nice to meet you."

"Saar van den Linden." My friend bats her lashes and stands up to get her hand kissed.

"You're Saar?" He frowns, but his question doesn't sound like he recognizes the famous model. "Hm." He shakes his head and then smiles. "Good to know."

And then he throws me off when he leans in to kiss my temple. "Have you behaved, darling?" He squeezes my shoulder.

I snort. "They're my best friends—they know."

At that, he drops his hand and nods to Celeste and Saar with his blinding, sincere smile. One that he doesn't give me before he leaves.

"Oh my God, he's hot. Like super-hot," Saar mouths.

"Cool down, you can have him in twelve months."

And while I throw the idea out there, the possibility squeezes at my stomach and spreads bitterness in my mouth.

She laughs. "You're such a good friend. I might be desperate, but not enough to grab your leftovers."

We move the conversation to other, inconsequential topics for a bit before I walk them out.

After shutting the door behind them, I hesitate at the base of the stairs. A part of me wants to go hide in my room, but I also want to face Baldo to see where we stand.

Why is it so awkward to be around him? *Because you got drunk and propositioned him.* Okay, I better address the disaster head on.

I find him in the library, sitting behind Mom's large desk by the picture window, opening his laptop.

"Your friends left?"

"Yes. What are you doing?"

"I'm going to set up here." He looks at me. "If you don't mind. I'm assuming you haven't been using this office?"

Because I don't work? "And why would you assume that?" I spit out.

Fighting wasn't the reason I came in here, but somehow I always find myself throwing verbal punches around this man.

"Because it's Mom's office and she only left a few days ago. Did you plan on using it?"

"No." I stand there and fidget while he ignores me. "I'll be upstairs."

Not sure why I feel the need to share that. It's not like we owe each other our whereabouts.

"Hold on." He gets a box from his briefcase and hands it to me. "I got you a new phone. Your old one is canceled and all data transferred to this one."

I stare at the box. "How?"

"I have people."

My heart speeds up. Another gesture to throw me off kilter. "Thank you."

"I got your old number ported to this, so you wouldn't miss any calls."

It's sad that I don't remember the last time someone did anything thoughtful for me.

Or what to do with the fact that this phone isn't the first, nor the only thoughtful thing from him.

Or how to accept it in light of his rejection last night.

"Thank you," I repeat.

He shrugs. "It's just a phone, sis."

Sis? Fuck him.

* * *

The next several days pass in a blur of work and tension. For the most part, we avoid each other.

I bury myself in my latest manuscript. Baldo is out of the house more than he's here, and when he is home he stays out of my way.

I can't decide how I feel about it. His distance is for the best, I try to argue with myself.

And yet, it's like getting a dose of rejection every single day. It seeps through my veins, poisoning me with foul feelings. And a bit of self-pity.

I hate all of it.

My latest book will feature an unprecedented amount of murder. And a lot of sibling hate.

Perched on my bed, I type away to finish the chapter. I'm hungry, but I don't want to go downstairs because I heard Baldo come home earlier.

As I finally reach a cliffhanger that satisfies me, I call it quits for the day. I save my work and create several backups.

Putting my laptop on the floor, I slide on to my back and stare at the ceiling. We have been married for a week. That leaves us with another fifty-one.

My phone pings with a message.

> **SYD**
> Vegas was amazing. We needed to get away.
>
> **LO**
> And elope (laughing emoji)
>
> **PARIS**
> Don't call it that, Lo.
>
> **LO**
> (eye-roll emoji)
>
> How is the honeymoon, Brook? (laughing emoji)
>
> Fuck off, a few more days and it might end in bloodshed.

> **PARIS**
> Play nice, Brook, it's for a good cause.
>
> **SYD**
> Not too nice. I'm still weirded out you married our brother.
>
> > Stepbrother
>
> **LO**
> Let's hope you don't get pregnant.
>
> **PARIS**
> (laughing emoji)
>
> **SYDNEY**
> (laughing emoji)
>
> > Refer to my earlier fuck off.

I drop the phone and consider calling Saar and Celeste. A dinner in town would be nice.

Normally I don't mind being cooped up while I'm working on my first draft, but with my housemate trailing the scent of coffee and *him* everywhere he goes, I need to get out more.

My phone sounds again and I answer without thinking.

"Brook speaking."

"Finally," the voice I really didn't miss drawls on the other side. "I thought you were screening my calls, baby doll."

"What do you want, Dylan?"

"Don't be so cold, doll. How are you?"

"I'm hanging up now."

"Okay, okay, just hear me out, please. Don't you miss me?"

"Like one misses hot coals in their ass."

He laughs. "You were always so funny, doll. I'm calling because my agent is trying to get me an audition in this pilot, and it seems like that bloke John Carver is involved. Isn't he your friend?"

John is my agent, but Dylan doesn't know that because he believes, like everybody else, that I'm just a rich socialite.

It says something about our relationship that we dated for three years and I never told him what I do.

But that was the least of our problems.

"Are you seriously calling in a favor, Dylan?"

"Baby doll, you skipped town so quickly we didn't sort out our last fight. When are you coming back, by the way? I miss you."

"You miss my bank account, and right now my connections."

"Don't be a bitch about it." His temper flares up. In his case, it never takes long.

"Fuck you. Don't call me again." I hang up.

While I recognize he's an ocean away, the memories of his tantrums rush through me and my body shakes despite my best efforts.

Suddenly feeling the need for some companionship, I dash out of the room and knock on Baldo's door.

I have a lot of my mental health issues under control, but I can't call my therapist every time something spooks me.

Besides, it's the middle of the night in England. It didn't stop Dylan, apparently.

When Baldo doesn't answer, I go downstairs. Light is coming from the library, so I veer that way.

I pause at the sight of Baldo seated at the table. He looks like he walked off the cover of a magazine, but what's new? Just seeing him calms me.

When we dance around each other in this house, it's easy to avoid looking at him. Lit only by the dim light of the desk lamp, his face looks relaxed.

His features, usually set in granite, are softer. Which is at odds with the sleek, metallic sheen of the gun he's cleaning.

The image is oddly captivating. I've written scenes like this countless times, but witnessing it in reality sends a shiver of intrigue down my spine. Especially when the main protagonist is Baldo.

"What are you doing?"

We've barely spoken since our wedding, and this is what I ask? Way to go, Brook.

His eyes lift to look at me. It's eerie as his whole body barely moves. "Cleaning my gun." He returns his focus to his activity.

I cross the large library, my feet sinking into the soft carpet, and stop across from him.

"What's that, a Glock 19?" My curiosity is piqued.

Baldo looks up, his eyebrows raising. "Yes, it is. I didn't take you for a gun enthusiast."

I shrug, moving closer to get a better look. "Just interested."

He chuckles, laying out the disassembled parts neatly on the cloth. "Know much about Glocks?"

"Favored for their reliability, they are lightweight, compact, with a good magazine capacity. It's the preferred choice for many law enforcement agencies." I recite the facts as if reading from a research folder.

"Correct."

I move around and watch him clean the barrel over his shoulder. "It's striker-fired, which is part of its reliability. No hammer to worry about."

He smirks and assembles the gun. Picking up the barrel, he holds it toward me. "Ever held one?"

I shake my head.

His tone is teasing, but his eyes are serious. "Feel the weight."

He stands up, that distinct musk of him invading

all my senses. I don't look at the gun between us, I stare into his eyes.

If I'm honest, I'm desperately seeking any sign that he's as affected by me as I am by him.

But he maintains a perfect poker face, bar the smirk challenging me to hold the gun. Like it's some sort of test. Or a metaphor. Here I am overthinking again.

Though it's hard to scramble a decent thought together when all my energy is consumed by his closeness. By my ragged breathing. By my pounding heartbeat. By my need to squeeze my thighs together.

"Why do you own a gun?" The words come out broken, struggling to get past the lump in my throat.

Why am I this affected by him? Why isn't he affected at all? I guess I really am only a sibling to him.

"Why do you know so much about guns?"

It feels like a challenge, like he's daring me to share a part of me. Am I ready to tell him about my secret career? It's the easiest of my secrets to unravel.

I want to tell the boy I used to love, but I don't want to share with the man who calls me sis. The rest of my family doesn't know.

Avoiding the question, I take the Glock from him. It's heavier than I expected.

"Are you sure you trust me with a gun around

you?" I know it isn't loaded, but the weight of it in my hands gives me a weird sense of power.

He licks his lip, and now I'm thinking about kissing him.

Tucking a strand of hair behind my ear, he smirks. "When it comes to trusting you, Brook, the jury is still out."

He traces the outline of my jaw with his hand and I lean into his palm, starved for his touch. My whole body comes alive under his caress.

Goosebumps spread across my skin. Heat burns in my lower belly. I'm having a really hard time breathing.

He looks at me with hunger and something akin to adoration, but I'm sure that's just wishful thinking.

Regardless, my body thrums with the need to be held. To be loved. To be owned by this man.

With a primal need for the second chance we never got. Perhaps it's just a need for closure, but it's visceral and relentless.

A whimper or a sigh escapes me, my lungs crying for oxygen.

The room is too hot. The gun is too heavy. The man is too dangerous.

But he's going to kiss me, and I part my lips to invite him.

Instead, Baldo lowers his lips to my ear. He puts

his hand on my hip, like he senses I might need the support because my knees are giving in.

"It's not an empty gun you'd hurt me with."

I shudder. At his words. At the unrequited desire. At the loss of... I don't even know what. I jerk away from him.

He is right. About our mutual lack of trust, and about our ability to hurt each other.

His words already hurt worse than a gunshot.

Chapter 13

Baldo

"Okay, Chloe, calm down. I'll take care of the mayor in Rome."

Fuck, living in the States is turning into a nightmare.

And not only because my business dealings are on occasions challenging over teleconference.

The biggest part of my current nightmare is living under one roof with Brook, jerking off to fantasies of her every night.

I fucking called her *sis*, just to put distance between us. It worked somewhat, but we can't sustain this for a year.

And the hurt in her eyes when I spat the word has been haunting me since then.

"You say that, but how are we going to have a discreet conversation about our liquor license over the phone? You know there is no way we can get it renewed the official way. Not in Rome."

"I said I'll take care of it," I snap.

"Someone is testy this morning."

"That would be you, darling."

Right then, Brook enters the kitchen and stops in her tracks.

"I got to go." I hang up.

I have no reason to feel guilty about calling Chloe darling, especially since it was sarcastic.

And Brook has no right to assume there are no darlings in my life.

Those are facts.

They have nothing to do with the annoyingly unpleasant feeling in my chest. Like I got caught doing something wrong. Or hurting her.

Brook glowers. "Good morning, *bro*."

Fuck. My. Life.

"You seem all sunshine this morning," I quip.

"No thanks to you."

She pushes around me to pour herself a coffee.

We both move at the same time and end up so close to each other that I can feel the heat radiating from her.

Moving to the side, we choose the same direction and end up pressed against each other again.

The coffee gurgles behind us. The birds chirp

outside. The vacuum is running upstairs where the housekeeper is trying to do her job.

Brook licks her lips, and my mind immediately imagines her mouth wrapped around my cock.

Even though she's glowering.

This dance we're trying to master is completely off, failing to follow any rhythm. And we're certainly not going to improve it unless we either fuck to release the sexual tension or find a larger house where we can avoid each other for the entire year.

The former has the potential to explode in our faces. The latter is stupid because even if I don't run into her, I will still know—my cock will still know—that she is around.

She raises her eyebrow, and I realize I'm still staring at her full lips.

It's been ten years and I remember their exact flavor. Having her this close makes all the memories rush back... some of them disturbing my composure, some of them just rushing straight to my groin.

The doorbell saves me from doing something I'd regret, because sometime in the last few days my dick has won control over my brain when I'm around her.

She frowns and pushes around me. "Are you expecting someone?"

I follow her, the hydraulic hiss coming from outside reminding me of my expected delivery.

Brook opens the front door, then snaps her head around to me. "What's that?"

"A tow truck."

The truck's winch groans as my favorite car is slowly lowered, its tires making a soft thud when they touch the pavement.

"On the truck." She huffs with exasperation.

"Maserati GranTurismo."

"Whose?"

"Mine, obviously."

"You bought a car?"

"I didn't buy it. I had it shipped from home."

Yeah, instead of shipping my clothes and other things I might actually need, I shipped something I want.

At least with my car, I'm in control.

"Whatever for? It's New York. You don't need a car."

"I need something enjoyable in my life. Especially since I'm stuck here for a year, sis."

Why I'm being such an asshole to her is beyond me. Yes, I need to protect myself from her siren song—one she doesn't even know she's singing—but I'm going above and beyond.

Am I proud of the way I've been treating her? No. But what's the alternative here?

I can think of one, but aside from her drunken

proposition the night of our wedding, I don't think she wants to venture down that road.

And I shouldn't want that either, because there is no way we would survive it unscathed.

"Yeah, I can see how only an overpriced pile of metal would put up with your charming personality, bro."

She pivots and marches away. I sign off on the car delivery, itching to take the car for a spin, but first things first. Let's behave like an adult.

I find Brook in the kitchen. "Do you want to go for a ride?"

Do you want to go for a ride? A dick-controlled brain, for sure.

She arches her eyebrow. "It's hard enough to share this large space with you. I'm not getting into the confines of your beloved car."

She leans against the counter, hiding her face behind the coffee mug. "But out of curiosity, what caused this peace offering?"

"I find the barking less than productive. Especially if it's going to last for a year." I shrug.

She sighs. "A year is a long time."

"And we're stuck together." *Come on, Brook, meet me halfway. Or in my bed.*

She lets out another sigh, loaded with resignation. Not my preferred way to charm a woman, but this relationship isn't ordinary, so I'll take her reluctant surrender.

"I'm busy this morning, but Saar and I are planning to go out tonight if you want to join us."

Checking out the competition might not be the worst way to spend my night.

"I have a gala to attend... Actually, it would be a great opportunity to snap a few pics as proof for Rupert. Why don't you and Saar join me, and we can go out after?"

Corm insisted we schmooze at this thing, to rub shoulders with local politicians and motivate speedy permit applications. And since he's so keen on getting Saar involved, I might just kill two birds.

"That sounds like a date. Send me the details, bro."

She saunters away and I regret ever calling her sis. What the fuck am I going to do with this woman?

* * *

"It's so nice to see you, Baldo." Gina, my oldest brother Massi's wife, gives me a hug. "The last time I saw you, you were like ten. God, you make me feel old."

"So Gio was right. You really are in New York." Massi pats my shoulder.

I didn't expect to run into my family at this event. I should have. Massi owns a restaurant and he's a Michelin-starred chef, so of course he is here. To network, like me.

"I heard what you did for Brook. That's quite a commitment. I can't believe Roberta Montgomery would do such a thing," Gina says.

"Though it's weird to marry your sister, even if it's just to stick it to the old witch." Massi makes a face of disgust.

Gina rolls her eyes. "It's not like they are blood relatives."

"I'm opening a club here in New York, so I guess I could make myself useful to the family." And suffer for a year.

"You should come for dinner soon. And we should get together with Gio and Andrea. It would be nice to catch up." Massi wraps his arm around Gina.

Those two first got married so young, and they got their second chance seventeen years later.

Is there a second chance for me and Brook? According to Massi's disgusted face, even if we overcome all the barriers we've built between us, we still would face an uphill battle with the family.

I've just returned and not even had a chance to rekindle my practically non-existent relationship with my parents and my siblings. I guess I couldn't care less about their opinions.

But Brook always wanted their approval. Having

lived away for so long, she's probably happy to finally fit in.

Our second chance would destroy her second chance with the family.

Why am I even thinking about it?

"We should get together. It's long overdue," I respond to Massi.

"It's really good to see you, bro."

My eyes keep darting to the entrance of this large, opulent banquet hall. Where is she?

Saar saunters in. She's dressed to the nines in a deep brown gown that makes most of the people in the room turn their heads. No wonder she is one of the highest paid models in the world.

I couldn't care less about the dress, because I'm focused on the fact that she's alone.

"Excuse me." I nod to my brother.

"No problem. We both need to mingle. Talk to you later, Baldo."

Gina sends me an air kiss, then I make my way through the floor full of tuxedos, gowns, clinking glasses and hushed conversation.

"Where is Brook?" I snap at Saar instead of a greeting.

"Hello to you too, jerk." She rolls her eyes.

I groan inwardly. "Pardon my manners, Saar, good

evening to you." Sarcasm laces my voice. "Where is Brook?"

"At home—" Whatever else she was going to say dies on her lips. "What the hell?"

"Saar." Corm appears by my side. "Nice to see you."

"I don't share the sentiment." She gives him a venomous look that probably turned most of the liquor here sour.

"You look ravishing." The fucker smirks at her, completely unaffected.

"If I knew you'd be here, I'd have stayed home. Oh wait, I can still leave." She smiles, this time with an equal amount of poison and honey.

She turns, but I grip her arm. "Leave if you want—"

"No, she should stay," Corm interrupts.

I shoot him a warning look. I'm not fucking interested in whatever sordid foreplay these two are having in front of me.

"It's a free country, Cormac, and I'm choosing not to spend time in the same room as you."

"You owe me a dance," he drawls.

She laughs.

"Okay, kids, as much as your verbal sparring is riveting, where the fuck is Brook?"

Saar snaps her eyes to me. "She is sick."

"Let's talk," Corm says to Saar, who steps back and looks at him with disgust.

"Sick?" All the hair stands up on my nape.

"Yeah, she got food poisoning or some bug. She tried to call you, but you didn't answer."

I turn to Corm. "I got to go."

"Me too," Saar adds.

"What the fuck, Baldo? I was going to introduce you to several people. People you must meet if you want to be taken seriously in this city."

"Next time." I turn and leave, tuning out his and Saar's protests.

It takes me an ungodly amount of time to get to Riverdale while I try to call Brook several times and keep getting pushed to voice mail.

God, I hope she's okay. I rush out of the town car without saying good-bye. The driver has been driving me for a week, so he should be used to my moods by now.

"Brook," I call as I enter the house.

The light is on in the kitchen, but I head toward the staircase. Taking two steps at a time, I barrel through the long hallway and barge into her room.

"Brook."

Her bed sheets are crumpled, but she's not there. A whimper comes from her en-suite bathroom.

"Brook, can I come in?"

She groans, and the sound hits me in the solar plexus.

Fuck it. "Brook, I'm coming in." I push the door open.

She's in the fetal position on the floor by the toilet. I squat next to her.

"Baby, let me help you to your bed."

Damp strands of hair are glued to her face. Even the T-shirt she's wearing is sticking to her glistening skin. I try to scoop her up.

She pushes me away. "Oh God." She scrambles to her knees and practically shoves her head into the toilet, gagging and then retching.

Fuck. I gather her hair and hold it while she heaves, stroking her back. She empties her stomach, but her body keeps convulsing with dry heaves.

A wave of helplessness and an overwhelming need to switch places with her constricts my lungs.

"I'm calling a doctor."

She raises her arm and wiggles her index finger. "It's food poisoning," she protests, sitting on her haunches.

Pale, distraught and ill, she smiles at me. It's a weak smile, but I swear this is the first glimpse of a genuine smile I've seen since I returned.

It hits me in my chest with a mix of emotions I don't want to contemplate.

We stare at each other, and despite the circumstances a sense of calm and peace descends on us. I don't know what caused it, but it feels like we've buried the hatchet.

She leans into me with a sigh. "You came."

Chapter 14

Brook

Did he come back for me?

Not that it in any way redeems him for the time when he didn't come, but tired, nauseated me is relieved he's here now.

Even though I don't want him to see me like this. God, I must look like a mess. And still, the way he's looking at me feels like he cares.

Like I'm not alone.

"Of course I came. Sorry, my phone was off." He scoops me up. "Let's get you to bed."

I put my head on his chest and let him carry me. I've been puking my guts out since lunch. I guess eating yesterday's takeout wasn't in my best interests.

"I feel like shit."

"You don't say." He sits me on my bed, and I immediately drop to my side.

He disappears into the bathroom and gets me a glass of water. "Take only small sips. I'm going to check Mom's medicine cabinet to see if I can get you something to hydrate you."

I close my eyes.

I shiver and squint. The house is silent and the light is dimmer. Did I fall asleep? Baldo carried me to my bed and then went somewhere... but now I'm covered.

Another wave of shivers runs through me, and I whimper, disoriented.

"I've got a bucket here for you." His voice is like medicine, lacing my insides with a security blanket.

For years, every time I got sick, I was all alone. I wasn't close enough with any of my so-called friends to call them when I fell ill.

My family was across the ocean. And my boyfriends? Well, they certainly didn't stick around for the *for worse or in sickness* parts of the relationship.

Baldo sits at the foot of the bed. He changed clothes. His biceps are bulging from his long-sleeved black T-shirt.

"Did I fall asleep?"

"You dozed off for ten minutes. Do you need to...?" He gestures to the floor.

I follow his gaze, and sure enough, he did prepare a bucket for me. "No, I think I got it all out. I feel like a steam roller ran over me. I'm sure I look like it." I groan.

"You always look beautiful to me." He runs his hand over my ankle. Even through the blanket, it sends shudders through my body.

You always look beautiful to me. I don't know how to digest his words. And not only because my digestion is seriously impaired now.

"Even when I cut my hair in middle school?"

He snorts. "God, you looked like a wet sparrow."

I giggle weakly. "What was I thinking?" I shiver.

"You need to change that sweaty T-shirt before you're strong enough to shower." He stands up and walks to my closet. I follow him with my heavy gaze.

You always look beautiful to me. Even in my poor state, the confession tugs at my heart.

"What is this?"

I blink to focus on his line of vision. My red strapless dress, with a slit down the entire length of the body-hugging skirt, hangs by the door.

"It's the dress I didn't get to wear tonight."

"Thank God," he mutters.

"You don't like it?" I'd be offended if I wasn't sick.

"If you think I would let you wear that to parade in front of other men, you're wrong."

I giggle. "Choosing my wardrobe for me now?"

He makes a sound deep in his throat like I'm a pain

in his ass, but somehow this little display of possessiveness negates his brooding.

He returns with one of my T-shirts. I try to push to a sitting position but collapse back on to the bed. "I'll change a bit later."

"You can't stay in your sweaty shirt. Let me help you."

"No."

Somehow the idea of him seeing me naked propels me to action and I sit up suddenly. My head swims and I gag.

"Christ." The mattress dips and Baldo's arms wrap around me. "Are you okay? I promise I won't look." He grabs the hem of my shirt.

"I'll do it." I try to find urgency in my weak state.

It's not that I'm a prude, but I'm not ready to face certain things that would require explanation.

He stills for a moment, probably done with me and my weird reactions. "Okay, I'm letting go and turning around to give you privacy, but if you faint on me, I'll be pissed."

I didn't even realize how heavily I was leaning on him. "That's kind of hot."

"You're delirious." He stands up and waits for a moment to see if I can sit by myself.

My brain swims, but only slightly.

When he sees I'm strong enough to sit, he turns around. "Hurry up."

I switch the shirts and drop back onto my pillows, pulling the covers with me. "I'm decent."

He nods, takes my glass and goes to the bathroom. "Mom had electrolyte powder. Let's try to get some in you."

He comes back holding the same glass, but the water in it is pink now and there is a straw in the drink. He helps me to take a few sips and puts the glass on the nightstand before returning to his spot at the foot of my bed, leaning against the brass footboard.

"Thank you," I whisper.

"It's okay. Let's hope the worst is over."

"Not just for this, but for staying in New York for me. Helping me with the inheritance nonsense."

His lips curve up slightly. He puts his hand on my ankle again but doesn't move it anymore.

It anchors me somehow, in this strange bond we are forging and fighting at the same time.

"There were times I imagined seeing you again, but I never thought it would be under these circumstances. Your grandmother had a sick way of showing love."

There were times I imagined seeing you again. So many times. And here we are acting like we never wished for it.

"She messed with our lives, did I tell you that?"

He shakes his head, and I recount what we learned from Rupert about Roberta's meddling.

"Wow, I guess buying you a Christmas present was too ordinary for the old lady."

"Right?" I chuckle. "But she got me thinking about my life. Like if I didn't get into the writing program on my own merit—"

"Stop it right now. Doubting your achievements is counterproductive."

"Oh, but I'm the queen of self-doubt."

"That's not the crown you should wear."

"You never doubt yourself?"

"Not really."

"That must be nice."

"I'm not saying I have no irrational blocks driving my life. I guess I've just accepted them, and I've learned to dance with my limitations."

Unlike me. I dance to outrun mine.

"Don't overthink it. Roberta might have influenced your admission, but she didn't write your assignments. If you were a mediocre writer, you wouldn't have finished with honors."

That startles me. "How do you know that I finished with honors?"

Something passes through his face, but it's gone

before I can recognize it. He shrugs. "I just assumed. Of course you were one of the best in your class."

A part of me wants to push him, to understand what felt like a slip on his part, but I'm too weak and tired to fight him. Besides, I'm enjoying this fluid coexistence that reminds me of the times we were truly close.

"You're full of compliments tonight. I should get sick more often."

"God, no."

"Can you give me another sip? I think I can keep it in."

He moves up the bed and holds the straw to my lips. After he places the glass back, he brushes my hair from my forehead. His fingers linger, and neither of us moves.

I wish I could tell him more about me, ask him more about him.

Tell him about that night.

Ask him about that night.

Fill in the blanks and find some sort of liberation from the past wounds.

His feather-like touch melts my insides, making my pulse spike. How is it that even in my depleted state, he can still ignite a spark?

But the fear that the truth would break us apart

prevails, pushing me toward my typical MO—avoid at all costs.

"Would you stay with me?"

"I married you, didn't I?" He wiggles his eyebrows.

I think he knows I was referring to tonight, begging him to fill the loneliness, but his commitment, even in jest, feels somehow significant.

"Scoot over." He lifts the blanket and slides in beside me.

He snakes his hand under me and rolls me on top of him. I tense, the feel of his solid body awakening every dormant cell in me. What's going on?

"Relax, Brook." He slides me to the other side of him. "Let's keep you on this side, near the bucket."

He manhandles me on to my side, so my back is to his chest, and covers us both. He's not exactly spooning me, but being this close to him gets my mind firing in all different directions.

Well, one direction really. My body is fully awake after grazing across his, feeling every dip and valley of his amazing anatomy. And the package. Holy shit.

For some outlandish reason, my mind goes to this morning, and as much as I told myself to ignore it, I can't. "Who is your darling?"

He makes a sound, like a snort or a disbelieving huff, I'm not sure. Not really the way to alleviate my insecurities.

"Good night, Brook."

Shit. Why am I seeking reassurance? It's not like we're in a committed, monogamous relationship. I can't expect that there are no women in his life.

Women would be acceptable, understandable, but if there is *a* woman... Does she know he married me? That he's here with me? I focus on that last thought.

He's here with me. He left the gala to care for me.

There is no way I can sleep now. I'm still tingly from the way he slid me across his body earlier. My mind is... confused, filled with feelings I don't want to feel, and those I don't understand.

* * *

A heavy weight is pushing me to the mattress and I'm so hot. Burning. I fidget under the burden, and a groan makes me look to my side.

Baldo's arm is heavy across my chest, our legs tangled together. His face is relaxed, peaceful. It's so outlandish to see him like that. He looks younger, like the boy who used to kiss me senseless in this bed.

He stirs a bit and I hold my breath. I don't want him to wake up yet. I want to enjoy this while it lasts.

For sure, once he opens his eyes, we'll find a way to spoil this rare moment of belonging.

He fidgets again, his hand instinctively finding my breast, cupping it. Okay then.

And is that...?

His hardness digs into my hip. Well, good morning to me.

Baldo flicks his finger back and forth over my nipple, and it salutes him eagerly. I stifle a moan and hold my breath.

"How are you feeling?" he rasps.

His eyes are still closed, but he doesn't stop his gentle grazing.

"I think I'm hungry, so that's a good sign."

"Give me a minute." His sleepy voice spreads through my chest and between my legs. "I'll make you some toast."

I squeeze my thighs together. Does he know he's playing with my nipple? And why am I so hypersensitive to his soft touch? I didn't even know I had erogenous zones around my breasts.

But then my body has been betraying me for years.

As if last night shifted something between us, Baldo kisses my temple, and while it's not a lustful display, it certainly doesn't feel brotherly.

"Okay, sweetheart, you really need to shower and brush your teeth."

I groan, covering my face with my hands, and

Baldo chuckles. He jumps out of bed and uses the bathroom.

"Don't move until I get you something to eat, and more electrolytes. I don't want you to faint in the shower."

Still mortified, I don't look at him, just hum something unintelligible, hoping somewhere on the way to the kitchen he'll lose his memory.

"Brook." His voice comes from the door, and I peek at him with one eye. "I'm glad you feel better."

I cover my eyes with my forearm and groan.

Was I hoping to sleep with Baldo? Ever since he entered the kitchen a couple of weeks ago, if I'm being honest. Despite my better judgment.

Was this the scenario I envisioned? Definitely not.

But here we are, and other than the embarrassing morning breath and sweaty skin, somehow this was better than any alternative.

But something tells me this is only a temporary ceasefire, not a peace treaty.

Chapter 15

Baldo

The music blares like there are at least two amplifiers booming in the house. Are we hosting a concert?

I drop my briefcase in the kitchen and glimpse movement in the sitting room. Through the open double door, I watch the performance.

Brook dances, gliding around the room and jumping up and down.

She props herself on her hands on the sofa and arches her back, throwing her head back, her hair cascading down.

She's really flexible. And now I'm thinking about the ways that flexibility could come in handy, and my cock stirs.

But before I can entertain all the things I could do

with her while she's propped up like that, she springs to her feet and glides to the side.

She looks so carefree and liberated that I catch myself smiling as I lean against the door frame and watch her.

The first time I caught her dancing, she had the music in her ears, so I couldn't appreciate how attuned she is to the rhythm.

I'm assuming the song then was sensual. Right now she is rocking to some serious heavy metal.

And fuck, she's adorable.

Until she notices me, and her peaceful expression turns into a scowl. She leaps to turn the music off.

"Seriously, you need to stop doing this."

"Doing what?" A smile tugs at the corners of my lips.

"Spooking me like this."

"Okay." I shrug.

"Okay?" she huffs, exasperated, panting after her performance.

"You're an excellent dancer."

My eyes trail her body clad in leggings and a tank top. Maybe I should buy her a new wardrobe that consists of oversize shirts that won't show her curves and skin.

"What?" She narrows her eyebrows.

She doesn't move from her spot beside the sofa, and I remain in the doorway.

It's like we're suspended in this territory where we dance around—pun intended—our unresolved feelings from the past, not knowing how to move forward.

"You look much better."

She smiles and walks to the kitchen. "You don't look too bad yourself." She gets a glass and fills it at the fridge door.

After gulping it down, she dons mitts and pulls a dish out of the oven, then rises onto her toes to grab plates from an upper cabinet.

"So how was your day?" She gestures to a seat at the corner of the island and sets the dinner there.

I frown. When I left her this morning, she ate a piece of toast and was feeling much better. But I still left on an awkward note, the night before lingering.

I didn't want to leave her alone, but I had to smooth things over with Corm after I bailed on the event.

Despite our bonding last night, and my realization that if something happened to her I wouldn't survive, I was dreading my return home.

It's like the distance helped me regain my control, and every fiber in me knew I'd lose it again the minute I saw her.

"What are you doing?"

"Serving you dinner." Brook bites her bottom lip, grinning. "Being a good wife."

Wife. Fuck me. Everything she does turns me on.

I prowl toward her. "Careful there, sweetheart. If you were my wife for real, I'd fuck you before dinner. And after it as well."

Brook tenses, but her eyes lock with mine, full of fire. She swallows and licks her lips and, fuck, if my cock doesn't feel it.

Yeah, I went there. And my dick is all too happy about that.

That regained control was just a pipe dream I keep stubbornly trying to fool myself into.

"But thank you for asking, my day was decent enough. It's a bit better now." I wink, and a flush spreads over her face. She's adorable.

"Aren't you romantic?" She ladles some sort of casserole onto my plate.

"Just being a good husband."

I try to hide my smirk. God, I enjoy teasing her a bit more than is healthy for this fragile relationship.

We eat in silence for a moment, but in the absence of the conversation I keep thinking about her lips, her body, those dance moves, and everything in between that turns me on.

Brook practically vibrates with energy, but I'm not sure if it's temptation or irritation.

That would sum up our current relationship. Equally tempting and irritating.

There is no question one of these feelings will dominate and explode soon. The question is, will we kill each other or fuck our brains out?

"How was your day?" I mimic her earlier question, desperately looking for some common ground.

"Fine."

She puts the fork into her mouth. And now I'm thinking about other things that would fit into her mouth, and no way can I stand up without her noticing the tent in my pants.

"What did you do?"

"The usual."

"So just sitting around and scowling?"

If she wants people to believe she lives off of her trust fund, I'll play along. Though I don't understand why she chooses to live like that, I'm not one to judge.

"You're hilarious." She rolls her eyes.

The energy between us is charged, as usual, but I'm not sure what she expects.

Did she cook to thank me for last night? Not that I needed or expected it. Because we're not that let's-have-a-dinner couple.

Fuck, we're not even a couple. I wish we could just have a meal without me searching for an ulterior motive.

"Sorry, let's rewind," I say. "I had a good day. My plans for the club here are moving forward."

"Do you have other clubs?"

"Yes, I have several across major cities in Europe, along with other entertainment businesses in Asia."

"Entertainment businesses? Like what? Karaoke bars? Those are popular in Asia, right?"

"Yeah, they probably are, but I own sex clubs there."

Her fork freezes on the way to her mouth, and I brace for her judgment. But instead she perks up. "Like strip clubs?"

"That's part of the services we offer, yes."

"Will you take me?"

I blink. Out of all the things she could have said, I did not see that coming. "No."

She pouts. "Why not? I've never been to a sex club."

And thank God for that. Yes, I'm a hypocrite. "They're geared toward a male clientele."

Over my dead body would I let her in that space full of horny men.

She rolls her eyes. "That's old-fashioned, but it's not like I want to pay for a lap dance. I just want to see how they look and work. Research, you know."

"Research?" I quirk an eyebrow.

"Okay, forget about it. Does Mom know you're a pimp?"

I almost choke. Coughing, I pound my fist on my chest. "What the fuck, Brook? I'm not a pimp. I provide a safe environment for sexual services."

She laughs. "I'm just messing with you. How did you get into that career?"

She tenses, probably realizing, at the same time as me, how this question hovers on the territory of our past. Of what happened after that night.

"I didn't plan on it, really. My first nightclub was an investment into an existing place in Rome. It happened by a lucky coincidence. The owner was on the plane with me, and we talked, and I ended up working for him at first. I won my first club in Asia at poker."

She widens her eyes. "You're kidding."

"I'm not. I won it fair and square, and since the business was thriving, I expanded it to other cities."

She cocks her head, a soft smile lighting up her face. "You enjoy what you do."

"It makes me a shitload of money. What's not to like?"

She snorts.

"But yeah, I love it. What about you?"

"As you know, I graduated in creative writing." She

pushes her plate away and I wait, but she says nothing else.

I try to ignore the pinch in my stomach. She doesn't want to share. Doesn't trust me enough to tell me. And can I blame her? Trust isn't something we've had a chance to cultivate.

"And you lived in London until recently?" I want to keep the conversation going.

"At first I stayed in Oxford where I studied, but I dated one of my professors, and... well, let's just say I moved after he didn't want to accept that we were over."

What a prick. But I'm unreasonably pleased she ended the affair.

"I returned here to help Paris. She came to see me when she was going through a rough patch with Finn, and I flew back with her. Long story short, I stayed because of Dad and everyone else, I think. It was so nice to be a part of the family again."

I know what she means. A similar feeling overwhelmed me that night I first arrived, after being away for years.

"And I guess partially because I was in a toxic relationship, so you could say I used the opportunity to run away." She sighs, the load of her life weighing her down.

Hearing her talk about the assholes she dated curls my hands into fists.

This marriage is certainly an unplanned complication, but I'm glad she was single and desperate to find a husband. Better me than one of the losers she kept around.

"And here we are," I say, taking a sip of wine.

"And here we are." She smiles.

There is a sizeable gap between us still, but last night and this meal has gotten us a bit closer. Maybe we can make this year bearable.

"It's strange to be in this house again like this." She runs her finger around the rim of her glass.

"It is strange."

"I feel like I know you and you're a stranger at the same time. There is so much we don't know about each other."

Why is she going there? What good would come out of it? As if our vows of "in sickness and health, for richer and poorer" didn't unearth emotions that should have been left buried.

"You know pretty much everything about me. I'm a club owner and a pimp." I grin at her. Let's not talk about heavy shit anymore.

But she doesn't smile. She slides from her stool, her thumb by her lips, abusing her cuticles.

The mood shifts between us. I knew tapping into the past would trap us like this. But could we avoid it?

I certainly would like to.

I slide down as well and, unable to help myself, I run my fingers up her arm. If I had even a sliver of self-preservation left, her subtle shudder kills it.

She puts her hands on my chest. Maybe she wants to push me away, but she doesn't.

Or maybe she just needs to anchor herself. Don't we both?

"Would you like some dessert?" she breathes.

I'm not sure if she intends the double meaning or if the innuendo is only in my head—correction, my pants—but by now I should just accept that I lost my mind the night I returned and proposed, so I go with that.

"You're still interested in consummating..." I'm giving her the chance to stop, but fuck, I hope she won't.

She frowns at first and then her eyes widen for a brief moment, but there is heat in them. "You didn't seem interested in the other night."

I step closer and her back hits the stool. She pivots, but now she's cornered, with the counter at her back.

"I didn't want to take advantage of you, but make no mistake, darling wife, there is only one thing I'd like as my dessert."

I lower my mouth to her ear, her scent of summer meadow, and... well, just Brook spreading through me like wildfire, igniting parts of me I didn't remember existed. "Only one thing I've wanted to taste since I kissed you the first time. That one taste I never got. And I think I'm done imagining it."

Her breath hitches. "Baldo," she whispers.

"That's a good start, baby, but I'll need you to scream it."

I hoist her onto the counter.

Our gazes lock. Her eyes mirror the raw hunger I feel, but there is also hesitation in them, or maybe shyness mixed with curiosity.

Is she nervous about this? Based on all the douchebags she dated over the years, I doubt it's a lack of experience that concerns her.

This is the first time we never got before. Perhaps I'm rushing her.

"Once I start, I won't stop. Are you sure about this, Tokyo?"

I don't even feel guilty about manipulating her with the name I used to have for her. She used to hate it openly, but I know she loved it.

Instead of words, she cups the back of my neck and pulls me to her. She wants my lips, but I slide away at the last minute and suck on her neck, then continue licking and biting down to her clavicle.

I can't wait to taste her, but I'm not kissing her.

That's too intimate, too dangerous. Lethal.

I squeeze her breast, and even through the fabric her nipple hardens, responding to me. Brook moans and throws her head back, giving my mouth better access to her cleavage.

My hands glide down her body as I learn her language, attuning myself to her reactions. To the way she sounds when she tenses and when she leans into me, how she shudders and arches.

Slowly I'm learning what makes her feel good.

But I'm too desperate to get to the holy grail to take this as slow as I'd like. There will be more time for that later. I need to taste her.

I hook my fingers in the waistband of her leggings and underwear. "Lift."

It sounded harsh, but she doesn't protest and hoists her hips up. God, what her obedience does to me. Fuck, she is perfect.

I shove both garments down so quickly she gasps and leans back on her elbows, watching me with mischief and desire in her eyes.

"Spread those pretty legs for me, baby."

Her eyes widen and she sits back up, pulling on my belt.

"What makes you think you're in charge here?" I grab her wrists.

She was wide-eyed before, but the shock is so hot now. It's adorable to watch how she fights this for a few beats, her expression morphing from glower to desire, and finally to surrender.

She drops back to her elbows and opens her thighs slowly.

"That's my girl." Without looking yet, I run my hands up her calves and thighs, slowly savoring the feel of her skin.

Her eyes are glued to mine, with anticipation and something else that I can't interpret.

I don't get to delve into it because my eyes drop. "Fuck, Brook, this pussy is prettier than I could have ever imagined." And imagine it I did, a million times over.

"Baldo, you're killing me here," she whimpers.

"That's good." I yank her closer to the edge and lift her legs over my shoulders.

Lowering my nose between her thighs, I take a long breath.

I fantasized about this pussy more than I care to admit, but this first whiff of her... fuck. "You're perfect. Just perfect."

"Baldo, you..." She squirms, as if she wants to recoil from me. "You don't have to—"

"Hush." I kiss her mound and she grunts. "Enjoy the ride, I'll go easy on you this time."

I wink and dive in, finally tasting the woman that belonged to me way before we embarked on this sham of a marriage.

Only she never did.

And still doesn't.

Chapter 16

Brook

His tongue. His breath. His mouth.

Oh, his dirty, filthy, talented mouth.

He nibbles, licks, devours. And my body arches, writhes, comes alive in so many ways that freak me out. Because this is too good. Too intense. Too painfully delicious.

Too much.

Too much.

Too much.

The buildup inside me is so unexpected and novel, I don't know how to handle it. I'm breaking into a million pieces, riding a blissful feeling that is such a new sensation it spooks me.

My heart thumps in my temples, overriding the waves of pleasure. Well, almost.

It's loud.

Deafening.

Unexpected.

I should be enjoying this. My body is savoring it. My mind is running a mile a minute and I can't silence it.

"Stop."

His breath is still hot and so pleasant on me, but the contact is gone. I realize it was me who screamed and I look down.

Baldo frowns at me, confused. He looks so beautiful and sexy with me glistening on his face.

I'm desperate to say something, to explain, but I'm drawing a blank.

And instead of taking charge and dealing with the unexpected brakes I put on his actions, I focus on my own vulnerability.

Spread on the counter like this, I want to trust him. I need to trust him. I should trust him.

I can trust him. I know I can—

He smiles, or smirks, I'm not sure. "You can take it, baby."

You can take it. Those words. Said with a different, kinder voice, but still those words. My body acts before my brain registers.

With my foot, I push at his chest. It catches him off guard and he stumbles back. I jump from the counter and run.

"What the fuck?" It's pure surprise in his voice, but I leave it behind me and dash upstairs to my room.

"Brook." Baldo's voice hits my frayed nerves, and I swallow a sob. "Are you okay?"

I lock my door, the click obscenely loud, and slide to the floor. Taking three deep breaths, I try to parse this unexpected outcome.

A soft knock startles me. Jesus, of course he wants to understand what just happened.

A lot of wonderful things, as evidenced by the arousal still glistening on my thighs. Plus one very embarrassing reaction to his amazing ministrations.

"Brook, are you okay?" he repeats, his voice laced with concern and confusion.

Another deep breath in, and a long breath out. "Yes, I just need a moment alone. I'm fine."

A beat of silence stretches, and I know I should just open the door and explain. But this is one of those moments where I need to sort out my thoughts and feelings before sharing them with anyone else.

"Okay, I'll be in my room if you need anything, Tokyo," he rasps.

My breath hitches and I fail to stifle the sob this time. Lowering my head, I hug my knees and cry.

Because of course, after delivering the best orgasm of my life, he would use his personal nickname for me.

It's official—I'll have to stay in this room

forever. There is no way I can face the man again and not die of embarrassment, or combust from desire.

His footsteps finally retreat and I slip down to lie on my side, letting the tears roll down my cheeks.

I'd call my therapist, but it's past midnight in London. And my phone is downstairs. So I cry.

Alone. Deserted. Isolated.

Just like I always end up.

Time moves while I lie suspended in my sadness and confusion. Until I have no tears left.

I push up on to all fours and eventually stand up.

God, this is such a clusterfuck of a situation. To explain why my brain shut this down would require other explanations and confessions, and I'm just not ready to go there yet.

Why not?

I can tell myself it's because I don't trust him, but that would be a lie. I'm scared.

I'm worried that once he learns how broken I am, he'll feel sorry for me. Once he understands the baggage I carry, he'll run. Why wouldn't he?

I shuffle to my bathroom and wash my face. I need a shower, but some perverse part of me doesn't want to wash away what happened. What could have been, before I freaked out.

Hoping Baldo is asleep by now, I venture outside.

Tiptoeing, I get to the landing and take one step at a time, trying to recall and avoid the creaky spots.

I make it downstairs and dash to the kitchen. In the absence of my therapist, I need to call Saar or Celeste.

I snatch my phone from the counter.

"Brook?"

I yelp before my mind registers that the velvet baritone isn't a threat. Despite all my inner conflict, it washes over me like a comforting blanket. Whiplash, anyone?

Baldo stands in the entrance to the sitting room, leaning against the door frame. Darkness blankets his impressive stature, but something tells me his casual stance is just a mirage.

He steps forward and his set jaw confirms my assumption.

"Jesus, you scared me. I thought you were in your room." Why do I lead with an accusation?

"I had an interesting evening that required a nightcap." He raises the glass with amber liquid.

He's not mocking or ridiculing me, but I almost wish he would. It would be so much easier to squash all my feelings and recalibrate if he was an asshole right now. Just like my exes.

I guess I'll just have to face this head-on. "Look, I'm sorry I ran away. It was a shitty thing to do."

"That depends on your reasons for that escape."

He steps closer, his face soft with concern, but also determined to get answers.

His earlier dominance flickers through my mind, and I want to be strong, but I take two steps back.

He's still a foot away, and my body tingles with recognition and need for him. Maybe sending money to immoral, illegal, horrible causes isn't such a bad idea. Fucking Granny.

"Look, Baldo, this was a mistake," I blurt out. *No, it wasn't.* Something is seriously wrong with me.

He narrows his eyes, his face unreadable. "That's the story you're going with?"

He doesn't believe me. Well, that makes two of us.

"Yes." A lie is the safest option. "And I'm sure you agree that sex only makes our problematic situation even more complicated."

"No, Brook, I think we're grown-up adults who are stuck together for a year, and we should untangle the complications."

"Well, maybe I'm not that grown-up," I lash out.

Definitely not a grown-up.

I regret my reaction immediately, but before I find the words to correct my course or apologize, because that would be the mature thing to do, Baldo shakes his head and puts his glass down on the counter.

Oh, and I'll never be able to look at that counter again.

"You're right, it was a mistake. Good night, Brook."

He leaves me in the kitchen.

Yet again.

And again, I deserve it.

> I fucked up big time.

CELESTE
> Yay. That's great. Finally.

SAAR
> @celeste, she didn't fuck, she fucked UP

CELESTE
> Oops. Sorry, chérie. Shall we meet?

> Yes, please.

SAAR
> Let's have late breakfast at your place.

> Love you.

It's almost ten when I drag myself out of bed. Not that I slept in. Or slept at all. But I bide my time, making sure I don't run into my husband.

However I slice the situation, there is no way the two of us can continue this ruse without either talking or avoiding each other. The latter is more attractive, but not exactly feasible.

But what if I'm the only one stuck with all the trauma from the past? What if he moved on and turned the page?

I embarrassed myself enough last night. Along with my drunken proposition, I probably turned him off forever.

I take a shower and deal with my emails. If my personal life continues with this turmoil, I'm going to miss my deadline. But I'm too tired to consider that.

When I make my way downstairs, I find Baldo in the kitchen. Dressed in one of his sexy suits, he is perched on the island's counter while he works on his laptop.

My life would be so much easier if the man wasn't so attractive. His broad shoulders tense, and he turns.

Our eyes lock and we stand there, as always, in the impasse of an unresolved past and an agonizing present.

"Good morning." I look away first and focus on getting my morning caffeine.

"I had better," he murmurs, and I hear his laptop slap close.

So this is how it's going to be. "Look, Baldo, I got overwhelmed last night—"

"As you said, it was a mistake." The ice in his voice

sends shivers down my spine. And not the good ones. "I have a meeting. I'll be back this evening. The housekeeper is coming today, and I asked her to prepare meals for the next few days."

Of course he knows the housekeeper's schedule. He's aloof and cold, executing his moves emotionlessly and with precision. Having everything under control.

He doesn't look at me as he washes his cup, dries his hands with a towel and packs his laptop.

I huddle over my cup of coffee, watching his every move.

He's so organized, so reserved. Is that the way he wants it? Or is it his coping mechanism?

Where I invite chaos to tune out the world, he brings order to feel in control?

If that's the case, we're doomed. Opposites might attract, but they don't last.

The doorbell snaps me into action. Baldo grabs his laptop case and I walk with him to the foyer.

It feels like I'm seeing him out, and a part of me wishes that were the case. That this was our morning routine.

I open the door and my friends rush in.

"Hello, traitor." Saar glares at him.

What's that about?

"Nice to see you too, Saar. Did you enjoy your evening with Corm?" He smirks.

"Fuck you. I left right after you. And there is no way I'd ever get involved with any ventures that have his name on it."

"Fine by me." Baldo shrugs. "It was his idea, anyway."

"Of course it was. Don't ever put me in the same room with him."

Baldo rolls his eyes. "Enjoy your day, ladies."

"What was that about?" Celeste frowns.

"His business partner is an asshole. Never mind. We're here for this girl." She wraps me in a hug, and I sniffle.

"Oh no, chérie, let's make you a cup of tea," Celeste suggests, and they usher me to the kitchen while my husband's Maserati revs its engine outside.

I need something enjoyable in my life. Especially since I'm stuck here for a year.

Stuck with me.

Chapter 17

Brook

"So he gave you the best orgasm of your life. With his tongue. And instead of begging for more—and there is nothing wrong with demanding what you need—you ran away?" Celeste leans back on the sofa and crosses her arms over her chest.

"I guess I just didn't expect it. I don't usually... Never mind. I guess it's the past, and what we could have been that came rushing back."

"But wasn't he your first?" Saar moves into a downward dog.

She missed her yoga practice for this emergency meeting, so she's adding poses into the conversation.

"He was my first kiss, and he'd have been my first everything, but—"

I watch my hands. I've never confided this to

anyone else, and maybe that's part of the problem. Keeping things locked inside doesn't allow them to move away.

Saar collapses to the floor, understanding the gravity of the moment. She crosses her legs. "You can tell us, sweetie."

Celeste rubs my back. "Whatever you feel comfortable with."

"We are the youngest of the bunch, and we were very close growing up. Like us against the world, we bonded over hating how we were always babied or ignored, or... you know, silly sibling stuff. It grew into something bigger, and I guess along with raging teenage hormones, we couldn't fight the attraction anymore. But it was weird at the same time because we were brother and sister.

"So we started sneaking around. I mean we're not blood relatives, but still... we knew everyone would judge us. One night, Baldo came to my room and we weren't careful, and my dad caught us. We were just kissing, but all hell broke loose, and our parents were so upset.

"But we couldn't stop. I loved him so much and he loved me, so we made a plan to run away. Baldo turned eighteen six months before me and he was able to access some of his trust fund then, so we decided to leave together."

"Chérie, that is so romantic," Celeste sighs.

"Hold your verdict, there is no happy ending." I chuckle humorlessly and then tell them the rest of the story.

How horribly our escape night went and how Baldo ran away without me, and I was left dealing with trauma no girl or woman should ever experience.

Somehow I get through the story without crying, and with every word I feel more liberated. Like my attachment to the unfortunate events is getting looser with every word.

I told the story once to my therapist, but that felt clinical, just giving the facts so she could fix me.

There is no judgment. No pity from the two women here. They just keep a safe place for me to share.

In sharing with my friends, something sets me free. Like the shackles of the past have been broken, not yet fully redeeming me, but disconnecting from me.

And I'm reminded that my past doesn't have to define me.

And there is one thing I know beyond any doubt, I need to tell the story one more time.

To my husband.

I fidget with the napkin for the hundredth time. Dinner is in the oven, our counter corner set up. Only Baldo is missing.

I considered calling him to find out when he's coming home, but after the way we left things last night, I don't want to nag him.

But if I'm stuck here waiting much longer, I might chicken out. Am I even strong enough to tell the story twice in one day?

Celeste thinks it would be easier. The longer I wait the harder it will be, and the farther apart I grow from Baldo. Not that we're together.

I pop a few Skittles into my mouth. My favorite comfort food is not doing it for me today.

The front door finally clicks, and I grab the bottle of wine and pour myself a glass, my hand shaking.

I take a fortifying sip. It tastes like shit after the candy. And it doesn't do shit—I'm only more nervous.

It's not so much that I want to tell him my side of our story, but that after the way we left things last night and this morning, there is another shitty conversation needed before we dive into the even shittier one.

Baldo halts in the entrance to the kitchen, a flash of surprise passing through his face before the typical arrogant, stony expression settles in.

"I ate in the city."

"It doesn't matter. I'm not hungry, anyway." I put another candy into my mouth.

"Obviously." He quirks an eyebrow, eyeing the small bag in my hand.

"Oh, do you want one?" Maybe we can bond over Skittles.

He makes a face like I offered him a poisoned pile of mud. "I don't eat candy, and I hate Skittles."

"What? That's grounds for divorce. Who hates Skittles?"

He looks at me unimpressed. Right. Stalling is not the way to go.

"I was hoping we could talk." My throat tightens with the words.

A loud beeping interrupts the moment and I jump, spilling the colorful round candy. Baldo narrows his eyes, puzzled by my reaction.

Great, he must think I'm crazy, and I keep confirming it for him.

My phone dances on the counter, and we both look at the screen at the same time. Rupert Montgomery.

I groan, scrunching my face. He's the last person I want to deal with right now.

Baldo looks at me and I shake my head.

I'm aware that I'm acting like a lunatic. Or a child. But I've been gathering courage all day, and this interruption would derail me.

Haven't the Montgomerys disrupted enough already?

Baldo gives an exasperated sigh, hits the answer button and beckons with his head for me to speak.

"Hello?" I squeak.

I guess all my reactions paint a pitiful picture, because Baldo steps closer and puts his hand on the small of my back. Despite our relationship being frozen in an uncomfortable limbo, he offers his silent support.

Because that's the man he is. Silent confidence with sincere kindness. Most of the time. He could improve on the execution though, because he can be a jerk.

But there is an undeniable compassion the man probably tries to hide. Actions speak louder than words and all that.

Like when he ditched an important event to hold my hair while I puked. Saar told me his business partner was pissed about that.

Or when he changed his entire life to marry me.

The heat from his hand curls through me, and instinctively I lean into his touch.

"Brooklyn, I've been trying to reach you all day." My great uncle starts with an accusation.

His attitude erases all my other thoughts. I roll my eyes and straighten up. "What do you need?"

Baldo nods his approval with my stance.

"I wanted to invite you and Baldassare to dinner on Friday."

God, I hate how he calls us both by our full given names. My great uncle would look great in a coffin with a wailing widow throwing herself at him, knowing she's the one who poisoned him. *Not the time for these visions, Brook. Not the time.*

We can't have dinner with him. Nooooo, I mouth, dropping my head to the counter and banging it softly.

We're nowhere near ready to fake it in front of my scrutinizing great uncle.

"Rupert," Baldo says jovially. "I'm here with Brook. Thank you for your invitation, but we'll have to decline."

A moment of silence descends on the other side of the line while I stare wide-eyed at Baldo, a smile tugging at the corners of my mouth.

"Why is that? As you know, I raised concerns about the validity of your marriage, and I think it's important we meet to clear any objections."

"Well, Rupert, I appreciate that you're trying to fulfill your duties as the executor of the will to the last ridiculous stipulation, but Brook and I are not available on Friday."

"I'd strongly suggest you make yourself available."

God, this might not be the best time to rebel. I chew on my cuticle, considering agreeing to the dinner.

"I don't appreciate your tone," Baldo says coldly. I don't necessarily love when he takes this tone with me, but it's fucking sexy now. "But since you're concerned about the validity of our marriage, you'll be pleased to hear we can't accept your dinner invitation because we're leaving tomorrow."

I bite my lip to stifle a chuckle, grateful for Baldo's no-bullshit attitude.

My glee turns to shock when he adds, "On our honeymoon."

Chapter 18

Baldo

"You don't have a guest room?"

Brook looks around at the open concept of my apartment in Lisbon.

It's a three thousand square feet attic room with one side of the roof made of glass.

My housekeeper hates the feature, but I love it. Not that in the middle of the city there is a chance to see the stars, but still.

"But you have enough room for your dancing." I smirk, but she glowers.

With the state-of-the-art kitchen in one corner and a custom-made bed on the opposite side, the room has been designed with a minimalistic approach.

Under the row of windows, near the bedroom corner, I have a desk, a sitting area in the middle, and a dining table beside the kitchen island.

I can see how there is no privacy anywhere in the cavernous space. Besides the bathroom and walk-in closet. But I never bring anyone here, so it's not like I need privacy from myself.

Brook doesn't move from the elevated entrance. We've been avoiding each other since I announced this trip.

The tension has lingered since I went down on her two nights ago. It's driving me mad that I don't understand what the fuck happened.

I want an explanation, but something tells me she needs time to get there herself. In the meantime, we're radiating with frustration, tension, and anticipation. I'm just not sure if we're anticipating the same thing anymore.

"Look, I have guest bedrooms downstairs. You can have this place to yourself."

I'm stubbornly ignoring the fact I offered her my personal space instead of one of the bedrooms on the lower level of the building.

I take her suitcase and roll it into the closet.

The silence is so pronounced that it feels like I'm drilling a ridge into the hardwood floor with the wheels.

It takes too long to get her luggage to the other side of the room, and suddenly I hate my own apartment.

I fucking hate this whole situation.

I worked on the plane to give her space. She seemed like she wanted to tell me something several times. She didn't. Instead, I got a lot of scowling and sulking from her.

Now I remember why I never got married.

And apparently, I'm lying to myself. Because let's face it, there is only one woman in the world who I would want to marry.

Fucking shame she is currently so unattainable. Even though she is my wife and she's only a few feet away.

I don't even know if I'm pissed at her rejection or at her bullshit.

"I'll get my housekeeper to fill the fridge. Let me know if you want anything specific. I'll text you the Wi-Fi password, so you can work if you need to. I have things I need to take care of downstairs. Call me if you need anything."

My apartment is above my business. The basement and first two floors are the nightclub, the third floor houses private gambling rooms, and the fourth floor has the offices and a couple of guest rooms.

The fifth, the attic, is where I live when I'm not traveling.

I push the elevator call button and turn. Brook moved to the sitting area, but she hasn't sat on the large

L-shaped leather sofa. She stands there, and fuck, she looks so small and lost in my large space.

"You'll be okay?"

Why do I have this need to make sure she's good? She's a grown woman and capable of taking care of herself, but somehow I feel responsible for her.

"It's my honeymoon." She spreads her arms, mocking the sentiment. "I'll be more than okay."

Fuck.

"I'm sorry I dragged you here, but I thought it was a good solution to get away from Rupert. It's not like he'd spy on us here, so we don't have to pretend. Besides, I wasn't planning on my temporary relocation, so this gives me an opportunity to take care of business."

And to regain my wits. On my home turf, and buried in work, instead of being exposed to her on a daily basis.

The elevator opens behind me.

"Of course. You're right." Her voice rings with bitterness.

"I don't know what your problem is. You said we're not a good idea. I'm trying to make this as painless as possible."

The elevator closes before I get in.

She opens her mouth and then closes it. Then she opens it again. "As I said, you're right."

"Fuck." I growl and hit the call button again. The door opens and I step in, ignoring the acid spreading around in my stomach. What is that even? Shame? Regret?

Get out of here now, idiot.

"Baldo."

I look at her, stopping the door with my foot. She steps forward, worrying her lip, but before she says anything my phone rings.

I pull it out of my pocket. "I got to take this." Not really.

"Sure. It's okay. We'll talk later." She smiles. It's tentative, but it's there.

And coward that I am, I take it as permission to avoid her and leave.

* * *

I'm an asshole.

Complete, despicable piece of shit.

I've successfully avoided Brook for three days now. Between all the fires I needed to put out in several of my clubs, the slot machine supplier in Budapest, a potential hospitality workers strike in France and a million other things, I've been too busy.

It's a partial truth.

But I wasn't that busy. So many times I entered the elevator then stopped myself.

Part of me is fucking mad at her rejection. Part of me is confused. And the sober, reasonable me knows that we're better off surviving this without poking at the past, or tempting the current attraction.

But I can't claim I'm being rational here. While I'm staying away, I'm checking on her even more obsessively than I used to before.

Like right now. My eyes trace the column of her neck as she sits at my dining table. The table where she's been taking her meals. Alone. Yep, definitely an asshole.

I should be concerned about my lack of boundaries, but this is the first time I'm really grateful I had the cameras installed upstairs.

When Art Mathison, my security consultant, suggested it, I didn't see the point. But I live so close to the club and the building is constantly full of strangers. Besides me though, only a few people have access to the private elevator. Brook is now one of them.

In the last three days, Brook has danced, worked on her computer—a little too much—and slept. She doesn't eat enough. She goes out once a day for a few hours and I have one of my bodyguards follow her.

According to him, she works at a cafe or takes a

walk, sightseeing. She texts me when she needs something but keeps it brief.

Right now, she's sipping wine and chatting with her friends, whose faces are stretched on her laptop with equally large glasses in their hands.

"Are you even listening to me?" Chloe huffs.

She flew in today to discuss... I don't even know what. Fuck. I pinch the bridge of my nose and turn to face her. "Sorry, I've been distracted."

"No way, I haven't noticed."

I sigh and lean in my chair, grabbing a stress ball someone once gave me that I've never used before. "You were saying?"

"What the fuck is going on, Baldo?" She stands up and starts pacing. "You extend your trip to New York without explanation, then you come back, but you're only half present."

"I got married." That fucking stops her.

Her expression would be amusing, but I'm more busy with the revelation. Why the fuck did I tell her?

I don't have friends. I'm on a friendly basis with some of my business associates, but I don't let anyone get close enough.

It doesn't pay off, as I learned early in my life. I never knew my father, my mother chose Micah over me, and Brook... well, that heartbreak still hurts.

But this fucking situation has been living in my

head and I need to get it out, so poor Chloe gets a dose of her boss's private life.

Fucking hell. It's not like I can take it back now.

Her reaction is less than helpful, because the woman dissolves in a fit of laughter, doubling over. She grabs the armrest of the chair and laughs while I wait impatiently.

When she meets my eyes and takes in my serious expression, she stops abruptly and drops into the chair.

I have to give it to her—she finds her typical professional composure fast, straightening her shoulders and flattening her pencil skirt. "I didn't know you were dating. Congratulations."

"Someone from my past I ran into in New York." I consider if I can—or should—tell her the truth about the pretend wedding, but decide against it.

"Oh, that makes sense. But you haven't been there in many... Oh, the one who got away." The smile that stretches across her face forces me to fist my hands.

Shit. I forgot I told her something along those lines when we hooked up years ago.

"Anyway, it's been an adjustment and kind of unexpected, but I need to figure things out as I'll be living in New York for several months."

Chloe clears her throat, but chooses not to share what she thinks about this recent development. "Of course. Let me know if you need anything from me."

"I think I'll need to travel back and forth, and I will need to reassign some responsibilities. Obviously I don't want to increase your workload, but I might need you to take on a bit more. Temporarily."

"Baldo, you kept my job and tackled all my duties when Mary was sick. I will get shit done. You know that. I might need you to deal with some of the misogynistic assholes who didn't get the memo that women are not objects, and God knows there are enough of them in this business, but you can count on me."

I did step in when her partner was ill, but I never thought of it as a reciprocal favor.

I glance at my screen. Brook is holding a dress in each hand in front of her computer. Is she getting ready to go somewhere?

Chloe clears her throat and I snap my eyes back to her. "Thank you, Chloe. I know I can always count on you."

I stand up and step round the desk so I'm in front of her. It's not the best move, but I need to get away from my screen if I want to focus.

Chloe fidgets and stands up. Of course she does, she wouldn't put up with any power games, though in this case my move was to stop myself from stalking Brook, not asserting my control over an employee.

We continue discussing the business in this awkward stand-off, but somehow the awkwardness falls away as we continue to tackle issues and brainstorm solutions. And eventually she paces, because that has always been her way of thinking better.

"One last thing. I know we're focusing resources on our New York location, but I heard about a club in Nice that is up for sale. Do you want me to look into it?"

I scratch my neck. "It wouldn't hurt. If it's a viable business, that wouldn't require much start-up effort, we can find the available cash. But let's not expand too fast. Especially with the looming strikes in France."

"Sounds good. If you don't have anything else, I may try to catch the last flight out."

I check my watch, pushing off the table and moving to the door. "I need to greet a group of VIPs in the poker room, but I wanted to talk to you about the declining revenue in Italy."

"Yeah, my brain is fried for that conversation. Maybe I should stay."

At that, she stumbles. "Goddammit," she squeals, and I catch her elbow before she falls.

Her arm flails and lands on my chest, but her fast pacing propels her sideways and I have to snake my hand around her waist.

"Those fucking heels of yours, Chloe."

We both laugh as she leans to take off her broken shoe.

"Stay overnight. We'll have breakfast together." I steady her.

Something strange crawls up my neck, and I snap my eyes to the door. It's closed, but I could swear it just clicked.

"Okay, I'll stay. I might see the Porto supplier tomorrow before I leave. One more thing off your list."

"Good." I open the door and we both exit.

"Is she here with you? I'd like to meet her."

A pang of guilt spreads through my digestive system, and I decide to ignore Chloe's reasonable question and steer toward the poker room without another word.

Chloe snorts. She's experienced me avoiding conversations before, and this is no different.

Only for the first time in... well, ever... I feel like shit about it.

Not so much about ditching Chloe's request, but about what I keep telling myself is me giving Brook some space.

Chapter 19

Brook

LO

Brook, are you in Europe?

SYD

Wait? What? Did she return to London?

PARIS

She didn't tell me she was leaving.

> You know I'm part of this chat?

> We're on a honeymoon.

LO

With your brother?

> Faking it, obviously.

SYD

Where did you go?

> (eye-roll emoji) To Lisbon, so he can work.

> **LO**
> Well, that's good. At least you're not sitting alone at home.
>
> **SYD**
> How are you feeling, Paris?
>
> **PARIS**
> Like a beached whale, but Finn loves pregnancy sex.
>
> **LO**
> TMI (puking emoji)

What an asshole!

I order a cocktail and scan the bistro. It's busy with business-people, tourists, and a Friday night pre-drinks crowd. People chatting in Portuguese and in English, laughing, having fun.

Apparently, Baldo is having fun as well.

He left me alone for three days. I could have slipped and cracked my skull on the bathroom floor, and nobody would have found me for days because my dear husband is avoiding me like the plague.

I guess my editor will be grateful that I channeled my boredom and anger onto the page. My newest manuscript will be the darkest I've ever written.

Baldo's neglect might make me a lot of money, after all. What a lovely honeymoon. Not that he was obliged to wine and dine me, but for fuck's sake, avoiding me completely?

After he went down on me and delivered a bliss I'd never experienced before then spooked me, I was hoping I'd get a chance to explain myself.

I wasn't able to on the night he announced our honeymoon, and now I don't feel like explaining myself to the aloof, distant asshole.

But I guess the failed consummation of our fake marriage was a good enough reason for him to fucking drop me like a dirty sock.

We haven't been married for a month, and I don't see us progressing to a year. Fucking Roberta Montgomery.

And what am I even expecting? Happily ever after? It would kill Dad.

Though I have to give it to Baldo, it's easier to fake it here, where we aren't under the constant scrutiny.

Lisbon is beautiful.

At first I feared Baldo's apartment would swallow me, but it's actually a wonderful home. The lonely wolf created a lair for himself that should feel cold, but somehow it doesn't.

Only a couple of hours in, the sense of belonging descended on me. Like we designed that place together.

The idea fills me like a bag of chips—delicious on my tongue, but sickening in my stomach.

And while I'm pissed that he abandoned me, I've been having a great time. Maybe the year would pass faster if we moved here.

But I just started bonding again with my sisters, not that they would miss me much. I could still visit Dad often.

I take a sip of my cocktail and catch the eye of a sun-tanned man across the bar.

He's checking me out, and not even trying to be subtle about it. His friend joins him with two girls in tow. I guess no flirting for me tonight.

Not with the freaking ruby boulder and simple wedding band on my finger. God, why do I even wear it? The thought stops me in my tracks.

Why *do* I wear it?

It's not like it has any significance.

I drain my drink, swallowing the feeling that coils in my stomach. I slide the set off and put them in the small purse hanging on my hip.

Easy. No significance.

"Can I have another one?" I smile and gesture to the bartender.

I need a drink to solidify the no-significance. Because if there was a ring that meant something, it definitely would be the one burning a hole in my purse.

If only I knew what it means. Baldo Cassinetti is an expert at giving whiplash to a girl, that's for sure.

In any case, it doesn't mean much to him.

After Celeste and Saar talked me into another seduction mission and helped me choose my outfit, I went to look for him.

Only to find him half-hugging a tall brunette. *Stay overnight. We'll have breakfast together.* Fuck him.

"Você está aqui sozinha?"

I turn, and I'm immediately blinded by the cutest smile. I guess the sun-tanned dude abandoned his group.

"Sorry, I don't speak Portuguese."

He grins, dimples and all. "Where are you from?"

"New York. I'm Brook." I extend my hand.

He kisses it, staring into my eyes. "Nice to meet you, Brook from New York. I'm Miguel from Lisbon, and I was asking if you're here alone."

I giggle. "Pleasure to meet you, Miguel from Lisbon. I'm alone here, but it looks like you have company."

I glance toward his group where his friend chats with the two girls, not minding us at all.

"The more the merrier." He winks. "Can I get you a drink?"

"Your margarita." The waiter places the drink in front of me.

I shrug. "You can buy me the next one if you're still around." I take a sip, smiling over the rim of my glass.

This guy is hot, and the way he's paying attention to my every move is a great self-confidence boost after the last few days. And yet, I'm forcing myself to enjoy his company.

He leans in and whispers into my ear. "Or maybe you can come dancing with us, and that way we make sure I'm around to order you the next one."

Smooth.

This could be fun, so why do I want to tell him I have plans? Why do I believe that going back to the large, empty apartment and curling up with my book would be more fun?

Because I'm hoping Baldo will come home. Can I be more pathetic?

Maybe I should go clubbing. It usually helps to numb my thoughts. It's fun. He seems like a decent person. Even flirting, he hasn't been creepy. Leaning in, but not touching.

There is nothing wrong with him or this situation, and yet...

He's not Baldo.

Fuck.

"I love dancing." I slide from my bar stool and down my cocktail. "Let's go."

***

SAAR
How is Operation Seduction?

I'm clubbing.

CELESTE
At his club?

Yes. With another man.

SAAR
Making him jealous. Good move.

CELESTE
Just be careful not to scare him away.

I don't think he cares.

SAAR
Where is your spark, woman?

I saw him with someone else.

CELESTE
Fucking?

Not yet.

CELESTE
Don't jump to conclusions.

SAAR
Or just have fun with the new guy.
Party away, my friend.

Not feeling it.

> **CELESTE**
> (crying emoji, kissing emoji)
>
> **SAAR**
> I'll be in Europe in a few days, I'll cheer you up.
>
> **CELESTE**
> And I'm stuck here.
>
> > Better than stuck alone in my husband's apartment.
>
> **SAAR**
> Go have fun @brook. @celeste wanna go out tonight?

Of course, we go to the best club in the city. Baldo's fucking club.

It's not even eleven and the place is packed. Miguel and his friends are fun, but I've been nursing my one drink, pretending to enjoy myself.

Being in Baldo's domain has killed the mood. I'm mad at him, but I'm even more upset with myself.

It's annoying to feel guilty for taking off my ring. It makes no sense. It's also annoying that a part of me wants him to find me here with Miguel and get jealous.

As jealous as I am over his long-legged brunette who—just my luck—is here, and very friendly with everyone.

Clearly she's a regular. Of this joint, and probably of Baldo's. What would she say if she knew he got married while he took his trip to the States? I bet he didn't share that with her.

"You're a cheap date." Miguel bumps into me with his hip.

We're standing by a tall, round table near the dance floor. The rest of the group is dancing, but I lost all interest as soon as I found out where we were going.

"Excuse me?" I cock my head, but Miguel is smirking.

"You've had this one drink since we came."

I laugh. "Sorry. It's not my kind of place."

It's so my kind of place. I love everything about it. The VIP rooms are upstairs, with glass overlooking the dance floor down here.

There are actually three dance floors, one on each floor, each playing different music.

The service is great. It would be fun, if this wasn't *his* club.

Miguel runs his hand down my arm and lands it on my hip. I don't want it there and try to step back.

He asks me something, but the DJ blares something in the speakers, so I yell, "What?"

"Do you want to get out of here?" Miguel repeats, and immediately jerks his head back.

"I'd take that question back and leave if I were you," the velvet baritone echoes behind me. Only its sound is far from velvet, more like scratchy linen.

I whip around, and the sight momentarily takes me aback. Baldo wears jeans and a black button-down, not his usual suit. His hair is messed up on top, as if he's been running his hand through it.

His sleeves are rolled up, and how did I not know his arms are inked? Somehow I absorb all of this in the blink of an eye, before I remember what's going on.

"What the fuck?" And just to make a point—not sure yet what kind of a point—I step closer to Miguel.

The wrong move, because Miguel decides to wrap his arm around my waist.

First, I don't want him to fucking touch me. Second, based on the fury in Baldo's eyes, the gesture might cost Miguel a limb.

Baldo steps forward, his lips curling into a smirk. "Let. Go. Of. Her."

Aside from the burning eyes, there is no sign of this being a disagreement. To anyone around us, he would look composed.

Or maybe just to me. So in contrast with my heart galloping in my chest.

I'm partially furious that he would dare interfere, and partially excited that he's jealous. I'm a lost cause when it comes to this man.

Despite that, how dare he?

"Who is this?" Miguel drops his hand and turns to me.

"The man who will break your arm if you touch her again," Baldo growls.

"Fuck you," Miguel spits. "I don't need this shit." He looks at me. "At least you were a cheap date." He shakes his head and turns to leave.

He doesn't make it far. Baldo grabs his collar, and now the people around us have certainly realized something is going on.

"Baldo," I yelp as his fist connects with Miguel's jaw.

The room around us erupts in gasps and cheers, while the rest of the club continues its normal flow.

Miguel stumbles, swearing, holding his chin.

"Mr. Cassinetti, we take it from here." A bulky man appears from somewhere and grabs Miguel. His colleague steps in front of Baldo and me.

"You're Cassinetti, the owner?" Miguel gawks, his lip already swollen.

"And you're banned from here." Baldo shakes off his hand and cracks his neck.

"You can't do that," Miguel protests as the two security guards crowd him.

"I can, asshole. Nobody touches my wife, or talks to her like you just did."

A few whistles and a moment of silence is all that happens before Baldo faces me, and everyone resumes what they were doing before the interruption.

"Was that really necessary?" I try to disregard the butterflies in my stomach.

I can't condone his behavior. However hot it was. Wait? What? Not hot.

Inappropriate. Aggressive. Panty-melting. Jesus. What was in that drink?

I don't know how to cope with the tug of war inside me. What the actual fuck just happened? And why is it equally hot and infuriating?

Baldo steps closer. I can't read his face. It's full of something.

Raw. Primal and kind of scary. "Where is your ring?"

Chapter 20

Brook

"What?"

He lowers his mouth to my ear. "You heard me, but just in case. Where. Is. My. Ring?"

I swallow and, fuck, he's intimidating, and why does it make me feel all giddy?

"*My* ring is in my purse."

He says nothing, just breathes near the side of my face for a moment, and I almost cower and tell him I didn't want to lose it, but fuck him and his Neanderthal ways.

After what feels like an obscenely long time, he straightens up, looming over me. "Put it on."

"Jesus." I'm relieved, and bereft at the loss of his closeness at the same time, and he is still very much in my face.

Rolling my eyes—to ascertain how above this I am, which is a fat lie—I unzip my mini purse and fish out the ring.

I take my time, while trying to ignore the warm feeling spreading through my chest and stomach.

This is fucked-up, but terrific. Terrifically terrifying.

He watches me like a hawk as I slide the ruby on my finger.

"Good. Now everyone knows." He nods, and he's about to turn.

I grab his arm. "Knows what?"

We stand in a silent, glowering duel for a moment, completely still, while the rest of the world dances, laughs, talks and drinks around us. But it all fades as my hand trembles, squeezing his biceps.

Somehow, this moment feels significant. I don't understand how or why it's this particular one, but I equally enjoy it and dread it.

Some deranged, insecure part of me really, really, really wants him to commit. As if right here, right now, it would even mean anything.

As if it would ever mean anything.

And yet if I was to choose between living my life before this moment, and being destroyed again by Baldo Cassinetti, I would choose the latter.

I want a fucking refund from my therapist.

Baldo shakes off my hand effortlessly and it's like a slap. While I'm craving the connection, he discards my touch.

But my unreasonable grief is short-lived when he snakes his arm around my waist and yanks me to him, whispering in my ear, "You're not a cheap date. Far from it."

Holy shit. I want to pull him down for a kiss and never let go.

As absurd as our relationship has been, I need him with such visceral urgency I don't think I can last another minute without him.

But I don't get that kiss, because Baldo hoists me over his shoulder and leaves the floor.

I punch his back with my fists, but it's a laughable effort. Groaning, I give up and just let him carry me away while several guests stare. Or that's what I think they are doing, because the club's raucous energy mellows around us as Baldo heads out.

"Let me down." I kick when we leave the sounds behind, entering some back hallway, but he only grabs me tighter.

We step into the elevator and he finally lets me slide down his body.

"You're behaving like a lunatic. That was embarrassing and unnecessary."

He shrugs and turns to face the door.

"You're such an asshole."

"You mentioned that."

"What's your fucking problem, Baldo? You left me alone for three days. I'm not property you can lock up."

The elevator jerks to a stop and the door into his apartment opens.

"You're my wife, and you shouldn't hop around with assholes who want to take advantage of you. What if Rupert has spies here?"

"You're incredibly invested in this ruse." God, I want to strangle him. And I want him to admit that the last ten minutes weren't for the sake of pretending.

"I call bullshit." I march across the room. As far away as possible from him. "You're having all the fun, but you can't stand me having some too. Hypocrite."

I drop my purse on the coffee table, the energy pulsing through me in bouts of anger and frustration.

"I've been working." He's so aloof and composed I want to throw something at him.

Opening a cabinet, he gets a glass and fills it with water. He leans against the counter, takes a sip and watches me patiently.

Fuck him.

"Working?" I snort. "I saw you with that long-legged hussy in your office."

I regret my words as soon as they come out. Way to

point out how unreasonable his jealousy act was by bringing out my own insecurity.

"I thought someone was at the door."

He's not even trying to deny it. That stinks more than it should.

He puts down the glass and walks over to where I stand. "I'm sorry I didn't get a chance to spend more time with you. I was trying to give you space."

"To give me space to do what? Go crazy in a strange city all by myself?"

His nostrils flare. "Okay, I was trying to stay away from you. Happy?"

He flails his arms in frustration and turns sideways. He tilts his head back, watching the sky through the glass roof.

I watch his profile, the statue of imperfect perfection.

Stay away from me. The statement hurts, and its poison spreads fast through my veins. "Wow. I'm sorry I'm such an inconvenience."

I march to the elevator.

Away from this.

Away from him.

Away from all these conflicting feelings.

He catches up with me so fast I yelp, but still I try to dash away. His arm weaves around my waist and he whips me around.

Fuck, this manhandling routine is getting really annoying.

"You're a goddamn inconvenience." He grabs my throat and my back hits the elevator door.

It's a violent gesture, but he inserts care into it, controlling himself. And as someone who's dealt with abusive assholes, I know the difference.

And I believe without a trace of doubt, in this moment, he's protecting me. Perhaps from himself.

Or from us.

"You destroyed me once already, Brook, and I swore I wouldn't be the idiot who lets you do it again. And yet, here I am, offering to marry you to help you out. You're a damn inconvenience, and I still can't stop thinking about you, worrying about you, spending my days wondering if there is anything I can do to make your life better."

He squeezes my throat and lowers his head to my ear, the warmth of his breath sprouting goosebumps on my skin. My breath hitches.

"You're a fucking inconvenience. The most painfully tantalizing, magnificent inconvenience." He punches the steel above my head and turns away.

Gasping, I circle both my hands around my throat. Not to soothe the hurt he caused, because he didn't really, but to keep the warmth of his touch confined, closer to me.

I recognize how fucked up this is, but I can't explore that further, because another, much bigger realization ripples through me.

I enjoy this. I enjoy his roughness. I enjoy the lingering fear while I know I can trust him.

Jesus. Fucking. Christ.

"I'm yours," I whisper.

Right now, I know that this has always been true. The enormity of it grabs at my stomach and my chest with a tight grip of fear. So I immediately have to protect myself and add, "For now."

He lets out a cruel chuckle and turns back to me. "We both know you can't handle me, Tokyo."

"Fuck you, Baldo. What is it going to take? Because you can hide in your office all you want, but we both want it. Or maybe the past versions of us need it."

He watches me for what feels like several lifetimes.

Years of longing, denying, and wondering all mount in the space between us.

"Careful, sweetheart, because there is nowhere to hide if you change your mind again."

Chapter 21

Baldo

"You're such an asshole," she snaps and slides past me.

Stopping by the dining table, she groans. *Yeah, there is nowhere to go, sweetheart.*

She turns to me. "It was humiliating enough, you don't need to poke into it constantly." The vulnerability in her eyes fucking guts me.

"Humiliating?"

What is she going on about? God, we can't find a common language here. Perhaps because we're both avoiding the real topics.

I walk to her, this time approaching gently because she draws the animal out of me, but I'm not an asshole who would get off on her insecurities.

I tuck a strand of hair behind her ear. "It was beautiful, fucking hot, and a perfect fantasy coming true building you up, almost letting you come. The next part was confusing, but you have nothing to be embarrassed about. I can be a lot to take."

She makes a dismissive sound. "You think this was about your sexual prowess? God, you're full of yourself." She crosses her arms over her chest and then frowns. "Wait? Almost letting me come? It was the best fucking orgasm of my life."

"Sweetheart, you didn't even come yet. Not by my standards, for sure."

She blinks repeatedly. "But I've... I never... It was so..." She keeps tripping over her words, and then she groans. "Okay, I need to tell you something, but... promise you won't judge me."

What's going on here? The furious pixie from earlier has changed into this shy, gentle fairy. "Brook, it's me. We used to share everything."

We both still, the tension that usually grips us at the mention of the past sweeping through us before she blows a raspberry, her shoulders hunching.

"I've never had an orgasm."

Now it's my turn to blink. "Come again?" Too late, I realize the poor choice of words.

"I've never had one," she snaps and fidgets, wiggling her shoulders like the words are ants crawling up her back. "And don't be weird about it."

"But you dated." Fuck, I'm making it weird.

"Yes, I guess there is something wrong with me." She wants to turn away, but I don't let her this time.

Grabbing her arm, I pull her to me. She hides her face in my chest. I give her a moment, but then I nudge her chin up, forcing her to look at me. This is not something I'm saying into her crown.

"There is nothing wrong with you, Tokyo."

She narrows her eyes, not believing me perhaps.

"Baby, I got a taste, and you've got the most tantalizing pussy. It's a severe offense to taste you and not finish the job."

"According to you, you committed that offense."

"I didn't get a chance to finish. But you were close, and I guess not ever seeing the meteorite shower, you thought that a falling star was it."

"Aren't you poetic? God, this is mortifying." She hides her face in my chest again.

"Hey, stop it. I'm glad you trusted me with this."

"I need a drink," she mumbles into my shirt.

"Another margarita?" I move to the kitchen and take out the blender.

"How do you know what I had?"

"It's my club."

She joins me and leans on her elbows across from me on the island. It pushes her tits together, practically spilling them from her stupid, tempting dress.

White, almost see-through; when I saw it on the

security screen I almost shut down the club to wash everyone's eyes with bleach.

I'm sure I wasn't the only one getting hard just from a glimpse of it. Though the current situation in my pants is a result of both her cleavage and, if I'm honest, her revelation.

I can't believe it. And a part of me is so fucking happy about it. Not that she's had such an unsatisfying sexual life, but that I can still...

I can't even think about that, because it feels like a commitment I'm not ready to offer. Not with her. Not again. I might be a complete idiot around her, but I still have some preservation instincts left.

She watches me as I mix the drinks and pour us each a frosty cocktail.

Brook takes hers to the table, but she doesn't sit, just leans against it. I put my glass on the counter and walk round it to stand on the other side.

I have never considered the size of my apartment a problem, but right now it feels so fucking large. Technically she is still in my kitchen, and yet she feels so far.

Taking out my phone, I use the app to dim the lights. When my eyes lock with hers, it's a sucker punch of feelings. Raw need. She's fucking perfect here in my space.

I could just... Nope, not going there. I drain my margarita in one gulp.

But the thought persists. In a sense, I could be her... Fuck. A level head and pragmatism are two things I've always been able to rely on.

But the depraved caveman who enjoyed his dormant status for years is up and ready to party.

I could be her first.

"Perhaps you were always meant to be my first," she challenges. It's not the shy, quiet *I'm yours* she threw at me before.

Her eyes dare me. Fuck. At least we are on the same page.

My cock takes her up on that offer immediately. When her eyes drop to the bulge in my jeans and she licks her lips, I abandon any and all restraint. Control. And common sense.

I pounce.

Grabbing her wrists and knocking her drink down, I whip her around and twist her arms behind her. I trap her hands between her lower back and my stomach and lower my mouth to her ear.

"This is how it's going to go down. I'm going to make you come as many times as I please, and you will let me. Is that clear?"

Her breath hitches and she bobs her head, nodding.

"Use your words, Brook," I growl.

"Jesus, you're bossy."

I push her, face down, onto the table and lift that infuriatingly short skirt of hers. I put my hand on her neck, my thumb on her pulse. An enchanting beat.

With my other hand, I trace a line up her inner thigh and cup her between her legs roughly, but not too rough.

She whimpers.

"Look at that, your pussy doesn't seem to mind. So wet for me already. What turned you on, Brook? My little caveman performance downstairs, or my hand on your throat earlier?"

Her pulse speeds up. "Both." The word is strangled. "But your hand more."

"That's what I thought." I kiss her shoulder and then take her ear lobe into my mouth. God, her body responds so nicely. "Let's start again, baby. I'll let you come as many times as I please. Is that clear?" I repeat.

I continue planting kisses down her exposed back. Fucking dress. I'm going to burn it tomorrow.

"Yes," she rasps.

"Good girl."

Even through her panties, and with her legs practically together, I can feel her core clench. Good to know that praise works.

I continue taking my time, kissing every exposed inch of her skin, slowly cataloging every reaction.

I enjoy coming like any other man, but this is my favorite part. Discovering a woman's body.

But with Brook it's somehow different. It's like I finally got the keys to the forbidden room. After years of yearning, discovering its every treasure now suddenly becomes my life's mission.

For the next part of the conversation, I need to entice her a bit. I'm a manipulative bastard, but there is no way I can stop at this stage, so here it goes.

I slide my fingers under her panties and massage her clit gently.

She moans, and while completely at my mercy, she still manages to push against me, seeking more friction. God, this is going to be fun.

"You relinquish control. I'm in charge completely."

She stiffens at this, but I don't stop with my hand between her folds, or with my mouth on her skin.

"Do you need to think about it, *Tokyo*?" Yep, pulling out all the stops here.

"Okay," she whispers, pushing into my hand. I smile against her skin, but falter after she adds, "I trust you."

Fuck. She shouldn't. She really shouldn't.

Not that I plan to hurt her, but I don't want the responsibility.

With her track record of loser boyfriends, she probably trusts easily.

In contrast with all my thoughts, my chest swells at her words. I'm a goner when it comes to Brooklyn Lowe, and it shouldn't surprise me after all these years.

"Okay, you need a safe word." I swipe my fingers through her folds and tease the opening.

She turns her head and looks at me over her shoulder, frowning. "Why do I need a safe word? Will you hurt me?"

"Not unless you want me to." She shudders at that. "But sometimes there is a very thin line between pleasure and pain. And sometimes even pleasure can be too much. My boundaries are probably wider than yours. We will figure it out together."

"Okay." She shivers in my arms.

"I love giving pleasure, but when it becomes too much, you might beg me to stop. I won't, because I have to take care of you. It's my kink. You need a safe word, so I know you really mean it."

She doesn't say anything, and I remove my hands, straightening up. She whimpers and bangs her head gently against the table.

I wait. I'm in no hurry. This is happening, but she needs to get on the same page as me.

Finally, she pushes off the table and faces me. "I have chased an orgasm all my adult life. If you get me where you got me the last time, I consider it a win. I won't be begging you to stop."

"Oh, I'm going to get you there, but it won't be a minor wave like before. It'll be a full tsunami, and you'll beg me to stop at some point."

"You're awfully confident. I can fake it really well. Years of practice."

She lifts her chin. Stalling.

"Safe word, Brook. Now."

She makes that cute exasperated face like she's annoyed with me. "Bossy—" But she shuts up, remembering that she agreed I'm in charge. "Skittles."

I chuckle. "Good girl. Now let's get you out of this hideous dress."

"I love this dress. It makes me feel sexy." She shimmies her hips, smiling.

"Baby, tonight was the last time you wore that dress."

"Jesus. Why do you hate it so much?"

"I hate every fucker who drools over you in this fucking excuse for a dress." I hook my hands in her cleavage and pull her to me. "You're being very disobedient, Brook."

I dip to grip the hem and kiss her neck while I yank it up, but she clamps my wrist. "Skittles."

I lean back, staring at her. Is she joking? This woman will be the death of me. "Skittles?"

She bites her cuticle. I don't even think she realizes it. I cross my arms over my chest. Fuck this.

"It's more a pause, not a stop. God knows, I want you to continue, to be in charge, but could I maybe keep the dress?"

"I'm not fucking you in that dress." And at this rate, I might not fuck her at all.

She looks nervous, though. Is it about the sex?

I've been so focused on getting her where I wanted, needed, her, that I didn't even consider that for her the two of us finally getting together is probably a big deal.

Fuck, it is a big deal. I just choose to ignore that fact.

"I'll change?"

God, I hate when she loses her usual gumption. "You don't need to be shy to get naked with me. I saw your cunt already."

She huffs, "You're such an a—"

"Asshole?" I smirk. "Okay. Do you have a silk camisole? Something to show some skin?"

She nods, looking at me curiously.

"Put it on. Keep the heels. No panties."

Brook shudders visibly, and it remedies the situation.

I want her to shudder.

To fall apart.

To unravel.

Chapter 22

Brook

By the time I emerge from the closet, I forget how to walk in heels.

I'm vibrating with an unfamiliar level of arousal and with an unhealthy dose of self-consciousness, along with something akin to anxiety.

I love giving pleasure, but when it becomes too much, you might beg me to stop.

I pause, taking a fortifying breath. I'm getting myself into a situation that will either mend me or break me. And that's before I take into account the doomed state of our relationship.

But then, if I'm to fight my demons, I want to do it with Baldo.

For the longest time, he's been the reason for all my pain, hate and resentment. Now it feels like he might just be able to heal me.

Perhaps we could move forward without addressing the past. But that's the problem, isn't it?

With Baldo, I can't pretend the past didn't happen. I can't outrun it like I've been doing. It's right here in my face.

With the man who could have been my everything.

One that never came back for me, and is now taking care of me in the most confusing way.

My heels echo loudly in the room. God, why am I so nervous?

I'm about to have probably the best sex in my life, and I feel like there will be an exam to pass or fail after. Or before? Jesus.

Over the clicking sound of the sharp stiletto tips, my mind registers sultry music softening the charged air in the room.

When I'm sure that I can indeed walk gracefully, I look up, and my steps immediately falter.

I don't know what I was expecting. That he would undress and wait on the sofa or on his bed?

But no.

Baldo stands in the middle of the room. His hands in the pockets of his jeans, he looks somehow larger, the confidence radiating from his casual stance. He's sexy and composed. So dangerous.

His rolled-up sleeves are the only skin he's showing. But even that is distracting, with all the ink, muscles and veins.

He smiles lazily. "Come here."

It's an order, and it spreads through my body like the best whiskey. Dizzying. Warm. A bit harsh.

I've always thought a man taking initiative was the way to go, but him passively standing there, making me bend to his wishes, is the hottest fucking thing ever. My stomach squeezes, speeding up my breathing.

Our eyes lock. His gaze is ravenous. Like I'm a goddess in his eyes.

That look is all I need to recall how to walk in heels. To remember I've been practicing burlesque for months now.

My midnight blue camisole barely covers my ass, and without my panties I feel quite exposed, but I walk to him with confidence and wanton grace.

It's a subtle sparkle in his eyes that tells me he likes what he sees. What a reward and confidence boost.

"Hey," he rasps when I stand in front of him.

"Hey yourself." I smile.

Just feeling the heat radiating from him, his gaze boring into mine, my earlier anxiety eases. Tentative excitement takes its place.

I reach out to touch him, but he removes my hand gently. Okay, no touching yet, I guess.

Irritation flashes through me, but I squash it. I've agreed to let him lead, and I trust him.

But when he doesn't move for what feels like hours, the sweet anticipation gives way to self-doubt. What is he waiting for?

I'm fighting the urge to fidget. Or hide. Or question him.

I distract myself by picturing how I would commit a murder. Not that I want to kill him. Not yet, anyway. Just escaping into the world of my fiction.

When he finally moves, it's the calculated step of a predator circling his prey, and God help me if that doesn't halt my breath. How him taking one step can ignite a wildfire within me is beyond me.

He's so close now that I can't breathe without brushing against him. My arm against his. My thigh. His thigh. My nipples. Shivers ripple through me, and he is still just standing there, studying me.

After what feels like another lifetime, he lowers his head to the side of my face. A shaky breath whooshes out of me. He hums at that, and then inhales, smelling my hair.

His hands remain in his pockets, and I'm about to explode from sheer anticipation. What the actual fuck?

"So pretty."

The reverence in his voice is like an aphrodisiac. A potent one at that.

"So fucking gorgeous," he rasps, and steps to the side.

I turn to follow, but he raises his finger. "Don't move, baby." It's a demand, but there is a softness to it, and in this moment I want to follow his every wish.

It's official—I've lost my mind.

He still doesn't touch me, just steps slowly behind me. He's so close, but not seeing him makes me feel alone. I don't know where to look. What to do. So I just tremble.

I stand here as he directed, my heart loud in my temples. He buries his nose into my hair again. "Like an angel."

Another shudder surges through me.

I jerk, yelping, when he finally touches me. It's just his fingers brushing my hair from my shoulder to the side.

"Shh, relax, baby."

With his lips, he traces up my shoulder to the crook of my neck. Butterfly kisses that somehow have a direct line to my core.

I'm shivering with need so raw I want to scream and beg him. It's been a minute and a half, and I'm literally crazy with yearning.

He continues planting kisses, his tongue swirling along my skin. Hot and wet, utterly disarming. I'm going to come just from this.

Or get violent, because this is pure torture.

Divine.

All-consuming.

Magnificent torture.

"Baldo," I breathe.

"Yes, sweetheart, tell me what you need."

He snakes his arms around me, and I lean into him, barely able to stand.

"You." The word turns into a moan as he brushes over my nipples with his fingers.

Suddenly, his touch is at my throat. Only it's not his hands, it's something smooth and cold. A silky fabric. He glides it up my neck and face to my eyes.

A blindfold.

My heart bursts into a galloping rhythm. And then there is darkness. Jesus.

He ties it gently at the back of my head. His mouth comes to my ear, the breath hot on my skin.

"I want you to only feel, baby. Can you do that for me?"

Only feel? As if the tornado of emotions swirling inside me, or the explosion of sensations over my body, weren't enough.

He traces my skin, taking his time, caressing my arms. From shoulders to hands, he is barely touching me, and I shiver with such primal craving it almost scares me.

How can one man have such a hold over my body when he hasn't even done anything?

"Baldo," I breathe again, not even sure if I'm pleading, praising, berating.

"You're perfect. My perfect girl."

Oh fuck, his praise quiets my brain.

He takes my hand and leads me somewhere. I don't think it's toward his bed, but I've lost all sense, let alone my sense of direction.

"Wait a moment," he rasps, and a jolt of panic grabs me. Is he going to leave? But then I hear sounds, moving something, opening a cabinet, I think.

Baldo comes back. I feel him before he touches me, and it's such a comforting awareness. I gasp when he lifts me effortlessly, but he puts me down immediately.

It's not the bed.

My naked ass ends on a cold, smooth surface. My hands land by my side. It's the glass table.

"Okay, sweetheart, I forgot one important rule." He kisses my jaw, his voice straining with effort.

While he's slowly unraveling me, he's coming undone himself. The thought is unreasonably empowering.

Like knowing this isn't just for me. To fix my problem. To help me with my frustrating issue. This is equally for him.

And yet he puts my needs first, and that's something that terrifies me. Am I worthy of that?

Ever so gently, he lays me on my back. The coolness of the glass contrasts with the heat of my body. I wonder if he picked this surface to ensure I don't burn, because I'm pretty certain I would.

He lifts my feet to the edge of the table, and a chair scrapes the floor before he breathes into my heat and my back arches, a loud moan escaping me.

"No kissing," he says, and pushes my knees open as wide as possible.

It takes me a moment before his words hit my brain and comprehension sinks in. The rule he forgot? *No kissing.*

I scramble to my elbows and want to push further, but his vise-like grip on my hips keeps me in place, and when he lowers his lips to my clit, I file my protests for later.

He sucks on the bundle of nerves, his hands digging into my skin at my lower stomach. I collapse back to the table and try to deal with the sensation.

"Okay, baby, I'm going to make you come quickly now, so you have a point of reference, and then we'll play a game."

My brain is too foggy to assign meaning to his words. They are just a murmur in the background of my heart pounding in my head. Of the fire licking my belly, and coiling pleasure up my spine.

Baldo devours me like I'm his last meal on earth. No wonder he picked the dining table for this part of the night.

Or maybe the bed is too intimate for him?

I gasp and my hips buck when he pushes what must be at least two, if not three fingers into me, erasing any further thoughts.

In no time, I writhe and squirm, but Baldo doesn't budge, holding me in place.

And then suddenly electricity zaps through me. My lungs heave and I chant his name, ready to jump out of my own skin.

My core clenches and my legs flex on their own accord, as wave after wave of bliss shudders through me.

"That's my girl." Baldo continues, moving his fingers inside me and rubbing my clit gently.

I may black out for a moment.

My body is weightless.

Boneless.

Fearless.

Tears pool in my eyes, and I'm grateful for the blindfold. I don't want him to see what he's just done to me.

My first love just gave me my first orgasm. How can I not assign any significance to that?

"How are you doing?"

He kisses my inner thighs. The right. The left. My stomach through the delicate fabric. For a no kissing rule, he definitely loves using that mouth of his.

"Brook?"

Oh, right. "What was the question?"

He chuckles. "How are you doing?"

"I want more."

Now he laughs. It's such a wonderful sound. I reach to remove the scarf because I want to see him.

But he grabs my wrist. "You keep that on, or there will be no more."

I groan in frustration, but fuck it, I'll gladly compromise if Baldo Cassinetti sweeps me into nirvana again.

"Ready for our game?"

"You mean your game?" I scramble to maintain a semblance of sovereignty.

"I'm pretty sure you'll enjoy it." His breath is by my ear, startling me. "Wait for me, Brook."

It's strange to lie on the cold table, my arousal dripping down my skin, but it's also arousing. Maybe it's the after-bliss. Or perhaps Baldo's undeniable talent.

And now I'm thinking about the women he honed his skills with. Before I can go down that particular path, his footsteps approach and a chair scrapes across the floor again.

He kisses my temple. "Hands above your head."

I don't understand how his commands shoot desire into every fiber of my body. But I obey, and he runs his hands up my arms to my hands. The chair screeches again and then I feel its backrest.

He closes my palms around it, making me grip it.

"I will make you come again and again, but you have to be a good girl and keep your hands there. Hold on to the chair if you need to, but when you move your arms, I'm going to stop."

"That's torture."

"That's surrender, baby. And the reward is worth it."

My brain misfires as he takes my nipple into his mouth. I almost regret not being naked, but even through the fabric, the sensation is electric.

I move my hands to hold on to his hair, but I stop myself. Good thing he gave me the chair. While I was holding it before, now I grip it with white-knuckled force as Baldo's hand joins in, paying attention to my other nipple, twisting and squeezing.

I'm a mess in no time. I moan, arch, and rub my thighs, seeking friction. Without thinking, my hand reaches for him and then he's gone.

"Fuuuuuck," I whine, and the bastard chuckles. "Come back," I snap.

"Hands on the chair." His voice startles me as it comes from a different direction than I expected.

Groaning, I grab the chair and immediately moan when something soft trails up my legs. A feather?

Oh my god. I'm going to die here. The best way to go.

The blindfold forces me to guess what's coming, anticipating, latently fearing and welcoming his next move, his touch, his ministration.

It's a perfect scenario for someone like me who normally stays in their own head when having sex.

Like often, I'd narrate intercourse in my head, but not with Baldo.

Here, spread for him on his dining table, I'm so absorbed by the game that I don't get a chance to retreat from the playground.

I lose track of time and space. I lose myself to his game. To him.

But his teasing goes on for what feels like an eternity.

"Baldo, I can't..." I whimper.

"Baby, we've just started. You can take it."

The phrase hits me like an icy ocean wave, erasing everything, and I kick with all my might.

Chapter 23

Baldo

"What the fuck, Brook?" She missed my groin by mere inches, but it's not the narrowly avoided pain that riles me up.

It's the utter confusion.

"You have a fucking safe word. No need—" The words die on my lips when I take in the scene.

Brook scrambled off the table and removed her blindfold, but she didn't run any farther. She's standing there, trembling, tears rolling down her cheeks.

The sight is a punch into my stomach and a vise on my chest. I'm not fucking sure what happened. Again.

My immediate instinct screams to take her in my arms. Should I? Can I?

"Brook, baby..." I approach slowly.

A sob escapes her, her shoulders trembling. "I'm sorry."

The sound kills any hesitation in me. Fuck that. I'll gladly have her kicking my balls if that makes her hurt disappear.

I erase the distance between us and open my arms. "Can I?"

She nods, and as soon as she buries her face into my chest, she starts crying.

I hold her and murmur her name, my mind misfiring and my heart hammering. I don't know what to do, because I don't know what happened.

I can't force her to talk when she is like this. But the agony of waiting to find out is excruciating. It coils around my spine like a poisonous snake. My hands itch, relentless energy zapping through me.

I ignore it, staying still for her. Fuck, it's hard.

I need to fix it. Whatever it is.

Selfish prick. She needs me to be here for her in whatever way she deems appropriate. I know that, and yet the helplessness drives me mad.

"You must think I'm crazy." Her shoulders continue to shake.

I press my lips against her temple and hold her.

And I wish I wasn't a coward and could kiss her.

She is a mess, at her most vulnerable, and here I am

protecting my fucking heart. Selfish and helpless. God, I have never hated myself more than now.

"You're not crazy. Could you tell me what I did?" I rein in my need for control and speak softly.

She sighs. "You said I can take it."

Okay, that didn't clarify much, but I sense she might continue so I remain silent. All the while I want to interrogate her and understand what triggered her reaction.

"I don't know how to say it."

Her admission fills the air with such gravity, I'm glad I'm holding her because it would knock me down.

Several beats pass as I hate myself, regret I ever went to New York, and feel grateful that I did.

Because I know I can fix it for her. Whatever it is, I'll fix it. Those loser boyfriends couldn't, but I can.

I must. Even if I have to burn the fucking world down.

Brook steps back and takes a deep breath. She squares her shoulders and looks at me, but her eyes are a void. Like she doesn't even see me.

I panic for a moment, because the vulnerable woman is gone and I can't stand to lose her. Not yet.

"Almost ten years ago, I was assaulted."

The words crash my world to the ground, dissolving every value, every security, every ounce of control I ever had.

I want to demand answers, draw blood, fucking kill someone, but all I do is stand frozen. The riot in my head prevails, as does the need to act.

The bitter, ugly, painful stillness of the moment is breaking me, but I need to let her lead this conversation.

That determination alone must be enough of an action for now.

She seems so far away, like she retreated to this other universe where she is strong enough to deal with the past.

"Give me a moment, please." She raises her index finger.

"Of course." The sound rasps through the lump in my throat. She can have all the time she needs to collect herself. Though she seems eerily calm.

She gives me a shy smile that I think is meant to reassure me. Of what I don't know. And then she surprises me when she walks away. To the bathroom.

I hear water running, and when she emerges she's wearing my black bathrobe. Of course, she won't have this conversation half naked. Idiot.

But on some fucked-up level, I'm pleased she chose to wear my robe. Like in the absence of my touch, I can extend my protection through the garment.

"Can I have some water?"

It takes me a moment to register what she's saying.

"Of course." Fuck, I have no other vocabulary. What I have is a growing chest pain, a lack of oxygen, and an enduring need to kill someone.

I fill a glass with water, and when I turn back she's sitting on the sofa. Through the mayhem in my head, I didn't even hear her move. I'm not ready to listen to her. The realization is like a knife in my intestines, carving.

Moron. Listening is exactly what she needs.

She takes the glass from me and folds her legs under herself.

When I don't move, she meets my eyes with an annoyed expression. "Sit over there." She gestures to the other sofa.

The wound in my guts bleeds more because that's too far from her, but I take the seat.

My ass barely hits the soft cushions when Brook starts talking. "Do you remember TJ, the checkout bagger at the supermarket who used to joke with us?"

I nod mindlessly, vaguely picturing the dude, but Brook doesn't look at me and launches into a clinical recount of the facts.

A gruesome, gut-wrenching memory that almost feels like a scene from a movie or a book, not a true recollection.

At one point, I can't stand it anymore and I jump up.

The moon casts a silver glow over the apartment, the dim lights mocking me as I pace, my blood boiling.

Brook speaks in a monotonous voice, void of emotions. Occasionally, she pauses to collect herself.

I don't know how she can retell this with such aloof coolness, but then she's lived with the story for God knows how long. How did I not know about this?

I'm still in the first stage of grief. The anger is real, burning at the base of my spine, spreading like wildfire.

When she finishes, she drains the water and puts the glass down.

"Where is he now?" I bark, and hate myself for that, but Brook is completely immersed in her detached persona and doesn't even flinch.

"I don't know."

"But the police got him." I continue pacing. It does nothing to calm me down.

"I never went to the police."

I almost tear a muscle as I whip my head to her. "What do you mean?"

She sighs. "I didn't want to go to the police. And please don't make me explain why. The reasons are irrelevant after all this time."

After all this time. She lived with this for... Did she say almost ten years? All my thoughts of revenge and rage come to a halt.

"When did it happen?" I force the words out, but I know the answer.

I know it.

With a clarity that lifts the doubt that has plagued me for a decade.

For years I tortured myself, trying to figure out why she hadn't come. Why she chose our family over me.

She didn't choose. The choice was made for her. Was forced on her.

We stare at each other as she nods slightly, confirming.

I fist my hands.

I punch the backrest of the sofa.

I pick up a large lamp from the side table and smash it to the wall.

I holler like an animal, almost losing my voice when Brook's words cut through all the madness to me.

"That man destroyed enough. Don't destroy your house because of him."

Our eyes meet again. Such contrast. A wild, rabid dog to a graceful swan. I need to do something. Anything.

Brook stifles a yawn. She must be exhausted. Fucking hell, I need to get out of my head.

"You're tired. Let's get some sleep." I sound lame, misplaced, even to myself.

"What about the night of orgasms you promised?" She stands up and sheds the robe off her shoulders.

"No, no, no." I dash to her and lift the robe. "Not right now, baby. There is always tomorrow."

She pushes me away. "Oh, so you were all eager to fix my orgasm problem, but now when you know just how damaged I am, it's too much work for you?"

I drop the robe. I can't recall if there has ever been a time when I was at such a desperate loss for words. For a reason. For a clear plan of action.

"Brook, that's not... I'm sorry..." I rake my fingers through my hair, squeezing at the scalp. "I don't know what to—"

"I don't know either, but you can't retreat now. I didn't tell you so you could treat me like a victim. I don't want you to feel sorry for me. I need you to fuck me."

I stare at her for the longest moment.

She lifts her chin, her eyes blazing with determination. She opens her mouth and closes it. She shuts her eyes and takes a long breath in. Then she looks at me with resolution.

"I can take it."

She says the words that triggered her before, and I understand her need to take over that narrative.

Not only to take it, to rise above it, to exorcise the victim in herself and reclaim her body.

I draw pleasure from pleasing others, but the form she needs is not in my usual arsenal. At least not before multiple orgasms. Then yes, then I fuck like it's nobody's business, to chase my release.

"Are you sure?"

She huffs in frustration. "Can you just fuck me? Not a pity fuck. Just take me like you only care about yourself. Be rough with me, so I... I don't know, so it's... you."

So I can erase any traces of him. Is that what she is saying?

I can give her that. I think.

I crack my neck and file the rage away for later. I've always been good at compartmentalizing.

"On your knees, on the bed. Now." I growl and, fuck, my dick welcomes the invite.

A jolt of desire flashes through her face, but instead of obeying, she lifts her chin again. "No."

I frown, but then it dawns on me. To achieve what she wants, she can't consent. Fuck, I hope she is right, and this won't break us all over again.

What turned you on, Brook? My little caveman performance downstairs, or my hand on your throat earlier?

My taunt from before flashes through my mind. *Both, but your hand more.* She needed this all along.

"Don't make me ask again." Fuck, this is the last

scenario I want to play tonight, but it's not me calling the shots right now.

"No."

I pounce, but she is faster and slips to the side, escaping me around the coffee table.

Reaching for her, I grab her hand and jump over the table. It cracks and splits, which gives her an advantage and she slips away.

She darts around the other sofa, her scent teasing my senses, pulling me deeper into the chase. My heart hammers against my ribcage, a relentless drum of adrenaline.

I kick at the shards of the coffee table and reach for her, but she jumps over the back of the couch, her figure a flash of desperation and grace in the vast room.

She glances back at me. Fear but also goading are etched across her face, and for a moment I want to stop this madness.

As if she understands my hesitation, she picks up a decanter from the cabinet beside her and throws it at me.

The chase is a language, every move a word, and she is determined to be understood. And I might not exactly speak the same language, but on some level, I need this too.

To chase her for all the years I longed for her. To

catch her and finally make her mine. Even in this fucked-up scenario.

My resolve hardens, and with a burst of energy, I close the distance and lunge at her. She yelps and tries to wiggle out of my grasp, but this time I have both my arms around her.

She kicks at me as I carry her to the bed. I drop her and immediately cover her with my body.

She lies on her stomach, trapped under me, fighting like a lioness.

My good girl.

She elbows me in the ribs, and I groan and twist her arms behind her, trapping them between us.

I kick her knees apart, gaining me better access. She struggles under me, but slowly loses her energy.

Holding both her wrists in one hand, I use the other to pull a condom from my pocket, unzip my pants and release my painfully stiff cock.

But I can't completely obey her wishes, and I first probe her with my fingers between her folds.

Fuck, she is wet.

Despite her struggling against me, I somehow sheath myself, lift her hips and drive into her with such force that it propels her forward.

I piston in and out of her with a punishing tempo. Like I can fuck the memories from her. From me.

Like I can chase not only my release, but all the

demons with every brutal thrust. Savage attack. Redeeming push.

"Harder," Brook cries, bracing her hand on the headboard.

My fingers are bruising her hips. Our skin glistens with perspiration. The slap of our bodies echoes through the room.

And then she tightens around me, her heat gripping my cock tight. And with my name on her lips, she comes, and I follow shortly after.

I collapse beside her, and our eyes lock. Spent and beautiful, she stares at me with a ghost of a smile lingering on her flushed face.

I'm spent and angry. But I keep the sizzling fire under control, because right now I can't leave her here. I'll wage my war later.

I should say something. I want to make sure she is okay.

Instead, I close my eyes, because this night has changed too much, and all the pieces are only now slowly settling in.

We've just redefined our mutual language, and I have no words. I'm not sure if I can... if I want to speak.

Chapter 24

Brook

"Please, Baldo." I writhe under him, desperately seeking release.

It's like he decided to catch me up on all the orgasms I haven't had. After the first cathartic fuck, Baldo brought me to the brink three more times.

But the man is a master of edging, and I now understand what he meant when he said I might beg him to stop.

I don't even know what I'm pleading for right now.

He's relaxed by my side, his head propped in his hand and his cock pressed against my thigh. But it's like he doesn't care about that steel rod at all. He's just leisurely pumping his fingers in and out of me.

"Please what, baby?" he rasps, and I'm glad for the effort in his words. He might look like he's just chilling beside me, but he's struggling to keep control.

I thrash my hips, trying to find more friction, or perhaps hoping to escape it. I don't even know anymore what would be better.

Skittles is on my tongue, but instead I cry out, "Just make me come, for fuck's sake."

He chuckles. "I thought you'd never ask."

The bastard.

But he crooks his fingers and does something else with his thumb, and bites my nipple, and it's like he's mastered my body in one single night.

An orgasm washes over me, and I'm coming and coming while he keeps finger fucking me.

And as I slowly come down, he's there, stroking my hair, planting kisses on my shoulder and handing me a glass of water.

One thing is clear. Baldo Cassinetti is an extremely generous lover.

We lie facing each other, just enjoying the closeness.

We're exhausted—well, I am. But I don't want to go to sleep. I feel like a new woman. Like tonight, the confession, the chase and the orgasms have fixed another broken piece in me.

A piece I didn't even know was still loose somewhere inside. A piece I never knew existed is now reattached.

And Baldo is tentatively a part of it. He always has

been, but I'm trying not to give it too much consequence because it scares me.

"Are you sore?" he rasps.

"In the best way possible." I don't think I'll be able to walk for several days, but it's not like I need to go anywhere.

"You should get some sleep."

"What about you?" I aim my eyes at the bulge in his briefs.

"Don't worry about me."

"I don't understand, though. Most men aren't this giving."

He keeps touching me.

Stroking my shoulder gently with the pad of his thumb.

Curling a strand of my hair around his finger.

And staring into my eyes. It's a bit unnerving. He must see into my soul, and I'm not sure that's a place I want to show him yet.

The world outside is in a deep slumber. The nightlife wore off hours ago, and the morning bustle of the city hasn't started yet.

"Taking care of women's..." He pauses, his jaw ticking. "Of your needs, gives me satisfaction."

Of my needs? It wasn't his first choice of words, and now I'm again thinking about all the other women he satisfies. About the long-legged brunette from his office.

But fuck it, he's with me, not with her.

Taking care of my needs.

I don't even do that properly most days, and having someone else put me first like this is unsettling. It makes me feel naked. More than I already am. Exposed. Discovered.

The feeling coils around my spine, settling in my chest, depriving me of oxygen. Baldo's full attention is on me, and I don't want him to witness another panic attack.

So I lean into sarcasm. "Like I'm a job well done."

He smirks, but shrugs.

"So it was mind-blowing for me and just a job for you?"

I need to lighten the mood, because everything that happened tonight is wonderfully liberating and special.

But also too intense, and I don't know where this level of intimacy leaves us. Or leads us.

It's all too much to deal with, so let's not.

"Mind-blowing?" He grins.

"And now I know why you have such a huge apartment." I punch his shoulder. "To fit your ego." I bite him gently.

He swats at me and smirks. "Mind-blowing."

"Just a job for you," I deadpan.

"Pleasing others is the sexiest thing. It turns me on. You turn me on. Fuck, Brook, you're the sexiest thing in the world."

Oh, what those words do to me. They grip at all my insecurities and traumas and turn them into dust.

It's dizzying. It's exhilarating. And yet, the primary emotion cruising through my veins is fear.

It's a familiar feeling, always lingering in the back of my mind. That's why I party, I go out, I surround myself with people and boyfriends—however unsatisfactory. To tune it all out.

But it has never been this loud when I'm with someone. It has a new cause, as if it replaced my former source of unrest.

What are we doing? How much is it going to hurt once we... no longer are? Because he has no reason to stick around.

Pleasing others is the sexiest thing.

Is that the reason he married me, cut his hair, got me the ring? It turns him on?

What's wrong with me? I'm lying here with the god of sex, blissfully satisfied, and my mind is sabotaging everything.

We used to be so close, soul mates, really. And now we're close physically and it should feel great, but it feels like I have more to lose. Which makes no sense.

"Maybe I was searching for something... some

special connection. Like if I give it my all, selflessly, I might feel..."

He plays with my hair, looking at me, but I'm not sure what he sees. Or contemplates. A hesitant smile lingers on his face, but there are clouds shading it.

"Feel what?" I croak, my mouth dry.

The soft silky sheet feels cold beneath me. The air is chilled as goosebumps prickle my skin in the stillness of the eyeblink.

It takes a lifetime before he answers. "Less. More. Something."

My heart hammers. He must see it pulsing in my veins, that's how relentless the beat is. "Did you find it?"

He said he was searching. Was. And while his words could have any meaning in the world, somewhere deep down I know. I know that I know that I know.

Like me, with all my unsuccessful relationships, he was searching too. In a very different, and perhaps less destructive, way than me, but we both were looking for that connection.

The one so familiar. The one we used to have.

"I'm sorry I left you here alone." It's not the answer to my question, but it is at the same time.

The apology fills the air between us. Heavy and

light. Redeeming and taxing. Welcomed but saddening.

Did he now find what he chased? With me? And it scared him, so he hid.

Or the connection didn't live up to the memory of us. The illusion we both cultivated over the years. Well, I did.

I have no claims on his time, but his apology feels significant. Like a commitment. Like he won't leave me alone anymore.

He left me once, a long time ago. Can I chance letting him in and trust he won't leave me again? God, I'm overthinking this. Making it way more than it really is.

"I got a lot of work done." I shrug, desperate to abandon the gravity of this conversation.

He runs his finger around my hairline. Slowly, gently, he tucks a strand behind my ear.

It's like he can't let go. Like he can't get enough. His gaze hugs me with reverence and adoration. I've never been looked at like this.

Correction. I have. By this man. But in many ways, it's not the same. His all-consuming, soul-caressing gaze is familiar and undiscovered.

"That's good," he rasps.

For the first time, I want to tell someone about my work. My family has always subtly suggested it's time to *do* something, because they all believe I party and live off my trust fund. I never cared.

But for some reason, I care about Baldo knowing I have a successful career. He doesn't ask. Maybe he doesn't care.

Like he married me, had sex with me, but sharing anything personal is above and beyond.

Like this fragile connection we forged tonight is all in my head. Perhaps all the orgasms have robbed me of perspective.

Of distance.

Of reason.

Where the fuck is this constant insecurity coming from?

"What's going on in that head of yours?" He uncoils a strand and takes another one between his fingers.

I roll on to my back, suddenly deflated by this pillow talk. He unraveled me tonight in more ways than one, and maybe I'm just temporarily emotional, but shit, I want him to care.

"I don't live off my trust fund, you know," I huff.

He chuckles. "Okay. It's not like it matters."

I turn my head to him, frowning.

"What?" He smirks. "I wouldn't let you pay for anything anyway, so what do I care if you make money or not?"

I rise to my elbows. Annoyed.

Patronizing bastard. And why is telling him about my career suddenly so important?

He's smart to draw the boundaries at the physical connection. Very smart.

"That's chauvinistic."

He laughs. "Whatever." He covers me with his solid body, heat shooting from his eyes.

His biceps frame my head and, God, this man is glorious. I haven't explored his naked body yet, and I want to.

He grinds his hard cock against me, and the unsatisfactory sharing conversation loses its power over me.

My eyes drop to his lips, and I think he's going to kiss me, but he lowers his head and nibbles on my neck, and down to my breasts.

The immediate shudder that ripples through me draws a moan from deep inside me. I close my eyes, reveling in the sensations so new to me.

So vital to me all of a sudden. Like my body wants to level the score after all the mediocre attempts before tonight.

I want more.

I need more.

All my insecurities bubble up, mingling with selfishness now.

"Kiss me," I whisper.

He tenses, it's only for a beat of a moment, and I almost think I imagined it before he resumes brushing his lips down my skin.

"I *am* kissing you." He takes my nipple into his mouth.

"On my lips."

Why am I so needy? The man already gave me so much tonight, and here I am, mourning that he doesn't offer more and demanding it.

He looks up, his eyes heated. "I thought I made it clear that I'm in charge. You can beg me to make you come, but the only demands here come from me."

He returns to my nipple, biting it hard through the silky fabric. My back arches at the sensation, taking all the fight away from me.

Clearly, one of us is sane enough to set strict boundaries.

It's a smart thing.

It's the safest thing.

It's the right thing to do.

So why does it hurt?

Somehow I can't sleep, my mind firing in a thousand different directions.

The chase and sex we had after my confession

seem to have unlocked something. It's like the years of therapy helped me to get so far, but there was a part of me that needed this to complete the healing.

I don't even understand where my need to be chased and fucked like that came from. I'm sure my therapist would have an opinion or two about that.

I let—forced—Baldo to take advantage of me, and it's like I reclaimed something I thought had been taken away from me a long time ago.

We can't get back what we lost that night, but we were able to mend some of it tonight.

I think.

I hope.

I worry.

But as I watch the darkness slowly giving way to a new day, I'm sure I'm the only one who offered intimacy tonight.

Baldo delivered what I needed, but he stayed in his shell, behind a tall, impenetrable wall.

And while he was ravishing my body all night, I didn't get a chance to consider what my confession meant for him.

One thing is what happened that night to my body, but that man didn't just violate me. He took something from Baldo.

A chance with me.

A chance for us.

I've never uncovered that layer of the tragedy before. I focused on my body, my emotional and mental healing. And that was all right at the time.

I know that, but tonight Baldo found out someone interfered with our future. And yes, he got angry, but I needed more from him, so I didn't let him express that anger fully.

I glance at the broken lamp and table. Shit. I should have forced him to talk to me. Tell me what it all unraveled.

But here I was, just taking and taking. Forcing him to keep his own reactions bottled up inside him.

Fuck. I turn to face him, ready to wake him up and make him talk.

His breath is even but not peaceful, and his face is in a frown like he's having a bad dream.

The shy dawn casts light over his body. The man is gorgeous. My eyes trail over his chest, rising and falling, his chiseled abdomen and his arms.

I take a moment discovering his tattoos. The symbols look like Japanese characters. I lean closer, relishing the scent of the man. It's a mixture of sweat, sex, and something earthy I vaguely remember.

I focus on his forearm. The symbols repeat. It looks like it might be one word on repeat in different size and type, but always the same.

Curiosity burns inside me, and I decide to let him

sleep and force him to talk and let out what my confession caused in him in the morning.

My phone has been charging on the bedside table, and I grab it and take a picture of him and his tattoos.

The stupid camera clicks and Baldo stirs. I slide the phone under my pillow.

He mumbles something and lifts his arm to cover his face with his forearm. The move uncovers another tattoo I didn't notice before.

My heart speeds up as I stare at the image inked into his skin, right on the side of his heart.

Not on display on his chest, but rather hidden—protected under his arm—is a map of Japan.

It's just a simple outline of the cluster of islands that form the country. And in the middle of it, there is a heart where the capital city lies.

Tokyo.

Chapter 25

Baldo

She's sleeping peacefully. That's good. That's good.

I want her peaceful. The selfish bastard in me hopes I brought some of that peace to her.

The peace I don't think I will ever find again.

For the longest time, I needed to know why she didn't come, and now I know. And fuck it. It brought exactly zero comfort.

I had always thought finding out her reasons would bring me closure. Fucking hell. Now I know, and I burn with vengeance. With rage. With the need to destroy.

That man stole from me.

He stole from her more. I know that, but my mind still goes to what I lost.

He stole her from me.

He rewrote our story.

And I want to fucking kill him.

I have to find him.

Brook stirs, stretches her arm and pats the sheets beside her. "Baldo?"

Her voice sleepy, she flutters her eyes open, a little disoriented.

"I'm here." I sit beside her.

She smiles. "You're here."

My chest hurts. There is no fucking oxygen in this cavernous space.

She blinks a few times and reaches for me, her hand landing on my biceps. She frowns.

"You're dressed."

"I have to take care of something. I didn't mean to wake you."

I don't think she is fully awake yet. Poor thing needs rest. And now a fresh wave of rage floods my bloodstream. At myself. I should have taken it easy with her.

"I was always jealous of your eyelashes," she says and yawns, curling up on her side, her hands under her flushed face.

I snort and pull the sheet up to cover her better. "My eyelashes?"

She closes her eyes and sighs. Her blonde hair spread on my pillow, and a ghost of a smile smoothing her features, she's a vision.

Mine.

For now, at least.

"Yeah." She yawns again. "It's unfair a man has such long, thick lashes."

I can't help it, I lean down and kiss her forehead. "I'll be back soon."

"Where are you going?" She's half asleep already.

"I have a quick breakfast meeting."

She sits up so suddenly, I almost topple from the edge of the bed. Not half asleep after all.

"With the long-legged brunette you were so cozy with yesterday?"

I raise my eyebrows. "Good to know I'm not the only one who's jealous."

"Prick. You really just fucked my brains out and you're going to have breakfast with another woman?" She scoots away from me, pulling the sheets with her as if seeking modesty.

She's fucking adorable, worked up over nothing. Her indignation makes me ridiculously happy. Not that there is much room for such emotion in my stormy mind this morning.

"Why don't you come with me?"

That stops her retreat. "What?"

"You heard me, Brook. Hurry up and get dressed." I stand up and walk to the kitchen, sweeping away the shards of last night by the sofa with my foot.

Fuck, I need to call my housekeeper to take care of this before Brook gets cut. I wish it was that easy to deal with the other broken pieces in the aftermath of our reunion.

"I need to shower." She scrambles out of the bed.

"No time for that."

"But—"

"I want everyone to smell who you belong to."

I hold her hand.

As if she's mine. I grip her tight, like that will somehow keep her by my side.

We walk across the street and down the block to a small bistro where Chloe waits.

I need to rein myself in and not crush her bones, her hand is so small in my paw. But fuck, the need to protect her, to own her, to make sure she's okay is so strong that I'm wild with boiling energy.

I walk down the street, ready to kill any man who looks at her. Christ, I'm even antagonistic toward women.

Closure? Fuck the closure.

I haven't been this unhinged for years. Yeah, for

about a year after that night, but then I got it under control.

Mostly.

Like having that ruby ring made years ago. I know that wasn't healthy. It digs into my palm now to mock me.

Now I know why she didn't show up, and I'm torn inside, barely keeping it together.

"Could you slow down a bit?"

Fuck. I've been dragging her behind me like a madman.

"Sorry."

"Are you okay?" She narrows her eyes, studying me as she tries to keep up at the same time.

"Sure."

Not at all, but that's not something I'm going to burden her with.

She needed the release last night, and I'd give it to her a thousand times over, even if it meant reliving her retelling the story again and again.

And the masochist in me wants to push her for more details, more gory facts, more hurt. Like I could make her tell me again, and with every word take some of her pain and swallow it to rot inside me.

"We should talk."

She means I should talk, but what I need is to act.

To turn every stone to find the fucking asshole and punish him.

But that's not happening this morning, so here I am, compartmentalizing again and putting on the Baldo Charming Cassinetti mask.

"We will, sweetheart," I lie and wink at her, pushing the glass door open.

The aromas of coffee and custard embrace us as we weave around the small tables in the busy place.

Chloe smiles when she sees us. If she's surprised I'm not alone, she doesn't show it.

"That was some exit last night." She applauds theatrically instead of a greeting.

Fuck. My caveman performance. Was it only last night, because it feels like I've lived another lifetime since then.

"Brook, this is Chloe Miller, my director of operations. Chloe, this is Brook. My wife."

Brook's eyes widen, and she stares at me for a moment before she blinks and extends her hand, and the women shake. "Pleased to meet you."

We take our seats and I grab a menu to channel the nervous energy somewhere. Not that reading the menu can consume a drop of the hurricane within me.

"The pleasure is all mine," Chloe says. "I'm so happy you two found each other. It was a long time coming for sure."

Fuck, Chloe knows more about my pining than anyone. In fact, she's the only person I've ever told about Brook. Not in too many details, but still.

Brook looks at me with curiosity, a smile lingering on her face. She says nothing. A part of me really hoped she would respond to Chloe and say she also is glad we found each other.

What the fuck is wrong with me? Where is my preservation instinct this morning?

The waiter comes to take our order.

"Try pastel de nata. It's a traditional dessert." I put my hand on the small of her back, because I simply need the contact.

"Okay, I'll have that and a latte." She leans into my hand a little, and I don't even want to think about how that makes me feel.

"So, what exactly did Baldo tell you about us?" Brook asks.

Chloe opens the linen napkin and places it over her lap. "That you're the one who got away. And as a helpless romantic, I'm so glad it worked out in the end."

Brook smiles. It's a satisfied smile. "When did he tell you this?"

Chloe looks at me like she's seeking permission to answer.

Time to hijack the conversation. "Chloe works

from our Paris location. We need to discuss a few things before she leaves, if you don't mind." I practically shut down the chitchat.

"Oh, I'm sorry. I didn't realize, since you invited me." Brook darts her eyes between me and Chloe.

"Actually, we don't have to work." Chloe looks at me, unimpressed. "Mary is flying to join me. We decided to go to Porto for the weekend. So, the two of us can talk shop later today, *boss*."

I fidget. The last thing I need is for the two of them sharing details about my occasional obsession with Brook over the years. Not that Chloe knows much about it.

The waiter fills our table with steaming coffee cups, aromatic pastries and water.

"I've never been to Porto," Brook says.

"The two of you should come with us. It would be like a double date." Chloe smiles.

"That would be great—" Brook says, looking at me.

"I can't this weekend. I have some business to take care of."

If Brook is disappointed that I shut down the getaway, she hides it well. She picks up the pastel with her delicate fingers and takes a bite, the pastry's flakes dropping to the plate. "Maybe another time. Is Mary your...?"

"My wife. She is a flight attendant, so we work

hard to align our schedules. She happens to work the flight to Lisbon, so I decided to take advantage of it." Chloe sips her coffee. "Unless you need me here."

"No, of course, go and have fun with Mary. You deserve it."

"We do." Chloe nods. "So last night was interesting. I hope nobody will be pressing charges."

Brook looks at me. "Could he?" A flash of concern in her eyes makes me unreasonably happy.

"You don't need to worry about that. I texted the chief of police this morning. If a complaint is filed, my lawyer will deal with it quickly."

"You have a texting relationship with the chief of police?" Brook's eyes light up like she's pleased to learn this, while most people would frown upon this blatant suggestion at corruption.

Chloe laughs, and several heads turn our way. "I like you, Brook. I like you very much."

Brook chuckles. "So, how long have you been working together?"

"Sometimes it feels like for too long," I say, swirling the spoon in my half empty cup of coffee.

I don't have time for this chitchat.

I came because I made Chloe stay last night, and I owed her this breakfast. I brought Brook to make sure she understands she doesn't have to feel threatened by Chloe. Frankly, by no other woman.

The danger doesn't come from any woman.

It most probably comes from me.

Because I'm feeling out of control, and that's a recipe for fucking everything up.

Brook puts her hand on my thigh, and it quiets the storm within me. A bit.

"We actually met before Baldo owned his first bar in Rome. I worked the floor there as a waitress. He's a decent boss," Chloe teases.

"I'm sorry. I thought the two of you—"

"Are fucking?" Chloe finishes her sentence.

I should have never introduced them. "Not anymore," I say, because there is no point in hiding this. Brook would find out eventually.

She drops her hand from my thigh, but I grab it back, squeezing. It's warm and small in mine. It fits. It belongs. And I don't fucking know what to do with that.

There are too many things we have to fix before we can fit.

And my heart might not survive that.

"For full disclosure, we hooked up. A long time ago. He was pretty fucked up over you, and I was trying to figure out who I was. The worst match ever."

"She turned to women after that."

Brook chuckles. "I guess the professional relationship turned better."

"Definitely." Chloe checks her watch. "I have a meeting with the wine importer, but I hope to see you again soon. It was nice to meet you, Brook."

Brook turns to me after Chloe leaves. "She thinks I'm your wife."

"Because you're my wife."

I suddenly need to prove it to her. Even if it's not a real marriage, our union is as real as they get.

Complicated.

Painful.

And too raw for pretense.

Chapter 26

Brook

Baldo drags me through the streets back to his house. I stumble, trying to keep up, but I don't slow him down.

He seems to be on a mission, and it's sexy. Fuck, the boy I used to know was playful. This man is intense.

He's hot and cold. Serious and playful. A man who, on his own terms, allows himself to come out to play, and then burns down the playground.

There are so many layers to him, and he isn't willing to show many of them. Or to talk about any.

If I don't count the confusing shows of affection, because I'm sure his caring gestures must mean something.

A car screeches to a halt as we barrel across a busy

intersection. The air is infused with this hectic foreign city full of vibrant colors and smiling people.

"I love the city," I pant.

I bump into the wall of muscles as he stops.

He looks at me and closes his eyes for a beat, before he exhales a heavy breath. "I'll show you everything later. I've been a shitty host."

"You made up for it last night. It's our honeymoon, after all. Shouldn't we stay in the room?" I tease, grinning.

The corner of his mouth tips up. "Right."

He resumes his crusade through the hilly streets, but he's slower, allowing me to take in the surroundings.

Occasionally he points at something, but otherwise we walk in silence.

I need to get him to talk before the tense energy pent up within him explodes—it might kill us both.

But if the time we spent together is any indication, Baldo Cassinetti keeps his thoughts close to himself and his emotions even closer, buried under the facade of a solemn exterior.

And if I learned anything this morning, those close to him respect him. It was obvious in the way Chloe spoke about him.

I like her. Even more now that I know she's in a happy relationship.

We arrive at the club and take the back entrance to the elevator.

As soon as we step into the cabin, Baldo pins me against the wall and buries his face in the crook of my neck. "I need you."

I wrap my arms around his shoulders, clinging to him and memorizing this moment.

I need you. The three words float through me, bleeding into every crevice of my soul, speeding up my pulse and spreading warmth in my chest.

I want to say something, but no words seem to match the intensity of emotions overwhelming me.

Last night we forged this new level of connection, and now everything is fresh and unchartered and so fucking fragile.

And it would be an adventure, but we've been there before, and it ended in misery.

Could we chance it again? Are we strong enough to survive?

And what about our family.

"Tell me you're mine," he urges, his chest heaving, his breath hot on my skin.

The shadow of vulnerability in his demand, the need to be reassured, cracks a dent in my heart, and I try my best to squash away the thoughts of my dad and sisters.

He skims my ribcage with one hand while he

supports himself with the other on the wall above my head and grinds his pelvis against me.

I don't know if his need is a replacement for words and feelings he should be expressing, or if it's just the first stage of opening up.

I don't know much about anything anymore, because his heat, his scent, his words, his touch... it all collides into that one urgent plea.

"I'm yours." And right at this moment, I am.

Unapologetically.

Unequivocally.

Unreasonably.

The door to his apartment opens and we stumble out. Baldo grabs my ass and lifts me up. Wrapping my legs around his waist, I start unbuttoning his shirt.

I want to kiss him so badly, but this is not the time or place to cross that bridge. This is for him.

For the boy who waited for me.

For the boy who had been wondering for years why I never came.

For the man who learned last night that another one—a monster—took what was his.

So I'm not going to kiss him. I'm just going to remember how his lips felt on mine.

Because I still remember. Because even if Baldo Cassinetti never kisses me again, I'll forever remember his kisses.

By the time we stumble to his bed, I'm yanking at his shirt, sliding it down his shoulders. He lays me on the mattress and lowers one knee beside me. He sheds the sleeves, dropping the shirt to the floor.

I undo my jeans and lift my hips. He yanks them off, along with my underwear.

I sit up to reach for his zipper, but he grabs my wrist and shakes his head.

"Baldo, I want to take care of you. You've done so much for me, and I want to reciprocate."

He cups my cheeks and lowers his forehead to mine. There is a war waging in his eyes, but his features soften. "Then be a good girl and do as I say."

His eyes flare with visceral need, and just the idea that he needs me to sate that hunger sets my heart to a gallop.

"Okay," I whisper, and lie down, spreading my legs wide. "I'm yours," I repeat, and he groans.

Staring between my thighs with so much admiration that it makes me shy, he puts his hands on my knees, applying slight pressure. My skin burns under his touch.

"So fucking beautiful, Brook. Your pussy is the prettiest thing in the world. And already glistening with need, you greedy girl."

I cover my eyes with my forearms. I'm no prude, but his words bring heat to my cheeks.

But of course, he pries my arms away from my face immediately. "Don't hide. You and your pussy are gorgeous."

He takes his time kissing each knuckle of my hands. First one, then the other.

He's kneeling between my legs, and I'm spread wide, on display, while he continues with his gentle routine of kissing my fingers. It's weird and arousing at the same time.

The man puts me into the most vulnerable positions, and I always feel more empowered in them, loving every moment.

And most importantly, getting out of my head minute by minute. And that is so new and scary. Wonderfully scary.

Baldo reaches into his drawer and pulls out something. He sits back on his haunches, holding a bottle of lube and a fairly large dildo. Oh my.

He squirts the transparent gel on the toy and a soft humming noise fills the air. He looks at me and I shudder.

Settling his face between my thighs, he gets to work with a dedication that will kill me one day. And what a way to go.

"Hmmmm," he hums. "You smell like me and sex."

Fuck, I forgot I left in a hurry this morning. "I should have showered." My legs jerk to close, but the man is relentless and pins them back down, spreading me even farther.

"Don't you dare. Stay like this," he commands. "Don't move, my dirty girl."

He swirls his tongue around my clit, while he nudges my opening with the vibrator.

What if I don't come this time?

What if last night was one of a kind?

Maybe my body acted on recognition from before, and now it remembers how broken it is.

"Brook."

I snap my eyes to him.

"Relax, baby. Let me take care of you."

His statement is matter-of-fact, like he can read my mind and knows I'm overthinking. But fuck, my body is all tense, and I force myself to let up.

"That's it." He sucks on my clit for a moment and changes the setting on the toy. It vibrates at my opening, but he doesn't move it any further.

I focus on relaxing, on wave after wave of pleasure, but I keep returning to my head. What's wrong with me, goddammit?

I groan with frustration and Baldo chuckles. He fucking chuckles, completely unfazed by my struggle.

"You're doing great, sweetheart. Such a good girl. You'll get there."

It might be a combination of his praise and the new action of his tongue when he circles and then moves it fast, pulsating, but I shudder, and the feeling building inside me gets so overwhelming, all thoughts leave my head.

My back arches, and Baldo moves his hand to my lower stomach and holds me down. He thrusts the dildo in slowly. He doesn't move it, just lets it vibrate inside me.

"That's it, baby, swallowing it like you would my cock."

I don't even recognize my body anymore. Tides of pleasure ripple through me, and I still don't have enough, knowing this is just the prelude.

"Baldo, please," I whimper.

"Since you asked so nicely."

He shifts his weight and reaches to tweak my nipple through my T-shirt.

A glimpse of recognition that he respected my need to be covered hits me right in the chest, but there is no time to ponder it because an explosion rocks through me.

My body convulses, and I'm flying or falling or something as Baldo continues to lick me, prolonging the bliss.

I'm still riding it when he climbs up. "I need to be inside you."

I wrap my legs around his waist, surprised I'm able to move.

Our eyes lock, but he reaches to the side. "Condom."

I clamp my feet together. "No. I'm clear and on the shot."

He studies me for a moment. "I've never..."

"Another first for us."

The words formed in my head as playful, but once they're out, the significance pulses through me.

"Are you sure?" he rasps, the struggle evident.

I nod, and he slides into me effortlessly.

Like he belongs. Like my body was made for him.

The thought immediately triggers the dread.

Because this level of belonging is painful.

I know from experience.

* * *

"Fuck, Brook," he cries, and collapses beside me.

I bury my face in the pillow, coming down and dealing with all the emotions.

Well, we fucked. We fucked a lot this morning. But we still didn't talk.

And now it's even harder, because I feel like we need more than to talk about what my revelation did to him.

Now I feel like we need to talk about us. About what this all means. For us. And for our family.

Ironically, we're on our fake honeymoon, but our relationship has never been this unclear. We either were or we weren't. Now we're lingering somewhere in between, and it feels in some ways harder than what was before.

"We should finally get you clean, dirty girl." He swats at my ass.

"Yes, please." I jump out of bed and pull the tee over my head.

I hesitate for a moment, but what the hell, I can't hide any longer. I don't want to hide any longer.

I turn in the doorway to the bathroom. "Are you coming?" I wiggle my hips.

Baldo rakes his eyes down my curves and swallows. "Are you sure?"

I bite my lower lip and crook my finger to beckon him to me. I'm showing more confidence than I feel.

Other men saw my scar, but they didn't have a story to go with it. Or the story wasn't in any way personal to them.

I mentioned the knife last night. I think I did, but it's still unnerving to have him see it.

I walk into the cubicle and turn on the water. It's a huge shower. I can dance on the white tiles around the glass walls.

While Baldo's apartment is all dark wood and earthy accents, this bathroom is almost exclusively white, chrome and glass.

I sense him coming in, but he doesn't step closer.

Submerging my head into the hot stream, I close my eyes.

With unwavering certainty, I know my maimed skin won't repulse him. I also know I can't hide it from him forever.

And yet, I'm frozen under practically scorching water because I want to delay the moment.

I don't want to see his sympathy. Or even worse, his horror. It would break me all over again. And I've been mending those pieces of myself for years.

"You're so fucking beautiful."

His voice washes over me like a warm blanket. I didn't even realize when he stepped closer. He's not touching me, but I feel his presence in my every pore.

He reaches for shampoo, squirts some in his large hands. "Tilt your head."

"You don't have—"

"Hush."

I lean against his solid body, and he massages my scalp and then lathers my hair. His hands draw a moan from me.

"Careful," he warns, and I want to ask what he

means, but then I feel his hardness between us and I chuckle.

Baldo twirls me around and washes the shampoo out of my hair. The air is filled with steam, and I'm feeling weak in my knees as he takes his time soaping my shoulders.

Hugging me to him, he does the same to my back, and then stepping only slightly back to clean my breasts and then—

Just sensing the ugly scar running from under my breast to my belly button under his fingertips, Baldo freezes.

I snap my eyes open. The lazy delight evaporates from the air as my gaze collides with his.

"Who did this to you?"

I sigh, but his mind is clouded with the brutality of his discovery.

"Who the fuck did this to you, Brook?" he demands, and then finally stills enough to read the answer in my eyes.

Understanding dawns on him quickly. But there is no sympathy or horror in his eyes. Compassion maybe, but mostly anger.

Fuck, I have had years to deal with my trauma.

I've done it while feeling sorry. I allowed myself to be angry. I hid from it all for several years.

I worked hard to channel my trauma into creating villains and plots that could swallow the darkness.

Baldo is discovering the gory details one day at a time, without much chance for reflection. Without even talking to me about it.

I know I can't take responsibility for his ability to cope, but I still want to.

"Fuck." He breathes heavily and grips his hair.

"It's my fault, mostly. It was just a nick of a blade. I don't think he even meant to use his knife."

The words roll off my tongue faster than I can think. Like taking the blame, I can make this better. Easier for Baldo to accept it. "I didn't want to tell Mom and Dad, and I neglected it and let it fester and it got infected—"

"Stop it!" He startles me. "None of this is your fault." He steps back.

I know—hope—it's not away from me, but rather away from the situation. And still I feel abandoned under the pelting water.

But the man who reigns over his control with a pathological precision once again tames the emotions, and looks at me with a reverence so unexpected, it takes my breath away.

Dropping to his knees, my fake husband who is yet to kiss my lips, kisses my marred skin with such devotion, that tears run down my face.

Chapter 27

Brook

He saw me.
 He finally saw me.
 And it broke us again.
Baldo worshiped my body in the shower, making me feel wanted and beautiful. Making me forget, come undone and put back together.

I fell asleep in his arms afterward, and woke up to a note from him.

Gone away on business. Be back in a day or two.

A day or two?

I pace the streets mindlessly, not sure what to do with myself. A housekeeper showed up and I decided to go out, but I have no interest in sightseeing or discovering the city.

I wanted to write in a cafe, but I'm full of pent-up energy. So mad at him for running away from the situation. Or maybe he really had a business meeting he couldn't postpone and forgot to mention it earlier.

I keep at my mindless traversing of the picturesque streets for almost two hours before my feet scream in protest, and I finally stop and sit in a small bistro near the water.

I order a coffee and the delicious sweet pastel de nata and open my laptop. I reread the last scene I wrote, but my mind keeps wandering to the events of the last few days.

I became a new woman, in some sense of the word. My first orgasms and Baldo's need to please me helped me reclaim my body.

I didn't even know I still needed that part of me to be complete.

In some way, I also got closure of my abruptly killed first love.

But my current relationship with Baldo is as unresolved as it's ever been.

He didn't find me repulsive, but if he doesn't address the issue and deal with his own trauma that I'm sure my revelation caused, he'll start to hate me. Not me, but everything I remind him of.

And maybe he already regrets everything, and that's why he disappeared. It's not like the man has shared one thought or feeling with me.

I opened up, but there was no time for him to reciprocate and speak up, or he skillfully diverted the topic.

I click out of the manuscript and click on video conferencing.

Saar answers quickly. "Give me a moment."

Wearing heavy makeup and an elaborate hairdo, she scurries into a corner of some hangar or warehouse, leaving people behind.

A heavy metal door creaks and she steps into the sunshine. "Hey." She smiles.

"Hey, where are you? Are you working? Am I interrupting?"

"Yeah, I'm in Madrid, I think. God, I'm so jetlagged I don't even know."

"That's not far from me. Maybe you can come and visit when you're done."

"I'm stuck on set till midnight, probably. Why don't you come over and we'll spend the day together tomorrow before I have to fly out in the afternoon?"

I almost decline, but fuck, why not? I'm here alone. And this is Europe, after all. Nothing is more than a two-hour flight.

"Okay. Send me the address where you're staying and I'll wait for you tonight, if I can find a flight."

She squeals in delight. "I can't wait to see you and hear everything about your fake honeymoon."

Groaning, I hide my face in my hands.

"Saar, get your ass back here." A male voice comes from somewhere on the other side.

"What's going on, Brook? Are you not faking it anymore? Are you together *together*?"

"Saar," the same voice yells.

"You better go. I'll tell you everything when I get there."

I pay and rush outside, making my way to Baldo's building.

"Brook?"

I turn and smile. "Chloe, I thought you'd be in Porto by now."

The woman beside Chloe rolls her eyes. She has short hair, and her height barely reaches Chloe's shoulders.

"Yeah, that got canceled pretty quickly. Is Baldo upstairs?" Chloe quips.

"He's gone. I thought you'd know." What kind of business would he need to handle without his second in command being aware?

"I thought when he made me stay here because he

had an *urgent* personal matter, that the said matter was you." Her tone is bitter.

I frown. "Oh."

She shakes her head. "Never mind, perhaps I misunderstood and assumed you left with him."

"I had to finish some work." I'm not sure why I lie. He doesn't deserve me covering for him.

Where did he go? So suddenly. And clearly lying about it to both of us. For all I know, he might have another wife somewhere. God, does he?

I'll poison him if that's the case. Stabbing or shooting would be too messy.

"Oh, this is Mary, my wife," Chloe says, snapping me out of that imagery.

"Very nice to meet you. I'm sorry your weekend plans got canceled."

"Well, we still get a weekend together." She smiles. "If I can get this one to stay away from work." She casts her eyes sideways at Chloe.

"I guess our spouses are workaholics, perhaps we should start a support group." I attempt to sound upbeat.

Mary snorts and Chloe jumps in. "I'm not the one constantly away."

God, the last thing I want is to be in the middle of their domestic dispute. "I'm sorry. I want to catch a plane to Madrid, if possible today, so I better go."

"Oh, why don't you get Baldo's concierge to take care of it?"

Because, of course, if I was his wife for real, I'd have access to that service. "Oh, great idea. Thank you."

If I was his actual wife, I'd also know where he is right now.

* * *

It's almost two in the morning when Saar comes to her hotel room in Madrid. I startle when the door clicks closed.

"Sorry, darling, didn't mean to wake you."

I stretch on the small sofa where I was writing—or trying to—before I apparently fell asleep. "That's okay. An hour more on this and I'd need a chiropractor."

"Why aren't you in bed?"

"My flight didn't get in till ten, so I wanted to wait for you."

She looks exhausted and stifles a yawn before she comes over and hugs me. "It's amazing when you're in Europe and we can just hang out like this."

"Are you okay?"

"It was a taxing day, but nothing unusual. I'm starving. Let's order room service."

"Comfort food after midnight? My favorite way to wrap up the day."

She giggles and orders way too much food and a bottle of wine. After she changes into sweats and a hoodie, she sits across from me with cotton pads and a bottle of makeup remover.

"Okay, so I saw the man, and oof..." She fans herself with her hand. "How is he, besides the obvious hotness?"

I snort. "Yeah, he's hot, I'll give you that. And extremely talented in the bedroom. He's successful and a good businessman from what I've seen. He's smart, brooding and aloof. I like it when he gets jealous, and he's also really caring. Intense and hard to read, but confident in that silent, dominant way that makes your knees weak."

Saar jerks the cotton pad away from her eye, cocks her head and studies me with a smile. Like she knows something I don't. "Are you falling for him?"

I groan and rest my head on the backrest.

"God, no." I'm not sure if that's actually the truth, but I can't let that happen. But then maybe I've been in love with Baldo for years. Or with the idea of us. I don't know anymore. "He is the best lover I've ever had."

She narrows her eyebrows, and I swear she can see my internal struggle. "Tell me everything."

And I do. I tell her everything that happened since we spoke the last time.

"It feels like you're together for real now. Are you?" Saar asks the big question and puts the cleanser bottle down, next to a pile of stained cotton pads.

"We haven't talked about it. The man is like a vault. I don't know what he's thinking or planning. He doesn't share. It's like he uses his generosity in all the other areas, and there isn't any left for words."

"The conundrum of every woman—how to force him to talk without spooking him. Men are hopeless creatures." She turns sideways and leans against the armrest, hanging her head backward, untangling her hair and massaging her scalp.

"And he hasn't kissed me. On the mouth, that is."

"What? He took care of your needs and had you thoroughly fucked, but no kissing?" She turns her head, her dark blonde hair cascading to the floor. "Well, I'm going to call it, but I think your dear husband is avoiding intimacy. Ironic, given all the action you guys have had in the bedroom." She wiggles her eyebrows.

A knock on the door announces room service. Saar signs the bill while I remove the cloche from the steaming paella. The scent of herbs and seafood fills the room.

We open a bottle of Chardonnay, then settle down to eat the mouthwatering rice dish and sip the wine.

"I don't know what to do with it all. I can't even blame him for retreating. He needs time to process, and it's probably best he does it away from me. But it's like I got closure and he got the exact opposite, and somehow I feel responsible for that."

"I know you do, but that's not healthy. He chose to leave back then, and while it sucks that he has this delayed onslaught of shit dumped on him, it's not your shit to clean."

"You're so poetic."

She chuckles. "But the question is, once you sort through the painful effects of the events from ten years ago, where does it leave the two of you?"

I slump deeper into the seat. "I don't know, because when I think about even a remote possibility of us, a real us, I want to pack my things and disappear."

"But you can't."

"But I can't." Though the reasons are blurred now.

"And is it because you're a good person who won't let her inheritance support evil, or because you're falling for the man?"

"Obviously I'm a good person. I think the girl in me never stopped loving Baldo. But the Baldo I married isn't the same boy. I'm not falling for him. I don't know him." My chest constricts at the words.

"And yet..." She finishes her glass and stands up.

I follow, unzip my jeans, kick them off and crawl

into bed. "There is no yet. I want to help him deal with the past, but if he's going to be a stubborn prick... I would miss the orgasms, but I'll just go back home and count down to the divorce." I want to joke, but that loss would hurt.

Rationally, I know he's not the only person to deliver orgasms, but he has been in my case. Am I healed now? Or forever dependent on Baldo's skills? I groan inwardly.

"That's still a year from now." She sheds her clothes and puts on an old tee. It must have sentimental value, because Saar definitely doesn't need to wear a threadbare shirt.

"Well, I literally survived worse. Whose T-shirt is that?"

I don't want to analyze my life anymore, because more spinning in circles will just give me a headache. And I'm already suffering from the early stages of heartache.

Or rather its remains from ten years ago. That should heal soon, though. And then I can move on. And if Baldo opens up and deals with the trauma, he'll be able to move on as well.

"It's just an old tee." But before she shrugs, she tenses for long enough to show it's not just an old T-shirt.

"You used to wear an extra large?"

She slides under the covers. "I think you need to talk to Baldo, and if he doesn't explain why he had an engagement ring on standby, why he never came back for you, and what is going on in his head now, you should set clear rules for your marriage, so you can survive the year."

Still curious about the original owner of that T-shirt, I snort. "You think clear, straightforward communication is the way to go? It sounds so adult and boring."

"It wouldn't make for good TV, that's for sure."

"In any case, there is no future for us. Dad would have a heart attack, and his health is feeble as it is. No need to add stress. I've just gotten back and found my place with them, and I'm scared the two of us together would shatter that."

"Brook, you're taking responsibility for other people's reactions again. You need to be more selfish. Yes, the two of you would be a shock for your family. But they would get over it."

"Like your parents?"

When Saar's brothers, Finn and Caleb, orchestrated a hostile takeover of their father's firm, Saar supported them. Their parents stopped speaking to all of them.

"That's different. My parents have always considered me and my brothers property to carve into their liking, to fulfill their dreams. They never loved me as much as yours. Love always wins."

"Do you really believe that about love?"

"God, no."

I chuckle. "Thank you for your pep talk, then."

"I've been fucked up by my family dynamics, but your parents love you and they will understand."

I sigh. "Life is unfair."

"But full of fun."

"I think if I'm with him for only one year, he can be mute, and I'll take all the O's I can. Why do I complicate things and want more?" I groan. "It's funny how he insists on clear communication when it comes to sex, but outside of the bedroom he's a closed book. I had to choose a safe word."

Saar groans. "I need to get laid."

We both giggle, then fall silent.

The problem is, I'm not sure I truly want Baldo to open up, because a part of me fears his rejection.

He wanted sex with me, but perhaps only because I opened that door with my drunken propositioning.

And as he pointed out, he is stuck with me for a year. Maybe sex with me is like his Maserati. Something to enjoy while he bides his time.

But his actions, the way he takes care of me... I can't be just an easy lay. Can I?

A woman's pleasure turns him on. Is his generosity just his normal MO, not special to me?

And where the hell did he go?

Against a background of Saar's soft snores, I stare into the night, waiting for sleep to claim me, while dark intense eyes, brawny arms and a rare but alluring grin flicker through my mind.

* * *

A sound drills into my brain with relentless tenacity. It infiltrates my foggy mind and I pull my pillow over my head.

But it does nothing to cease the ringing attack.

"What the fuck?" Saar's voice pulls me to reality. "Is that your phone?"

I groan. Of course it is. What time is it?

"Make it stop," she pleads.

I push up on to my elbows, blinking, unable to locate the offending sound, when it finally stops. I drop back, but my relief is premature and the ringing returns.

Trying to untangle from the sheets, I manage to stand up, stumbling around the room before I find my phone on the charger beside the bed.

I glance at the caller ID. "John, this better be good." I plop back onto the bed, yawning.

"Shit, sorry, I thought you were in Europe."

My agent is based in London.

"I am in Europe. What time is it?"

"It's ten o'clock here, so I guess eleven in Portugal."

"I'm in Spain... never mind... What's going on?"

"I can't believe you sidetracked me with the time conversation—I have great news, Brook. They finally signed off."

I sit up so fast my head spins. I blink a few times, my heart hammering against my chest, and then I squeal.

"Jesus, what's going on?" Saar sits up in her bed, her hair sticking out in all directions.

"Congratulations," John says in my ear.

"Thank you."

"What happened?" Saar mouths.

"They agreed to all my requests?" I ask John.

"Mostly. I'll email you the contract and the dates I need you to be here. They want you to meet the main protagonist."

"Yes, of course. I can be there anytime."

"We did it, Brook. Talk to you soon." John hangs up.

I fall back and kick the air and pump it with my fist at the same time. "My book is becoming a TV series."

Chapter 28

Baldo

Guilt. Overwhelming guilt.

This heavy load of guilt has been weighing on me since Brook told me what happened to her that night.

I should have been there. I should have never asked her to run away with me. I should have left the house with her, not before her. I should have...

My head has been spinning with all the bitter, nauseating remorse swirling inside me. The endless *should have*s stripping me of control.

Sleep, food, and less whiskey might stop—or slow—the spiral, but they wouldn't negate one fat truth.

I failed her.

I haven't done this many transatlantic flights in...

ever. There was an obvious benefit to not doing business in the States.

Not that I'm here for business. Though the trip is turning out longer than I planned. Fucking Mathison is on vacation, but at least I tricked him into talking to me.

So here I am, my plane taxiing yet again, en route to the Dominican Republic.

Chloe is pissed because she had to cancel her weekend getaway due to my unexpected trip. If she could shred my balls over the phone, she would have.

Another candidate to castrate me is probably Brook. It was a dick move to sneak out while she slept.

I had to act.

I couldn't sit around and pretend her story didn't impact me.

It's our story, after all.

Not that she didn't bear the brunt of it. Fuck, how I wish I could have taken all her pain and suffering.

I had to act.

As I watched her sleep, I realized how strong she has been. So resilient.

Yes, she had more time to deal with everything, but fuck, I'm proud of her. And the selfish bastard in me is pleased I could help her at least with the last pieces.

She was already put together and healed, but she

needed me to seal the wounds, and I'm so humbled by that, I can't even decipher what that means.

Her confession puts all her partying and living on the edge in perspective. How many times did I judge her way of life? Told myself I dodged a bullet not ending up with her?

Idiot.

"What can I get you, Mr. Cassinetti?" The flight attendant smiles at me.

"Whiskey, Tamar. Thank you."

She brings it over and lingers. "Are you sure there is nothing else?"

I never fuck my staff—well, not since Chloe—but that doesn't mean some of them don't try. "Thank you, Tamar. I'm good. I need to catch up on some work."

Her smile turns saccharine. "Of course, but if you need to relax later—"

"That'll be all. Thank you."

She finally leaves.

I should have called Mathison before I boarded my plane in Lisbon. Since when am I this impulsive? Goddammit.

Since Brook Lowe waltzed back into my life.

I've been obsessed with her since childhood, and having her around for real now is a challenge. Even before we unraveled the past.

Fuck.

It was easy to keep her at arm's length before. When I was still blaming her for never showing up. But now?

Now I'm not so sure anymore. But first things first, I need to avenge Brook.

After we land, a car waits for me to take me to the address Art sent me. My phone pings with several messages.

> **CHLOE**
> Personal business? I ran into Brook. You owe me a getaway with Mary.

I check my watch. It's way too late there, but Chloe might still be on the floor at the club, so I call her.

"You're such an asshole. You don't cancel my plans via a text. And here I thought you needed time with your lovely wife. Where the hell are you?"

I guess she's still up.

"What did you tell Brook?"

"You're going to fuck this up, Baldo," she warns.

It's a fake marriage. But maybe she's onto something. "What did you tell Brook?"

"She thought you were away on business, so I pretended I must have misunderstood. I don't think she bought it. Maybe you shouldn't have lied to both of us."

"If you see—"

"Baldo, if you want to talk to her, call her. Not me. Besides, she went to Madrid."

What the fuck is in Madrid?

"Why?"

"Again, call your wife. I have to go." She hangs up.

I almost hurl my phone across the car, but I'm not adding another thing to my list of inexplicable behaviors. I rake my fingers through my hair. Madrid?

The car passes a large gate and pulls to a stop in front of a modern cube-like mansion. A red Ferrari and a sensible family-size Mercedes are parked to the side.

I tell the driver to wait for me, and before I reach the door, they are flung open. A blonde woman with bewitching brown eyes glares at me.

"Hello, I'm here to see Art Mathison."

"I don't appreciate you intruding on our family time. Art does *not* do business when we are here, and I hope your *emergency* is a matter of life or death because you don't want me to be your enemy."

I guess that's his wife. She steps to the side, and I enter a huge open space. Across the room is a wall of windows that are open, merging the exterior with the interior. In the infinity pool, kids are jumping and splashing.

No wonder Art was unwilling to take this meeting. Shit. "My apologies for the intrusion, Mrs. Mathison. You have a beautiful home here. I'm Baldo Cassinetti, nice to meet you." I offer a smile and my hand, but my manners don't placate her.

She frowns and folds her arms across her chest. "Related to Andrea?"

"He's my brother." Not sure how she knows him, but maybe it will score me some points.

"He's an asshole, so I guess it runs in the family." She shakes her head. "Forgive my lack of hospitality." Her statement leaks sarcasm. "I really don't like Art working when he's here. His office is down the hallway to the right."

"Thank you. And sorry, again."

I follow her directions and knock on the door, but don't wait for an answer. The office is a stark contrast to the rest of the white, airy house.

The blinds are drawn, swallowing the room in darkness, the only light coming from several monitors at a large desk.

The reflection illuminates Art's face. His expression makes his wife's welcome a pleasant experience.

"Art." I nod and take a seat without him offering. This looks like an uphill conversation. "You have a nice place here."

"Not to be intruded upon."

"I'm sorry I insisted on seeing you in person. It's a sensitive matter."

He raises his eyebrow slightly, but keeps looking at

me with a murderous expression. "Why do you think I took this meeting?"

I drum my fingers on my thigh. "Because I threatened you."

I was desperate when I didn't find him in New York, so I pushed for a meeting, suggesting I would expose his past to the media. A bluff.

I know little about his past, nothing tangible. I really took a risk with my threat to expose him.

"You have nothing on me."

"Yet here I am."

He scrutinizes me in silence, while an imaginary clock ticks off what feels like hours, not minutes.

"So I can say to your face that if you ever threaten my wife's peaceful mind again, I will destroy you." His promise is definite, and I have no doubt he means it. But if he finds the piece of shit, it's all worth it. "With pleasure," he adds.

Perhaps I went too far, threatening him. I have a feeling not many people dare to, but I doubt he invited me here just to deliver this threat.

Especially since I can hardly outsmart his skills. Which stinks a bit.

"What's brought on your desperation?" he asks.

Ah, so it was curiosity that got me the invitation.

"A woman was assaulted. My woman."

Not that I have a claim on her, but that's irrelevant now.

Saying the words is like swallowing acid. They burn my throat and down my esophagus, slowly spreading into my already nauseated stomach. I haven't eaten since I left Lisbon. Well, since breakfast with Chloe.

The calories in whiskey are not nutritious enough, but I'll deal with that later.

He pinches the bridge of his nose. "I'm listening."

I summarize all I know from Brook's retelling, which isn't much.

"That's all?"

Art Mathison is the best when it comes to security and surveillance. Rumor is he got his billions as a hacker, but now deals in legal contracts only. Well, some are questionable.

Besides being the cyber security consultant for my business, he also takes care of the odd surveillance and information gathering project here and there.

Some of the people I deal with need encouragement before deciding what's best for me and my business.

I've known the man for years, and never have I heard him say more than two sentences. He rubs me the wrong way with his entitled attitude, but he's the only person who can get the job done.

Besides, the lack of information is a thrilling challenge for him, I'm sure. But I'll indulge his bullshit for now. This isn't the time for a pissing contest.

"Unfortunately, I don't have more."

"The victim—"

"Brook Lowe."

"Is the subject we stopped following six months ago."

"That's correct."

He cracks his knuckles. "Old flame?"

"My wife."

The jerk of his eyebrows is nearly imperceptible. He's surprised. It's good to catch him off guard.

"Congratulations. That's why you stopped the surveillance."

I nod. No need to tell him I stopped checking up on Brook because I finally decided my obsession with her was counterproductive to my efforts to put the past behind me.

In hindsight, I would have known she was in New York and never traveled there.

"Women don't appreciate being watched."

He addresses the words to his keyboard, already typing away, and something tells me he's speaking from his own experience. Did he spy on his wife?

He finishes typing and looks at me, folding his hands behind his head, his huge muscles bulging. A former illegal fighter, he still keeps in very good shape.

"I'll do my best." He glances toward the door, dismissing me.

"Thank you." I stand up and extend my hand.

He shakes it, but before I turn, I can't help it. "Why is she in Madrid right now?"

He smirks. "Interesting."

The fucker. I glower at him, and he chuckles.

"You would have it in your monthly report," he taunts, but runs his fingers over his keyboard. "She took an evening flight and went straight to a hotel where she joined someone in their room."

I should be concerned how quickly he got that information, but I'm too riled up by the facts to contemplate that.

"Whose room?"

He smirks. "You should talk to your wife."

The flight back to Lisbon is fucking long. Too long. My blood sizzles with unanswered questions.

It will take time before Art finds Brook's assailant. If he finds him after all this time with no police reports. If the nickname doesn't lead to the real identity, I might never face the man.

But that was something I anticipated.

Brook sneaking to Madrid, on the other hand...

By the time the pilot announces our landing, I'm practically vibrating with energy. And not the good kind.

I want to murder someone. It doesn't help that I haven't slept well for almost three nights. Or eaten properly. My lovely wife will be the death of me.

My driver pulls up to my building. It's before lunch, and the crew is probably just finishing the club's clean up.

Normally I'd check on everything and head to my office first, but today I take the back entrance and head upstairs.

She's not here. Fuck. For all I know, she's still in Madrid.

I trudge downstairs to my office, hoping for some quiet time to collect my thoughts.

"Well, look who's back." Chloe smirks from my chair.

So much for peace and quiet. "Get out of my seat."

"Oh, and he's in one of his famous moods. Lucky me." She tilts back into the leather backrest and puts her stilettos on my desk.

"Chloe," I growl.

To her credit, she reads the room and stands up. "In case you're wondering, everything ran smoothly in your absence. I took the meetings you decided to miss, and I hope I can go back to Paris now."

She rounds the desk with a fake smile.

"Have you seen Brook?" Yes, I'm that desperate.

She quirks her eyebrow. "She has a phone. It's a mobile, by the way, which by definition means she probably has it with her. You should try to dial it."

I sit behind my desk. "Have a safe flight home, Chloe."

"You're welcome. It was a pleasure to cancel my plans so I could step in."

"Okay, I hear you loud and clear. I'm an asshole."

"Spa certificate and an extended weekend for me and Mary." She drops her demands and saunters away, slamming the door behind her.

Fucking hell. I rub my temples and force myself to look at some spreadsheets. But it's a lost cause—I'm tired, fucking mad, and constantly listening for the goddamn elevator.

Why don't I call her? If only I knew the answer to that. It feels like something people who trust each other do.

People who have a normal relationship. Not people who sneak out on each other during the night.

It's almost nine when the elevator rumbles in the background. I take a deep breath, lock the office, and punch the button as soon as it stops on the upper level.

When I step out of the steel car, lights are on everywhere, but I don't see Brook.

I drop my keys and phone on the dining table beside her laptop.

"Oh, you're home."

Her voice startles me.

Whipping around, my gaze collides with hers. She is in the bathroom doorway. Breathtakingly beautiful. She has the kind of presence that is heart-stopping.

I want to tell her I missed her. That I'm sorry I didn't explain where I was going. I want to tell her I'm glad she's back in my life.

"What did you do in Madrid?" is what I say instead. *Yep, protect your heart, asshole.*

She frowns. "How do you know I was in Madrid?"

"Chloe told me."

"When?"

She eats the distance between us. Her scent infiltrates my mind, and I want to kiss the shit out of her. Fuck.

"When I called her."

She glowers and throws her arms up in exasperation. "So you had time to call Chloe, but you didn't bother to call me?"

"What did you do in Madrid, Brook?"

She grabs her phone. "You're such a hypocrite." She marches to the elevator. "Since I'm here mostly alone, I went to meet with Saar. She had a shoot there."

Fucking Mathison.

Exhaling, I scratch my nape. "Brook—"

"I'm going downstairs to have a drink. Don't bother joining me unless you're ready to talk. To really talk, Baldo."

Chapter 29

Brook

The steady beat of music fills the air, but the club is still half empty. It's too early. The crowds start in an hour, and then it'll be full of dancing bodies, clinking glasses, laughter and blaring music.

I swirl the paper umbrella in my cocktail and sulk. What an asshole. He disappears and then dares question my whereabouts? Especially after he lied about his trip.

Determined to drown my frustration, I put my glass to my lips, but end up only wetting them.

The idea of partying my thoughts out of my head is unappealing. It worked before, but Baldo gives me a headache without inducing one with alcohol.

Sighing, I put the glass down.

"Trouble in paradise?" Chloe slides onto the seat beside me.

I snort. "No trouble. And no paradise."

"Oh, I'm sure it's not that bad. You guys are still in the honeymoon phase."

I don't look at her, because I'm sure she would see on my face how wrong her statement is.

I like Chloe—even though I've just met her—and I don't think I can pull the pretense off at the moment.

To my utmost annoyance, I'm also jealous of her. Not because she slept with Baldo way back when, but because she got to be with him throughout the years when I tried and failed to forget him.

The young bartender takes someone's order and turns her back to us. She pulls a lighter from her pocket.

Holding it close to her hip, hiding it from view, she flicks it a few times, her eyes darting around in the mirror. That's odd.

"He cares about you, Brook. He cares about you a lot." She pats my shoulder. "I have to greet a VIP and I'm leaving for the airport in an hour, but I hope to see you soon."

We hug and I return to my drink.

> He returned and made a scene about me being in Madrid.

> **SAAR**
> Your man is jealous, bask in it.

> Why are you my friend?

> **SAAR**
> Because I'm amazing and you cling. (heart emoji)

> I miss you.

> **SAAR**
> See? Clingy. (devil emoji)

The girl behind the bar drops a glass and jumps. She leans down to pick it up, her eyes constantly scanning the room. For what?

She pats her pocket again, the outline of her lighter bulging slightly.

My imagination sparks with interest, already conjuring several scenarios, but maybe she's just a heavy smoker, eager for her break.

I turn to watch as the club fills up, but my eyes keep landing on the staff entrance, hoping Baldo comes down in search of me.

Nursing only one drink and not partaking in the clubbing, I observe the crowd and wonder why I used to enjoy it so much.

I mean, I love to dance, but on the floor of Celeste's studio or at home it brings me peace. At clubs, it was more about quieting the loud voices in my head.

But that noise has fallen silent since... since Baldo returned to my life. The man is infuriating, but I want him around.

And it's not just for the orgasms. I groan inwardly.

I'm just going to force him to talk. I slide down the chair. Jesus. We haven't even been married a month, and I'm exhausted from all the emotional whiplash.

I don't make it far before a shrill alarm slices through the music. For a split second, everything freezes—the dancers, the bartenders, even the very air seems to hold its breath.

And then, as if the heavens themselves have opened up inside this dimly lit room, water cascades down from the sprinklers overhead.

Panic ignites faster than the fire that must have triggered the alarm. The crowd surges, pushing and shoving.

Water soaks through my clothes, plastering my hair to my face and turning the dance floor into a slippery mess.

My first thought, absurdly, is that Baldo is going to kill someone for ruining the polished wood.

I need to find him.

He must be somewhere here, trying to evacuate the club safely. My heart pounds as I push against the flow, my eyes scanning faces for him.

He's nowhere.

My throat constricts, panic clawing its way up.

I glance toward the bar and realize that's where the fire started. It seems contained already, but the image of the flickering lighter in the hands of the young woman behind the bar stops me in my tracks.

"Ma'am, you need to leave. Now!" a bulky man urges. I recognize him from the other night, throwing Miguel out.

His voice cuts through, authoritative and impossible to ignore.

I shake my head, water flinging from my hair. "I have to find Baldo," I shout back.

He doesn't listen—or maybe he can't hear me over the noise. With a gentleness that belies the urgency of the situation, he wraps his arms around my shoulders and starts guiding me toward the nearest exit.

As we move, I look over my shoulder, searching the chaos for a sign of Baldo.

The night air hits me like a slap when we finally emerge outside. It's hot, but I'm shivering, drenched.

The security guide sheds his wet jacket and wraps it around me. It doesn't help, but I appreciate the gesture, tucking the wet fabric closer to me.

"Stay here." He runs back inside.

"Where is Baldo?"

I stand there, my heart hammering in my temples.

The question, a mixture of worry and frustration, remains unanswered.

Baldo is always in control. For a second, I don't believe the chaos has swallowed him tonight.

What if he fell asleep upstairs and can't get down? What if... I force myself to stop overthinking.

As the crowd spills into the night, I keep searching for him, and my eyes land on a group of employees huddling by the side, the bartender among them.

She looks scared, still glancing around as if she's expecting something else to happen, or someone to arrive—

"Tokyo." The voice is a whisper of relief behind me, and I whip around.

"I couldn't find you." I wrap my arms around his waist. "I couldn't find you," I repeat.

"I'm here. Are you okay?" He pulls back, inspecting me.

I nod. God, I'm so happy to see him. "The bartender. She had a lighter she's been playing with all night."

He frowns and then looks above my shoulder, assessing the situation. The police have arrived and people are dispersing, but I'm sure there is a lot of work for Baldo.

"I'll be fine. Do what you need to do. Let me know if I can help."

He smiles at me, but then narrows his eyes. He removes his jacket and tugs at the one over my shoulders. "Don't wear another man's jacket."

He wraps his dry, thousand-dollar suit jacket around me. It swallows me in the warmth and scent of the man, and instead of rolling my eyes at his caveman display, I smile at him.

"Relax, it's your ring I'm wearing."

The door of Baldo's office clicks and I scramble to sit up. I fell asleep on his leather sofa.

He brought me here, got me dry clothes, and put a bodyguard at the door despite my protest before he left to deal with the police and the early investigation.

"Sorry, I didn't mean to wake you." Baldo looks at me, his gaze cold. "We need to review the security footage. Let me take you upstairs."

"I'd rather stay here. I won't disturb you."

"Let her stay." Chloe pushes in behind Baldo.

He studies me with hooded eyes, a line marring his forehead. His eyes look darker with circles of fatigue under them.

The way he's looking at me squeezes at my stomach, worry souring it. He's retreating before I even got him to open up.

He shakes his head ever so slightly and sits behind his desk. Chloe stands beside him.

I guess her plans to leave were postponed yet again.

I want to join them, but somehow I feel I have no right. So I sit there with an uneasy feeling.

Baldo's jaw ticks as he drums his fingers on the desk. Other than that, he's in complete control.

Dressed to perfection—he must have changed—his hair is perfectly mussed, his features tired but composed.

I can't claim I know the man anymore, but I'd bet my yearly royalties the composure is just a mask.

After a few clicks on the keyboard, they both lean closer to the monitor and Chloe swears.

Then they turn to me, and I swallow. What the actual fuck? There isn't accusation in their eyes but there are questions.

"How do you know Miguel Oliviera?" Baldo asks.

"Who?"

"The man you came in with a couple nights ago and Baldo had thrown out?" Chloe asks.

"I don't know him. I was having a drink at a bar, and he came over to talk to me."

Baldo lets out a long sigh and Chloe rolls her eyes. "So I guess it checks out, and it seems your jealousy cost you, boss." She pats his shoulder and walks to the door. "I'm going to oversee the cleanup. You look like shit. I'm not sure when you last slept, but fucking do it now because I want to go home. Good night, Brook."

When the door closes behind her, I stand up. "Is Miguel—"

"The arsonist? No, you were right—the bartender started the fire. He paid her to do it. It was supposed to be a diversion, so he could rob my safe."

"I don't think she wanted to do it. She was so nervous..."

Jesus, I brought this to his door. Not intentionally, but still. No wonder he's looking at me like I'm a nuisance. *Inconvenience* he called me before. "Baldo, I'm sorry."

He rounds the table and pulls me to him, holding me close. "You have nothing to be sorry about. He blackmailed the girl, and he didn't succeed with the other part of his plan because I intercepted them when I was coming down after the alarm."

"You faced them?" I jerk back, the vise on my insides gripping tighter.

"I wasn't alone. My men were still here. He didn't time it very well." He kisses the crown of my head. "Let's go to bed."

We head upstairs in silence that speaks volumes. I don't understand what it's saying, only that it's loaded with pent-up energy.

We exit the elevator and Baldo picks me up and

carries me to his bed. He takes off my clothes, and then his.

I watch his every move, enthralled by the sight of him and panicked by his aloof presence.

He climbs in beside me, nudges me to my side, and pulls my back to his chest. Wrapped in his arms, I feel slightly better.

Our breath synchronizes quickly and Baldo's evens out. While my mind is swirling with uncertainty, the fatigue is stronger.

The heavy hands on my hips.

Warmth between my thighs.

A shiver of pleasure startles me from my sleep.

"Baldo..." I sigh and arch my back as he does that thing with his tongue that has my entire body trembling with need.

"Good morning." He continues his delicious assault, adding two fingers. It takes no time before I get there, screaming his name.

He climbs up and positions himself at my entrance. I'm still dizzy from sleep and my orgasm when our eyes meet.

There is determination and adoration in his gaze. He moves slowly. Too slowly, but I don't dare argue or demand. If this is what he needs, this is what he gets.

The least I can do after causing—unintentionally—

so much damage to his club. And he's in charge in the bedroom, after all.

But this slow pace and his disarming expression are too much. Too intimate. Too dangerous.

And somehow eerie. It's like he's saying goodbye.

"Stop it, Brook. Let me make you feel good."

As if he could hear my thoughts. Jesus.

"Harder," I challenge.

And he obeys me, which should feel like a win, but it doesn't, because Baldo not reminding me he's in charge is only further confirmation that something is broken.

But his pace gets relentless, and soon I can't think anymore. Only feel. My body thrashes in a tornado of sensations, battling with my heart that weeps at the contrasting emotions.

I come and Baldo follows me shortly after, my name on his lips as he pours himself inside me. He rolls off and leaves for the bathroom.

I prop myself against the headboard.

He comes out, dressed in his robe. "I have the plane ready to take you back to the States."

Chapter 30

Baldo

I march to the kitchen, distracting myself with the coffee maker. I'm the asshole who can't even look at her.

She could have gotten hurt in the fire last night. She did get hurt ten years ago. I have a security detail on standby to protect her, but she can't stay with me.

The sheets rustle and her small feet pound across the room. "Take me to the States? What about you?"

I pause, almost snapping the stainless steel coffee pot in two. "I need to stay to take care of business. I'll join you as soon as I can, so we can have dinner with Rupert."

"I'm not going to the States."

Of course, she would argue. Nothing with this woman is easy.

"You can't stay here." I pour the beans into the container of my state-of-the-art coffee maker.

"Look, I'm really sorry I brought Miguel here. Though if you hadn't thrown him out..."

Fuck. Now I've made her feel guilty about Miguel fucking Oliviera. "Don't worry about him. He will rot in jail."

I don't understand what happened the night I threw the douchebag out of my club. He was only talking to Brook when my restraint started slipping, and when he leaned toward her and whispered into her ear, I snapped.

I know she's only mine temporarily, but fuck Miguel. He's got balls, I'll give him that. It took courage to mess with my business.

Brook remains silent for a moment. Or I think she does, but I'm too close to the roaring coffee grinder to be sure.

Yes, I'm still the asshole who hasn't looked at her. Fucking coward.

As soon as the ruckus stops and the machine hums with the coffee preparation, Brook says, "You don't decide where I go. You don't just send me away because you don't want me around."

I whip around, and the sight in front of me startles me.

She stands on the other side of the counter. In my fucking shirt. Kill. Me. Now.

Her chest heaves, her hair is in disarray, her lips are swollen and her eyes are a bit puffy from sleep. I catalogue every detail, searing the moment into my memory.

The cocktail of emotions tugging at my heart is potent. I want to hold her forever. I need to have her. I want her to be mine. To protect her. Well, without failing at it like I have been.

All that mixes with all the opposite feelings. I don't trust her. Perhaps it's childish to still hold a grudge over the past, but she didn't choose me back then.

Or any day after, when she could have reached out and explained why she didn't show up. It took her almost ten years, and being forced into marriage with me.

Circumstances influenced her honesty, and if circumstances change, who knows if she would stick around.

Fuck.

"You need to leave," I growl.

She flinches, but then straightens. "Where were you for the past two days?"

My eyebrow jerks up, but I contain any further reaction. Whiplash, anyone? Where did that fascinating mind of hers go?

The way she stands there, a woman on a mission, is so fucking hot. "I don't think you want to know."

"I asked, didn't I?"

I close my eyes and bow my head before I take a deep breath. It's not very fortifying, but being around Brook throws me off my game. "Okay, I don't think you'd like the answer."

She huffs. "Why don't you tell me? Because you don't trust me?"

I drop the coffee bag, beans spilling across the counter, and round the island. This shouldn't have triggered me, but fuck her taunting.

She steps back, hitting the table. I drop my hands to the glass surface on each side of her, caging her.

"Trust *you*? I don't trust myself around you. Ever since you waltzed into my life, I can't find peace of mind."

My lips are so close to hers. Just an inch and we'd kiss.

No fucking way.

"I didn't waltz into your life. You waltzed into mine. With a proposal, no less."

"You needed my help." I smack the tabletop with my palm, making her jump.

Stepping back, I run a hand through my hair.

I don't know what we're even arguing about. But I'm losing control, and I don't like the feeling. I hate it.

Frustration and irritation pulse in my temples. Why the fuck is everything so complicated?

"Where did you go? Is there someone else?"

I snort. "No."

"So why are you sending me away?"

I shake my head. *To protect you. To save you. To save me?*

"How did you get this ring?" She raises her hand, wiggling the fingers in front of my face. The ruby catches a sun ray from the window above and sparkles with red vengeance.

Fuck. "I had it made."

"That's obvious. But there is no way this ring was made in the time between the unexpected proposal and our wedding. How did you have an engagement ruby?"

"I had it made a long time ago!" I grab her hand, closing my palm over the ring.

Her eyes widen, and I can practically see the comprehension setting in. Yes, my obsession with Brook runs long and deep. Too deep.

I had it made when I made my first million. I never understood why. It's not like I was planning to seek her out.

Okay, perhaps I was. I've fucking carried it with me ever since. A therapist would have a field day with this.

And this is why she needs to leave. I can't think when she's gone, but I'm a complete idiot when she's around.

"Why?" she croaks.

Her hand is so small in mine, the ruby burning a hole in my skin.

"Stop the interrogation. You fucking know why." I drop her hand and rake my hair again. This is what she does to me. I want to pull my hair out dealing with the onslaught of feelings. "What do you want from me, Brook?"

She raises the hand I've just dropped to her chest, holding it by her heart. "I want you to talk to me. To tell me where your head is. We've both been seeking closure, but—"

"There is no fucking closure for us, Brook. You might be on the other side of the world, hating my guts, fucking assholes that don't deserve you, but there is no closure. You will always be a part of me. Whether I like it or not."

"Clearly you don't."

"You want to know how I feel? Like I failed you." She winces like I slapped her. "I'm drowning in guilt. And if last night proved anything, it's that you're not safe when you're around me. You were fucking assaulted because of me, and yesterday you could have been..." I hit the counter with my fist, turning my back to her.

"Is that why you're sending me away? For my safety?" Her voice is just a whisper.

She puts her hand on my back. Electricity zips through my body at the gentle contact.

What am I thinking? I missed her the past two days —almost ten years, if I'm honest—so why do I keep expecting it to get easier? It won't.

"Yes," I admit, knowing very well I'm exaggerating. Overreacting.

"So there is no other woman?"

I turn and pivot her, so her back is now toward the counter.

Brook gasps and I wrap my hand around her throat. Her pulse gallops against my fingers. "There has always been only you, Brook."

"Then cancel the flight."

Her breathing is labored, but so is mine. We stare at each other, like we can fill in the blanks we're unable to say with our eyes.

It's the worst idea to give into this lust. Because that's what swarms through my veins. With a hefty dose of the obsession I've been nurturing for years.

"I'm scared too," she says. "But I don't plan to hide. I'm not going anywhere, Baldo. We owe each other a chance."

"I don't believe in second chances."

If I did, I would have sought Brook out a long time ago. I would have visited my mom way before this month.

Fuck, Miguel Oliviera wouldn't have been arrested for burning my club, and a few made-up charges I manufactured to ensure he stays away for a long time.

A tear rolls down her cheek. "Okay, I'll believe enough for both of us for now."

I pull her to me, wrapping my arms around her and holding her so close that she might suffocate.

This wonderful, slightly crazy woman with the overflowing imagination is a hundred times braver than me.

I kiss the crown of her head and lift her up bridal style. "Let me take care of you." It's not a command like I usually issue. It's a plea.

I don't know how to let her know I'm in it—whatever the *it* is—with her, even though I'm scared shitless.

How to thank her for putting up with my indecision.

How to ask for forgiveness for everything that has happened to her. For what I caused, and what I never prevented.

She wraps her arms around my neck and hides her face in the crook of my neck. "I'm yours," she says, granting me permission.

And I accept the sweet lie and take my wife to my bed.

"You're obsessed with my hair."

Brook lies in my arms, naked and sweaty. I play with a lock of her hair, circling it around my finger.

I'm obsessed with *her*, not just her hair.

As we lie there in a post-orgasmic coma, I catch myself smiling. I'm happy. It surprises me. And scares me a bit, but fuck, I enjoy basking in it.

Give it to Brook to crawl under my skin. Just like she did when we were just kids.

Or perhaps she never left, engraved in my heart and a part of my soul since the day they moved into our house.

"Your hair is my first memory."

She stills and then raises her chin to look at me. When I don't look at her, she grips my jaw and forces me to do so.

"Baldo?"

"Your hair is my first memory. Has all the fucking impaired your hearing?"

Yep, I can't deal with her adoring—and somewhat puzzled—look. And I fucking hate talking.

She cups my balls, gently. "Explain, because my

impaired hearing should be the least of your worries."

I laugh. "You need my balls more than me, baby."

She scoffs and moves to roll off, but I don't let her, tightening my hold on her. "When you moved into our house with all your annoying sisters..." She elbows my ribs and I chuckle.

"Okay, I actually don't remember you moving in, but I remember this angel. You had curly hair, and it was lighter than it is now, and I was in awe. It's just a glimpse, a souvenir of the past a long time ago, but I don't remember anything before that, so I guess your hair is my first memory. I believed you were an angel my dad sent me."

I don't remember my father. I was too little when he passed.

"Your memory plays tricks on you. I've never been an angel." Despite her barb, she fails to conceal her emotions.

"More a devil, or a witch."

"Hey." She swats at my chest. "But you might be right."

"A rare moment of self-awareness. God, I need to fuck you more to get this much honesty." I chuckle.

"Dick."

"It's all yours, baby."

She snorts and then looks at me. The moment stills and we gaze into each other's eyes, speaking that wordless language that seeds hope inside me. But it's also open for interpretation.

"Why can't you kiss me?"

I wonder that myself lately. Fuck.

I'm not ready.

Kissing is intimate. Kissing is commitment. Kissing is trust. Something I decided ten years ago I would no longer give to another person.

"It's not you. I don't kiss."

"Never?"

In contrast to my words, I trail her chin with my lips, kissing down her neck and to her clavicle. "Never."

She shudders when I reach for her nipple. "But you kissed me before."

As soon as she says the words, she tenses, her entire body rigid with the realization.

Brook is the only woman I've ever kissed.

"Stop overthinking it and let me fuck you now." I cup her mound and slide two fingers through her folds. "Look how wet you are for me, baby. I can't ignore that."

Chancing a look at her, I push both fingers inside her. While her body is still stiff from the revelation, her face is lit up, her eyes shining. Fuck, she's radiant.

I bury my face between her breasts, wondering why I still can't kiss her. She arches her back and moans, and all my thoughts evaporate, giving way to pure instincts and desire.

I bring my fingers to my lips and suck at them. "Your taste is addictive."

She groans. "Stop with the poetry and fuck me already."

Throwing my head back, I laugh. I haven't done that much, and the sparkles in my chest feel foreign but not unwelcome.

I return my hand between her thighs, pinch her clit and drag my finger around her heat, down to her tight rim. "Will you ever grant me access here?" I press gently and she gasps.

A blush spreads across her cheeks as she worries her bottom lip between her teeth. "I've never—"

God, the information cracks something inside me, like I could get a do-over for the first that never happened between us. Yeah, I'm a simple creature.

"Who else would you let there if not your husband?" I wink and return to her clit. As much as I want to, she is not ready, and I might be dominant, but I'm not an asshole.

Brook grips my hair and forces me to look at her. Her eyes shine with challenge this time.

"Dear husband, I'll grant you access the day this marriage becomes real."

My world tilts on its axis.

Chapter 31

Brook

The end.

The exhilaration from typing those two words hits me, bittersweet. It's relief and grief wrapped together.

A sense of accomplishment along with a sense of loss. Like the characters lived with me for months and now they've moved out, and I already miss them. Happy and scared to share them.

I lean against the chair, stretching my neck to the side. It's a good thing I've finished, because continuing to write in coffee shops or at Baldo's dining table, like right now, would soon result in a chiropractor visit.

He went to Italy, but he'll be back tonight. He left at the crack of dawn, promising to be back as soon as possible. And telling me he's leaving for a change. Progress.

I miss him, but I'm glad I had the chance to work. After the night of the fire and the following morning, I was finally able to focus on the story I was writing.

We didn't say everything, and he didn't open up completely, but we're moving in the right direction. Now I just hope we can maintain the course.

I'll believe enough for both of us.

What a bold statement. I don't even know where it came from.

He had an engagement ring made for me. How long did he have this ring? A ring that a silly girl dreamed of back then.

He never came back for me, but at one point he was planning on it.

What stopped him?

We might not have survived if he had come for me. I was broken, in full-blown PTSD mode.

Years healed me to an extent, and what was still festering I successfully tuned out with work and social life. The louder, the better.

Would I have healed better and faster if he had returned? Probably not. Our parents would have suffered, our siblings would have hated us.

They were just establishing their own names in the world, and they wouldn't want us tainting it.

Out of eight of us, as the two youngest, we were

always the closest—we were like a real brother and sister. Our stepparents were our real parents.

Our family might be supportive, but this would have been a bit too much for them. And society would have gossiped to no avail.

Dad would have suffered. He already did.

What's to say it would be different this time around?

I'll believe enough for both of us. But can I believe that the rest of the world would be happy with us? That is, if we find our own happiness. Because as we stand now, it's all fragile and tentative.

As temporary as our marriage certificate.

And yet I hope. I hope we can overcome our trust issues. That we can grow stronger and heal each other.

That we can uncover the hidden parts of each other and make them shine. That our families will support us.

The last one scares me. Just the idea of upsetting Dad in his frail state. Maybe the idea of us is not the right one.

Maybe the timing would never work for us.

Or the geography. Wrong place, wrong time, and all of that.

Because clearly Baldo needs to be here, and I want to be with my dad as much as possible.

So can we even make it work? Would he resent me

if I make him move? Would he travel so much back and forth that we'd grow apart?

And once the TV production starts, I'll need to be in the States. I insisted on being involved as an executive producer.

Though we might resolve some of our issues as a couple, the world outside is a very different ball game.

His work. My work. Our families. So many variables where not even the two of us are a constant yet.

Depressed by all my thoughts, I try to distract myself by re-reading the last chapter I just finished.

I save the file again then email it to myself and upload it to the cloud. As always, I need to make a copy. I don't know why I fear losing my manuscript so much, but better safe than sorry.

I rummage through my purse for my USB key, but I can't find it. I flip through all the gazillion compartments of my computer bag.

I re-save the file again and dive into my purse one more time. Nothing.

My phone chimes with an incoming message.

> **BALDO**
>
> Finished in Rome, making a quick stop in Milan. I should be back by 8 pm.

I grin at the message as if it's a love note. In his

strange Baldo way, he's giving me an update, which is significantly better than him disappearing.

> I miss you too.

Three dots dance on my screen.

BALDO
There is a delivery on its way. Let me know when it arrives.

Jesus. The warmth seeping through his messages is arctic.

> Not a fan of sexting then?

BALDO
My meeting is starting...

I roll my eyes, but before I can respond, my phone rings with an unknown number. I answer to speak with one of Baldo's men, asking for permission to bring up a package.

Within minutes, I'm staring at a sleek black box.

> Your package arrived.

I don't expect an answer because of his meeting. I save my file again and go to make my tea. A message pings again.

> BALDO
> Open it.

> Me: I thought you had a meeting.

> BALDO
> Open it.

> Jesus, you're bossy.

> BALDO
> Brook!

God, I can almost hear him growl. Dominant bastard.

I take off my shirt and bra and pose, licking the rim of his favorite espresso cup. It takes me several takes before I'm satisfied, but I finally get a pic that I'm happy with. Salacious but tasteful.

I send it and get dressed, waiting for his reply. Instead of a message, my phone rings.

"Brook speaking," I say innocently.

"What the fuck, Brook? I dropped the phone and now I have to bleach my associates' eyes," he says with urgency, but softly.

I guess he is still within earshot of his current company.

I laugh. "Sorry. I didn't mean to impede your business negotiations, but you were so strict and businesslike in your messages I needed to make sure your personality didn't get lost on your flight."

He snorts. "I have to get back. Have you opened the package?" His voice is more relaxed now, and it rumbles through me like a symphony.

"Let me do it now."

"Are you still topless?"

"Maybe."

He groans and I giggle.

With a knife, I slice the tape at the edges, then lift the lid and remove the pink tissue paper.

"You didn't want me to feel lonely?" I drawl, pulling out a vibrator and a silk gown so skimpy it will literally cover nothing. It's more of an accessory.

"Wear that when I come home. I'm arriving at eight. You start playing with it at seven, and don't stop until I arrive."

He hangs up. What the hell?

Goosebumps sprout all over my skin and I clench my core, squeezing my tights together as if that will stop the heat his words sparked.

I check my watch. It's only noon. Argh. I press the button, but the toy remains off. I fish the cord from the package and go to the bedroom to plug it in.

The outlet is behind the nightstand, and as I move it, the drawer slides open.

I put the toy on the charger and am about to close the drawer when I notice a small USB key. Bingo.

I go to my computer. I'm sure Baldo wouldn't

mind. I won't erase anything, just back up my file until I can find my own USB or buy a new one.

Pushing it into the slot on my laptop, I wait for the new window to open. When it does, I pause.

I'm not sure what I'm seeing, but I can't unsee it anymore. Nor can I keep my curiosity contained.

Why does Baldo have files called *Project Tokyo*? They are numbered with six digits, looking like a date stamp.

I click on one of them, killing any thoughts about invading privacy or breaking trust. I'm *Tokyo* after all.

What I find is a report by the Mathison Corp summing up my life that month, along with a few pics. Me with my ex, Dylan. Me on the street, leaving a nightclub. Me entering the building of my agent's offices.

The written summary gives notes about my whereabouts, my routine, and even about a new deal with my publisher.

No wonder he never asked what exactly I do. He knew.

Like a woman possessed, I keep opening other files. It's like reading a very clinical personal diary. It's my life condensed into one USB key. No emotions, just pure facts.

Hours pass as I read and review the visual depiction of my last seven years.

Some of it is strangely comforting. Like the one time when Dylan really got out of control and the police showed up.

I always assumed it was my neighbor who called them. Turns out it was the shadow hired by my guardian angel. Or the man who obsessively invaded my privacy.

The files end shortly before Paris came to visit. Maybe they didn't fit on this flash drive anymore. I rush to the nightstand and rummage through it, but I find nothing.

Returning to my laptop, I stare at all the Project Tokyo files.

Numbness and an odd elation course through me, and I'm utterly confused about my discovery.

What was he thinking? I knew he didn't just forget about me. He had Tokyo tattooed near his heart, after all.

His tattoos!

I scroll through my pictures and find the one I snapped that morning when I admired his artwork.

It doesn't take long to find out they truly are Japanese characters, spelling one word only.

Tokyo.

It wasn't just one map outline with a heart. He inked his body with the name he used to tease me and please me with.

I open a few more files, weirdly obsessed with the details of my life as if I didn't live through them.

Diving into my story is easier than thinking about what all this means. The man has been obsessed with me. He invaded my privacy.

But he—or rather his people—intervened on a few occasions when I would have gotten into trouble, or could have been hurt.

I groan when I read how my shadow got me into a cab when I was plastered at a club one night. Jesus. How embarrassing. What did Baldo think about my lifestyle?

The elevator dings and I jerk my head up. God, I didn't realize it's a little past eight already.

Baldo steps inside and frowns. His expression darkens as he rakes his eyes up and down my body. My heartbeat drums in my temples.

"I thought my instructions were clear," he warns.

Putting his hands into the pocket of his pants, he saunters down the three steps and crosses the vast space toward me.

He's so handsome and commanding, prowling to me like the predator he is. I almost want to forget about my discovery and just enjoy this hungry version of him.

But something propels me forward and I yank the USB out and hold it in front of me.

The hunger in his eyes disappears, replaced with an unreadable expression. A mask he wears so well.

His dominance solidifies though, and I step back. Not that I fear him, but his natural authority is too overwhelming.

"You went through my things?" His voice is cold and calculated.

If my discovery disturbed him in any way, panicked him, annoyed him, there is no trace of it in his countenance or his voice.

The man is unreadable. No wonder he won a club at poker.

"I didn't go through your things. But even if I did, my invasion of privacy would pale in comparison with years of files about me."

I have been strangely stunned, mostly perversely engrossed in reading about myself for hours. But now when he's standing in front of me, I'm mad.

I'm upset with him.

He never let me go. Yet he never came back for me.

Should his obsession horrify me? Perhaps. But I'm more concerned about him keeping in the shadows, letting me wonder for years why he abandoned me.

"I can try to paint it in a different color, but the reality is I used to have an unhealthy obsession with you."

He delivers this statement with no emotions. It's

simply a matter of fact. He is not trying to apologize or explain. Or I guess the admission of his obsession explains somewhat.

"Why?"

He lets out a loaded breath and pinches the bridge of his nose. "I don't know."

That answer hurts. It disappoints me more than anything I found today. "You don't know?" I spit the words.

Is he lying to me or to himself?

"As I said, it was an unhealthy obsession. I don't think there is an explanation for those. I lost you, but the need to protect you remained."

I think about the drunken cab ride, or the police saving me from Dylan's antics. In his own unorthodox way, he did protect me.

Only that one time, he wasn't there.

I've never blamed him for what happened to me, so I'm not going to start now, but my wounded heart, or perhaps perplexed mind, goes there for a moment.

"Did you come home last month because you knew I was there?"

"I didn't know you were there. I stopped the surveillance six months ago." He doesn't move.

He doesn't try to touch me. To make excuses. He handles this exchange with no pleading, and somehow that makes it worse.

"Why? You realized protecting me wasn't your business anymore?"

"You were always my business." His nostrils flare. Finally, some reaction.

"You have a funny way of showing it. Carrying an engagement ring and watching me from afar, but never fucking coming for me."

"Well, one rejection was enough. You made it clear you didn't want to have anything to do with me."

What the hell? All the contrasting feelings collide inside me, exploding.

"If you really cared, you would have come back for me. You would have returned home to see why I didn't show up. You would have been there to help me."

"I did come back!"

Chapter 32

Baldo

Brook follows her sharp intake of breath with a soft, pained whimper, and jerks her head as if I slapped her. "What are you talking about?"

I was half hard all afternoon, thinking about finding her in the lingerie and playing with that damn toy.

The day has been torture, thinking about her constantly. If I don't focus on my job, who even am I?

I have two obsessions in my life: Brook and my work. But somehow once the first one became part of my life, no space has been left for the other.

We stare at each other in a silent duel. Confused and hurt. That's how she looks. And if I'm honest with myself—not that I've been practicing that much—that's exactly how I feel.

"I'm talking about you choosing the family.

Choosing your dad." She flinches at each word. It gives me no satisfaction, and yet I can't help myself. "Giving up on us before we even had a chance."

It's like I want to share the heavy load of guilt. To blame her, so I can absolve myself. It's not working. Not even a bit, but I can't take the words back.

Her bottom lip quivers, but she straightens her spine. "I chose you."

Could I have it all wrong? "I stayed in the hotel overnight, then I paid for another night. You weren't answering your phone, so I went back home."

She plasters her hand over her mouth and gasps. "You came back?"

A steamroller of realization flattens all my previous assumptions as that afternoon plays in my head.

"Where have you been?" Dad demanded, not even letting me past the threshold.

"I'm back, aren't I?" My teenage self responded, annoyed by his treatment. He hadn't been hostile, but certainly reserved since he had caught us kissing.

"You're not welcome here," he whisper-yelled at me.

I looked over his shoulder and my eyes met Mom's. A couple of feet behind Dad, she had tears brimming in her eyes, both hands clasped to her chest. But she didn't interfere when Dad stepped outside and closed the door behind him.

"What are you doing? This is my house."

He stared at me with a mixture of regret, pain and anger. "Not anymore."

"Let me see Brook." I didn't care about his opinion anymore. I needed to see her. To find out what happened.

"Son, she doesn't want to see you. I think it's best for everybody that you stay away."

"No, no." Brook shakes her head. "Dad wouldn't..." Tears roll down her cheeks. She keeps shaking her head, as if denying the truth might make the outcome digestible.

"He did. And Mom let him."

The words are final, as painful said out loud as they were silent, spinning in my head for almost a decade.

"No, no, I can't believe..." She doesn't finish the sentence, her eyes pleading with me, but also becoming resigned to the bitter truth. "Baldo, oh my God. That's why Mom didn't want Dad to know we got married. They never approved. They kicked you out. They will never approve."

"I don't need their approval."

Taking off my jacket, I hang it on the chair. I

should have pushed more. I shouldn't have let Micah shove me away.

Brook slams down into her chair. She's too quiet, and I hate that I don't know if she needs consoling or if she needs time alone to absorb this fucking revelation.

I don't know what to do with that either. Over the years, when I always considered she might not have made that choice, or she might have changed her mind, I locked it away as wishful thinking.

It's not like her life looked to be filled with grief.

"Talk to me, Brook."

She snorts. "Says the man who keeps his cards to himself. Why didn't you tell me when I told you about that night?"

"Really? I don't think there was room for it that night. If I mentioned it then, it would have been an accusation. I believed Micah when he told me you didn't want to see me."

"Is that why you did all of this but never approached me?" She points at the computer.

Outside, the world is waking up for the night of partying. Laughter, cat-calling, music and roaring cars flow by on the street below.

My old habits call for me to go downstairs and check that everything is prepared for the night ahead.

I should make a few phone calls to deliver on the commitments I made in Italy today.

My desk is overflowing with paperwork that I'm sure Chloe didn't tackle.

And while I think of it all, I don't have an iota of desire to go through the motions.

Not that I particularly want to discuss the past or my obsessive surveillance with Brook, but I would still rather be here with her than anywhere else.

Even when she is mad or heartbroken—I don't know how to handle drama—I still want to be with her.

What that means, I'm not ready to contemplate. But somewhere between our pathetic wedding ceremony and tonight, my subconscious decided for me.

I belong to this woman. I belong with this woman.

I'll believe enough for both of us for now. For now, she said. For her, this is still a temporary arrangement. A means to an end.

Well, fuck that, I wanted to protect myself from the pain, but I had no chance from the beginning.

From the moment I saw her in the kitchen of our Riverdale childhood home, I was desperately destined to get hurt. No matter how much I believed I was in charge.

"I almost did once. It was more to confront you, to find out why the fuck you gave up on us. I was in London, and I looked you up."

I sit down across from her at the table. With Brook

behind her laptop, there is an offensive gap between us. Like this is a formal interrogation.

Perhaps she needs some answers. I want to put all this behind us.

Start afresh. If that's even possible.

"You did? What happened?" She slaps the notebook closed, leaning forward.

"I caught you leaving your building with that fucking D-list actor you'd just started dating."

"Dylan..." She groans, and lowers her head to the glass tabletop and taps it with her forehead.

"Yeah. You were laughing and looked so happy, I decided to let it go. I thought it was perhaps only me who regretted what could have been."

Lifting her head, she stares at me, pain and fatigue marring her beautiful face. "So you just left, but continued watching me from afar?"

"For another two years, yes, then I gave up."

"I'm glad you gave up."

"You have every right to be upset about my invasion of your privacy."

"I think I'm too stunned from all the revelations to even be mad at you. But I'm glad you gave up, because if you didn't, you wouldn't have come home. You would have continued to avoid me?"

She phrases it like a question. Like she's daring me

to confirm or deny, and hoping at the same time. Not sure what she's hoping for.

"Perhaps not, or maybe I would have. We will never know. I was shocked to see you there, but in some strange way also relieved. Even happy."

"I was pissed." She snorts.

I chuckle. It's a sad rumble, but I can't deny it feels good to shed the layers of resentment we've harbored against each other for so long.

"Frankly, I'm shocked you didn't give up a long time ago. It's not like my life is anything to be proud of."

She scoots her feet up, resting her chin on her knee. Her blonde hair frames her face in that angelic way I remember from our childhood.

"What are you talking about? You became a bestselling author. I read your books. You're really talented."

Her eyes widen. "You read my books?"

"Of course. I'm very diligent in everything I do, including my obsessive stalking."

She snorts. "There is something really wrong with me, because the dumb girl in me is thrilled you kept tabs on me."

I give her a lopsided smile. "We're both fucked up."

She grins, and we stare at each other for a moment, and then her stomach growls.

I stand up. "Get dressed."

She reaches for the box I sent her earlier, left on the table, and pulls out the skimpy garment from it. "This?" She arches her eyebrow.

"Later. Now get that sexy ass into a dress, so we can go for dinner."

"It's late."

"It's Portugal. We'll be among the first guests."

We walk to my favorite restaurant, Brook's hand a treasure in mine. The contact is comforting and odd at the same. Like we're a genuine couple when it's never been true.

We don't talk. There has been too much of that. Every conversation between us lately has been fucking life-changing. I don't think I can handle any more.

And yet, the idea of banal topics feels too unattainable for us. She was right when she said we used to be able to talk a lot.

It was easy back then, when we were trying to figure out who we were.

Now? Now it's like every new bit of information opens a can of worms and unravels something. And that's before I even consider that I'm helplessly falling for her.

Yeah, it's official. I'm a glutton for heartbreak. Because that's where this leads.

I have never judged Brook for her irresponsible, wild life. I understand her behavior better now. Her way to escape the trauma she carries around.

But after all that, life with me would quickly bore her. She's looking at us through a temporary lens, and soon she'll move on to live her grand life, instead of sticking with the man who buries himself in work.

And that's before I consider the inevitable pressure that our family would create, causing friction between us. We simply can't last.

That doesn't stop me from enjoying the moments we still have.

As we walk, the silence is comfortable. The temperature is still bearable, not too hot yet, but not cold either.

We pass around vendors and tourists, and Brook looks at everything with such enthusiasm.

I'm enjoying myself. I don't even recognize the feeling anymore, but I find myself grinning at her when she admires a handmade necklace or homemade soap in a small shop.

Outside Mimi's, the lights glow warmly through the windows.

"Wow, I like this place already." She smiles at me, and it hits me right in the chest.

Everything about her this evening is somewhat new, painting life in high definition.

I have confirmation that she never chose to abandon me, and the heavy burden of doubt and hurt has dissolved at my feet.

It liberates me, allowing for a sliver of joy.

I kiss the crown of her head. "You seem to be liking everything tonight."

"Shocking, I know."

I return her smile. My stupid grin spreads as the effortless flow between us grows in my chest.

"Come, let me introduce you."

We walk inside and Mimi, the plump, motherly owner, greets us. "Baldo, mio caro, it's so good to see you." She kisses my cheeks. "And who is this beautiful senhora?"

"Mimi, this is Brook, my wife."

Chapter 33

Baldo

Mimi swats at me with the white towel she carries over her shoulder and wipes her hands with it. "Nice to meet you." She pulls Brook in for a hug.

"Lovely to meet you." Brook welcomes Mimi's intrusion with a warm smile.

Their exchange tugs at my heart, but it also reminds me we won't get the same reception at home. Not as a couple.

It's not fair to Brook.

"I can't believe I wasn't invited to the wedding." Mimi huffs.

"It was in New York." I squeeze Mimi's shoulder. "Brook, Mimi's cooking is the best in all of Portugal."

That placates our host. Beaming, Mimi leads us to a cozy corner table.

The aromatic scents of garlic, tomatoes and herbs waft through the air as we sit down.

"I'm not even giving you menus. Tonight, you eat the best food in the world and drink the best wine from my cellar to celebrate your wedding."

Mimi shuffles away, swatting at me again with the towel. I guess I'm not forgiven for getting married without her blessing.

"I must say, I'm surprised. I'd never picture you in a place like this, but I love it." Brook looks around with her typical curiosity.

Mimi's restaurant exudes a rustic charm. It's a well-kept secret among locals, not yet infiltrated by tourists.

The interior boasts an eclectic mix of mismatched wooden tables and chairs. Walls adorned with black-and-white photographs capture Lisbon's timeless beauty, while handwritten menus suggest dishes prepared with love and tradition.

"Mimi and her husband are talented cooks. Please don't make this place a crime scene in your book."

She laughs. "I can't promise that, but I might send my hero on vacation here."

"I like Waldo Rivers." Her main character, a PI, is a well-written, flawed hero.

She covers her face. "God, I forgot you read my books."

"Why haven't you told the family you're a writer? I get the secret behind the pen name your publisher has been milking, but sharing your success with your family?"

She purses her lips and moves them to the side, thinking. A gesture I remember. "I never felt like I fit in, you remember that. Being a rebel had been my cry for attention. One I never outgrew. I know it's stupid, but I kept telling myself that if they were truly interested, they would find out."

"Are you going to tell them now?"

I want to ask about us, not just her career, but maybe we can have an evening where the conversation isn't tainted.

"I don't know." She smiles at me, and for the next few beats we just stare at each other, pretending we have no worries in the world.

"I hope you like fish and seafood." I break the silence.

"Of course I do, especially fresh. But my favorite has always been Mexican food. There's something about the blend of flavors that I find really exciting. Tacos, enchiladas, bring it on."

I chuckle. "You lost me at tacos."

She gasps in mock offense. "You take that back. Tacos are a primary food group."

"Steak is a primary food group."

Brook narrows her eyes, grinning. "We may have to agree to disagree on that one. It's Skittles all over again. Who even are you?"

We stare at each other for a moment, wondering who even we are.

Well, I'm wondering, because as much as I'm sensing the long-lost connection, I'm also realizing we've grown up, had experiences that changed us, and this is almost like our first date.

Rediscovering.

Uncovering.

Wondering.

The server brings us water, wine, and a bread basket.

"Oh my god, I haven't eaten all day." Brook tears a piece of white loaf.

"Why?"

"I was too busy revisiting my life. Thank you very much." She rolls her eyes.

"I'm sorry you found those files, but it's not like there was anything earth-shattering there."

She munches casually. "I partied, shopped, and dated abusive assholes."

I wince at that. I hate those men, and that's before I acknowledge how poorly they treated her. "Stop putting yourself down, or I'll put you over my knee until your ass is burning."

Her eyes widen, and there is a spark in them before she catches herself and covers the reaction with the wineglass.

"This is delicious."

"My company is delicious."

"Sappy much?"

I throw my head back, laughing. God, I haven't done that in years as much as in the last few days.

And just like that, the walls are cracking. They have been cracking for weeks now, but I haven't admitted that to myself openly.

Mimi arrives with two plates of prawns pil pil, knowing it's one of my favorites.

"Mmm, this is divine." Brook sighs. "The garlic just melts in your mouth."

"Told you, Mimi's the best. She knows all my weak spots." I wipe my mouth and watch Brook eat.

It's addictive. Just like on the street, when she admired everything she saw, she eats with an enthusiasm that is contagious.

Maybe she partied and shopped a lot, but she certainly grew into enjoying life with open arms.

"Maybe I dated assholes because I craved the adrenaline of it."

"I can give you enough adrenaline, baby." I lick my lip, steering the conversation, because no fucking way I'm talking about her fucking exes.

Our eyes lock and she opens her mouth, but changes her mind and returns to her food instead.

"Brook," I warn. "Talk."

She straightens the napkin in her lap and takes a sip of the wine. "Would you chase me again like that first night?"

For a second, my mind goes to that night when I didn't save her. Will the shadows of our past always define every moment between us? Mark our intimacy?

But then I look at her, really look at her, and what I find isn't the ghost of the past, but genuine desire, primal need. Her pupils are dilated, and her breathing is rushed.

"Is that what you want me to do? To force you?" There is nothing I wouldn't do for her.

"Yes," she rasps.

"Okay." I smile, and my cock twitches in my pants. "You have your safe word."

She bites her bottom lip, excitement flashing across her face.

"Fuck dessert. Let's go use my gift."

"How was Italy?" Brook asks, taking a bite of the pastel de nata.

We're sitting in the same bistro I took her to with

Chloe. Our small table is one of the few that line the front windows along the sidewalk.

Her eyes are glassy in that dreamlike way, and her face is flushed. She wears the just-fucked look beautifully. Her blonde hair is in a messy bun on top of her head.

No makeup. No frills. Nobody would guess this woman's net worth is formidable. It's funny how I know so much about her, but only this morning I learned how she takes her coffee.

No surveillance report could ever get me a taste of the real woman behind the bravado. Getting under all her layers is exciting. And dangerous.

"Boring." I cross one leg over my knee and lean back, enjoying the view.

There are moments—fluid, silent moments like this one—when I still can't believe I have her. That she is mine.

For now.

She cocks her head. "I thought you loved your work," she mocks.

"Yeah, but your tits distracted me."

Fuck, when she sent me that picture... I don't think I've ever conducted a business meeting with a semi in my pants. And I own sex clubs.

She laughs. "I'll keep them to myself. I wouldn't want Baldo's empire to crumble because of my boobs."

"It would be a worthy fall." I pick up her hand and kiss her knuckles.

Electricity zaps between us. I almost throw some bills on the table and drag her back to my lair.

"Where did you go before Italy?" She licks her finger, the creamy custard sticking to them.

I don't particularly want to have this conversation. Fuck, I don't really want to have any conversations, but the glimpse of her tongue distracts me. I'm a simple man, as the bulge in my pants attests.

"New York, and then the Dominican Republic."

"Wait? Do you have clubs in the Caribbean?" She takes a sip of water. Her lips pressing against the glass. Why is her every move so arousing?

She's drinking water. *Get your fucking head out of your ass, idiot.* It's like I'm seventeen all over again. Pure infatuation.

"Cayman Islands, yes, but I went to the Dominican on a personal matter."

"Oh." She glowers at me, and then turns in her seat as if people watching was her intention instead of getting more details.

Fuck, she's adorable.

"Brook," I warn, and she looks at me, unimpressed. "I told you already, I don't think you'll like it."

"How would you know if you're keeping it a secret?" She scoffs, folding her arms.

"Brook, leave it."

She huffs, and this time she turns the whole chair. Such a dedicated people watcher.

We sit in silence, but this one isn't comfortable like before. She folds her arms and glowers at the pedestrians. Not that they are the target of her annoyance.

"Tokyo." I sigh.

She snaps her head to me, her eyes narrowed. "Don't Tokyo me."

I smirk. "You're still jealous?"

"Fuck you." She grabs her phone from the table and pushes off her seat.

I grab her wrist. "I've only been with you since we got married, darling wife."

She drops back to her seat, but yanks her hand away. "Why should I believe you?"

"Because I wouldn't lie to you." I have never spoken a more honest truth.

The statement sits between us, heavy with implied commitment. Maybe not to the extent she would like to hear, but one that I'm willing to give at this point.

Brook stares at me and then shakes her head, like she can't agree with herself. "Okay, I trust you."

Fuck. She awarded me her trust with her body already. But this... this feels like more.

More significant.

More binding.

Essential.

We both startle when her phone dances on the table.

"It's London." Brook tenses and picks up. "Is Dad okay?"

Shit. I watch her for any signs, hoping the news isn't too bad.

"Oh my God. Yes, yes, we'll get back as soon as possible."

She's smiling as she says that, so I relax. Though I'm not particularly keen on returning to the States.

"Paris had a baby boy. It's a bit early, but they are both doing well. Mom and Dad are returning from Florida. We should go back."

She's radiant with excitement, but her smile dies as soon as she utters the words.

We don't need to say it out loud—the implications are obvious.

Are we returning as siblings or as a couple?

They will never accept us.

Chapter 34

Brook

"Where are we?" I yawn and blink a few times, stretching my limbs.

I couldn't sleep on the flight. We landed at the crack of dawn, and I must have promptly fallen asleep in the town car Baldo hired.

I'm so excited about meeting my little nephew, and spending more time with Dad. But our return is clouded.

Baldo and I are together. We're a couple. We're married, and while we're both hesitant about full commitment—the man still hasn't kissed me—we can't pretend this is fake.

But Dad doesn't even know about the fake marriage.

It's all too overwhelming, and we are both evading the topic. I'm avoiding to the best of my abilities—it's a superpower of mine—and I left all the travel arrangements to Baldo.

As if having someone else booking the travel meant I didn't have to face the return. I didn't want to think about coming back to our Riverdale home.

But as I look up, we're not in the Bronx.

Baldo helps me get out of the car.

No, definitely Upper East Side.

"We're home."

I frown at him, but he's busy overseeing the luggage. A uniformed bellhop appears with a trolley and starts loading our suitcases.

Why do we have four of them? I only had one. Is Baldo planning to stay longer?

"Home?"

He takes my hand, and we follow the bellhop. "Temporary, until we find our own place."

"Is this a hotel?"

"Yes, but the rooms are only long-term rentals. No tourists, thank God."

I snort. "I thought the hospitality industry was your bread and butter."

"Entertainment is my bread and butter. I hate fucking tourists."

I snicker, elbowing him.

We enter the lobby, where the floor is a polished

expanse of marble, reflecting the soft, ambient light from exquisite crystal chandeliers above us.

A large, intricately designed mural on the wall across from the entrance captures the essence of the city.

Every detail speaks of refined elegance, full of grandeur. Even the air is subtly scented with what I guess is a bespoke fragrance. Soft, classical music plays unobtrusively in the background, adding to the serene ambience.

Home.

"Mr. and Mrs. Cassinetti, welcome to Emporio Suites." A man in a sharp suit approaches. "Here are your key cards. My name is Pietro and I'm here to assist you in whatever way you need. Let me give you a tour of our—"

"We're exhausted after the flight, Pietro, so we'll order room service and rest." Baldo gives the man a hundred-dollar bill. I guess we're now tipping for not getting the service.

"Of course, of course, please let me show you to your private elevator. We'll have your luggage there in a few minutes."

The moment the elevator door closes, silence and tension descend on us. We should talk about the way we're going to handle the family, but I'm not eager, and I guess Baldo isn't either.

A petty part of me regrets Paris having the baby early, interrupting our honeymoon. A fake honeymoon that helped us grow closer. But definitely not close enough yet.

It's like we didn't get fully grounded in our relationship, and now we have to face yet another challenge.

"Private elevator?" I break the silence.

"I booked us into a penthouse suite. It's large enough so we can each have some privacy."

I turn to him. "Privacy?"

What the hell? When did we take several steps back after we'd just made forward progress?

"It has an office where you can write." He keeps looking at the numbers above the doors.

I hate the unspoken challenge hanging above us. But it's like neither of us knows how we want to handle it, so while we're figuring it out, we can't talk about it.

But shouldn't a couple face challenges together? Discuss them? I'm worried I made Baldo talk so much in the last few days that he might be out of words for years to come.

"An office, I see. It almost sounded like we're getting separate bedrooms."

The door opens into a large living space, but I don't get to see much of it because Baldo grabs my wrists and yanks me to him, twisting my arm behind me.

Not hurting me, but locking me in. He wraps the other hand around my neck, forcing me to look at him. "Only one bedroom. You have no choice in that," he says darkly, and I shiver.

There is a retort on my tongue, but it dies as I feel the bulge in his pants.

We pant and stare at each other, our lust igniting the air around us.

We shouldn't be fucking instead of talking. That's not a solution to our problem.

That thought is a fleeting frivolity.

Our relationship is like the tide. Retreating and advancing. Let's hope we don't get tumbled by an unexpected big wave.

God, but I want this man.

"Let go of me." I kick his shin.

He grunts and loosens his grip. A jolt of excitement electrifies my spine and I run.

The penthouse sprawls before me. I glimpse the floor to ceiling windows, featuring Central Park bathed in the first rays of sun.

Marble floors stretch beneath my feet, slick and slippery.

The opulent decor blurs into a dizzying rush of colors and shapes as I dart through the open living area.

The problem is, I don't know the space. Every

choice is a gamble, every door a potential trap. But the thrill... the thrill of the chase ignites me with wild exhilaration.

What's wrong with me? I don't understand the part of me that revels in this twisted game of cat and mouse.

And yet, adrenaline courses through me like an awakening, a dark and perverse revelation of my true nature. And with Baldo playing along, instead of judging, I'm growing to accept this side of me.

I don't sense him behind me, but when I chance a look over my shoulder... He hasn't moved, but his eyes follow me with an aloof coldness. Like the predator waiting for his prey to tire out.

Jesus, he is hot.

My breath comes in ragged gasps.

I stop behind the sofa, gripping the backrest like I could throw the furniture at him. He advances with cat-like grace, prowling in my direction.

No rush.

Just calculated precision.

In control, as usual.

He rounds the love seat and a glass coffee table. There is only the sofa between us.

My eyes dart toward the large double doors to my left, and then to a hallway to my right.

The moment I return my attention to him, I know I shouldn't have distracted myself.

He lunges over the backrest. I yelp, but without thinking I react and slide to the side.

He grabs me around my waist.

We lose balance and collapse to the floor. I fight with everything I have, like a woman possessed.

Baldo grunts as I elbow him, but it doesn't slow him down at all. I kick my legs to no avail. The man has straddled me.

I graze his cheek with my finger, drawing blood. He hisses and seizes both my wrists, forcing my hands above my head.

We pant, glaring at each other.

"Your luggage—"

We spring to our feet, emerging from behind the sofa probably looking like we just fought. Which would be accurate.

The bellhop blinks a few times. "Is everything okay?"

"Of course." Baldo casually steps around the sofa, approaching the bewildered young man whose eyes stay on me.

Good man, making sure the lady isn't in peril.

I force a smile, and as soon as my lips curl up, the absurdity of the situation hits me and I giggle.

Baldo gives me a warning look, but his lips quiver as well. He pulls money from his pocket and tips the guy before he's even unloaded the suitcases from the cart.

The hop's eyes drop to the bill, and then back at me. I nod, encouraging him to take it. And leave, for fuck's sake.

He reaches out for his tip. "You're bleeding, sir." He points to Baldo's face.

Baldo flicks his finger over the laceration from my nails and shrugs. "A shaving accident."

I snort, and my reaction calms the young man enough. He gives us both one more puzzled look and rushes to the elevator.

As soon as the door slides closed behind him, I release the laugh, regretting the interruption but having fun at the same time.

My laugh freezes when I meet Baldo's eyes. The hunger in them is back, perhaps tenfold. His pull has me transfixed, vertigo tugging at my senses.

As if the interruption never happened, my heart goes from a murmur to a thundering in my chest.

Baldo cracks his neck. His cock is straining against his zipper. Jesus, did the bellhop notice?

"Where were we?" he rasps.

I bolt, veering right, then left. I somehow avoid him and dive through the double doorway.

I stumble into the bedroom, lavish and vast, with floor-to-ceiling windows offering a dizzying view.

For a split second, I'm transfixed by the sight, and Baldo catches me from behind.

Wrapping me in a vise-like hold, he lifts me. I struggle, but without much effort he carries me over to the huge bed.

One powerful arm still around me, he fists my hair and yanks my head up. "You're mine now."

Oh, what those words do to me. No longer just prey, I'm a participant in this wanton dance.

Baldo pushes me to the mattress, bending me. My face hits the silky sheets and I try to wiggle away, but I'm exhausted, and he's so strong.

"Move and you'll regret it," he snaps.

With his hands, he pulls my pants and panties to my ankles in a quick move. But it frees my hands and I try to push off the bed.

Not a chance.

He lurches over me and covers me with his whole body, wrestling my arms into submission.

He grips my wrists, twisted at my lower back, with one of his hands, and uses the other to free himself.

He kicks my legs apart and runs his cock through my folds. "Hmmm."

There is so much praise, so much reverence in that sound, I moan.

"So ready for me. Good girl."

He impales me so suddenly I lurch forward, gasping. Filled by him. Knowing he plays my lewd games without questioning me.

He understands me.

He cherishes me.

He adores me.

Maybe not always in words, but in so many actions.

It takes no time before my walls clench and my muscles tense. "I'm there."

"Thank God."

And then we're coming, swept by a wave of pleasure, in unison.

Baldo collapses on top of me, kissing my hair. "Are you okay?"

"More than okay." I turn my head to face him.

He is only an inch from me. His eyes drop to my mouth. My lips part, and my heart hammers against my ribcage so fast that he must hear it.

The moment stretches, and fuck it, I close the distance between us.

Chapter 35

Baldo

I jump back and scoop her up.

We almost kissed, but I chickened out.

I've fucked her. I've made love to her. I would kill for her, or happily die for her.

Yet I'm a scared asshole who can't give her that last symbol of her power over me.

Am I aware this is a pathetic attempt to maintain the upper hand? Yes.

Do I realize the upper hand is not what relationships are built on? Also, yes.

Am I willing to take that last step and savor her? No. I'm not.

Why?

Fuck if I know.

Rounding the bed, I lay Brook gently on the covers,

kissing her forehead. Like she needed a consolation prize.

I remove her pants and underwear from around her ankles and drop them to the floor. Yanking the sheets from under her, I tug them to her shoulders.

"Let me clean you up."

Fuck, I don't know where the bathroom is. I open a double door, only to be confronted with the shelves and empty hangers of a walking closet.

Okay, the other door it is. I enter the spacious bathroom and let the water run.

What's wrong with me?

They will never accept us.

Brook has been so excited about our nephew and coming back to be with her dad, it's like I'm losing her all over again.

But this time, she's still here with me. Just being drawn away by her loyalty to them.

To our family.

The rational businessman in me knows that we need to sit everyone down and tell them. Hope for the best, but adopt the outcome whether they accept us or not.

The scared man in me fears that if it comes down to a choice, Brook would choose me, and then hate me for stealing her from her family.

Or worse, she wouldn't choose me.

No, I need her to work through it and realize what she really wants. What she's willing to give up.

Fuck. I left her waiting there.

I take off my clothes, wetting a hand towel before I return to the bedroom.

She smiles at me, but it doesn't reach her eyes. "I should shower."

I kiss her forehead. "Baby, you didn't sleep on the flight. Let's catch up on sleep, and then we can deal with other adulting tasks."

Gently, I wipe between her thighs while she watches me with hooded eyes. There is sadness in them, but maybe it's just fatigue.

Fuck, I'm tired to the point of not being able to think.

I get us both bottled water.

I draw the curtains closed.

I feel like a robot, just executing the motions while Brook follows me with her gaze.

She gulps down the bottle and turns to her side.

I slide under the sheets and take her in my arms, pulling her as close as possible. She melts into me.

Her shoulders tremble and then shake. I tense. Is she crying?

"Brook?"

She turns to me, chuckling. "The poor bellhop."

She gets the words out and bursts into full-blown laughter. Fuck.

It's contagious, and maybe we're just delirious from exhaustion, but we both dissolve into hysterical cackles.

Brook wipes her cheeks, still grinning. "God, it feels good to laugh."

"It does."

She turns to me now, her face shadowed by the darkness in the room, but her eyes glow.

She cups my cheek and traces her fingers around the scruff of my jaw.

My heart hammers against my chest. Just fucking kiss her, asshole. Take the risk.

"You got us a beautiful place here." That's not what I expected her to say, but I focus on the *us* in that sentence.

"Only the best for my wife," I tease her, but a part of me is begging her to choose me. To become my real wife. To tell the world.

That part is overwhelmed by the very firm belief that we found some tentative happiness in Portugal, but it can't last here.

Because while I wish she'd choose me, I don't want her to have to choose.

Maybe if we stay around longer, everyone will accept us naturally.

Maybe we can visit the baby and then return to Europe.

All the options seem unfair to Brook, who is already snoring softly beside me.

Despite the impending doom, she feels like mine. I watch her sleep, wondering just how long I get to be with her.

How long before I lose her again?

"That's not acceptable, John." Brook's voice cuts through the air, reaching my sleepy mind.

I roll in the unfamiliar bed, missing the warmth of her. I don't know how long I slept, but I finally feel more myself.

Still unsettled and hating our current predicament, but at least I'm rested.

"Then I pay the penalties and rescind the contract. There is no way I'm working with him."

What the hell is happening? I get up and find yesterday's boxers. Fuck, we need to unpack.

The bedroom is dark with the thick curtains closed.

I follow Brook's voice, finding her standing by the glass wall of windows in the living room. The strong light blinds me momentarily. How long did I sleep?

Her back is to me. Her hair is all messy, and she is wearing only a shirt.

My black shirt. I haven't lost her. Yet.

Her hair is wet, and the shirt falls almost to her mid-thighs. She looks edible. Delicious.

But she is tense on the phone. Who is John?

I remember that name, I just can't place him right now.

"Tough shit. Talk to them, but my decision is final." She nods a few times. "Okay, John, thank you. Keep me posted." She drops her hand and sighs.

"Good morning." I walk across the sun-bathed room to her.

She pivots. "Good morning? You slept like a log. It's two in the afternoon."

"Well, that won't help with the jetlag." I snake my arms around her shoulders and kiss the crown of her head. "Did you sleep well?"

"Yeah, I just woke up half an hour ago." She looks up at me, smiling. "You look rested. It suits you. Did I wake you?"

"No. What happened?"

Her shoulders slouch and she groans. "I got a TV series deal."

"That's wonderful, baby. Congratulations."

"Yeah, but they want to cast Dylan Sinclair as the lead."

Annoyance swipes through me, and, if I'm honest, jealousy too. "Over my dead body."

She chuckles. "That's what I said. I have an executive producer role, but my agent isn't optimistic my influence is enough. Someone must have pulled strings."

"I'll take care of it."

She snorts. "No, you won't. I can take care of my own problems."

"Dylan Sinclair is my problem."

As I said earlier, she'll work with her ex over my dead body.

She rises on her tiptoes and kisses my cheek and walks away. "That is very chivalrous, and a bit unhinged, but let me fight my own battles."

I follow her to a room opposite our bedroom, and we enter a fully equipped kitchen and dining room. "Wow, this place is huge."

She puts her hand on her hip. "Baldo Cassinetti, you had no idea what you were renting, did you?"

"Not really, but it will work for now. Back to Dylan."

She waggles her finger. "No, no, no, we've already said his name too many times today. I'll wait for my agent to find out more, and then we'll see."

Oh, yeah, John is her agent.

She pours two cups of coffee and hands me one.

Mindlessly, I take a sip and spit it back immediately. "I need to buy a coffee machine."

"You're such a snob."

"I'm a coffee connoisseur, sweetheart." My eyes drop to her nipples. "You showered without me."

I take her cup from her and sit her on the counter, filing the Dylan issue away for later. She grins at me, wrapping her legs around my waist.

"I talked to London." She runs her fingers through my hair.

I unfasten the three buttons holding the shirt together. It falls open and my cock hardens. "Hm." Cupping her left breast, I lower my mouth to taste her nipple.

Her breath hitches. So responsive.

"Paris asked for a few more days to get settled before we visit. Lo and Dom are having dinner at Casa Cassi and suggested we join them. Tonight."

She moans, arching her back and tilting her pelvis to get closer to me.

"Okay. We could do that. But I'm having my appetizer now."

"Your stamina is endless."

"Are you complaining?"

She smiles and lifts her feet to the counter, spreading herself for me. I groan.

She leans onto her elbows. "Dinner is at eight."

I guess we're still talking. Not really about important things, but I'm not complaining about this sexy domesticity.

"And I thought I'd go visit Dad before?"

I still. Is she asking for my permission? It certainly doesn't sound like she's inviting me.

Our eyes lock. There is a tentative plea in hers. Definitely not inviting me.

"I'll meet you at Massi's restaurant. Now stop distracting me."

I lower my lips to her nipple again, burying my disappointment in the taste of her.

* * *

I'm the last to arrive at Casa Cassi. Mostly because I spent two hours at the gym in our building and still didn't release all my pent-up frustration.

Lo and Dom are sitting across from each other, and Brook is between them, which doesn't leave room for me to sit beside her.

I wonder if she chose the seating arrangement to stay at a safe distance from me. Our current company believes our relationship is fake, after all.

"Hey, sorry I'm late." I kiss both women on the cheek and shake hands with Dom.

"No problem, we just got here as well. The traffic was brutal from the Bronx." Lo gestures for a server.

"You were in Riverdale?" I glance at Brook, whose eyes are downcast, playing with the butter knife.

"Yeah, we all went to see Bianca and Dad. The few weeks in Florida really did him well," London says.

Brook looks at me and averts her eyes, darting her gaze around the table like there's something to find there.

So, it wasn't just her visiting her dad.

It was me not visiting with her. *Don't be an asshole. Give her time.*

"I'm glad to hear that." I adjust my cufflinks.

The server pours me a glass of water and retreats. I look around for the menu. He didn't even recite the specials?

Lo picks up on my hesitation. "Oh, Massi will serve us whatever he wants."

"But no worries, you will love it." Dominic leans back in his seat.

The room bustles with cutlery clinking, conversations humming, servers running. I want my wife to fucking look at me.

London leads the conversation, asking about my business, recounting what her charity achieved, sharing the new endeavors she and Dom are starting for orphaned kids. It's impressive, and the two of them seem like true partners.

My eyes meet Brook's, but she looks down again. Guilty? Or has she already retreated to a world where there is no space for me?

In the middle of the main course, London picks up on the tension.

"What's up with the two of you?"

Brook wipes the corners of her mouth. "What do you mean?"

"What happened while you were in Europe? Please don't tell me you fucked." She makes a face, like that would be the most unsavory thing.

"And what if we did?" Brook counters, dropping her fork.

"Whatever, you're both adults." London surprises me with her dismissive stance, but then she adds, "Still weird. It would kill Dad."

"Did you know Paris and Finn named the baby after him?" Dom says.

I think he's trying to divert the conversation, but a baby named after Brook's dad only emphasizes how all the sisters are respecting their father and creating memories with him, while Brook is poised to give him a heart attack because of me.

I drop the napkin and excuse myself before I strangle someone. I rush to the bathroom and wash my face, hoping to cool down the hot blood coursing through me.

When I open the door, my gaze clashes with Brook's. She is leaning against the wall opposite the men's room.

"You're mad at me."

It's not a question, it's a statement, but there is hurt behind her tone, and I hate it. I hate that she's struggling, and I hate even more that I don't know how to fix it for her.

These are her decisions. She doesn't want me to help with the Dylan bullshit. This is way bigger. While I don't give a fuck about anyone accepting us, she does. I need to respect that, give her time.

But I can still hate the situation.

"We should head back." I turn to leave.

She grabs my arm. "Baldo, I'm sorry. I didn't know Lo and Syd were bringing Dom and Hunter. I would have invited you to join us."

"Would you?" I accuse. So much for giving her time to decide.

She sighs. "Please, don't... You cared when I showed you all the ugly pieces of me. You helped fix them all. And I wish I could somehow fix this for us. I'm worried about Dad, but he's doing much better, and I'm sure with time he would grow to understand. Can you be patient?"

Chapter 36

Brook

While Baldo reluctantly promised his patience, Uncle Rupert proved to be a very persistent bastard.

We put him off for a whole two weeks. Two weeks while we resumed some sort of existence in New York.

Me editing and arguing with the TV network.

Baldo mostly spending time on the phone, monitoring his business. Or in his club. He didn't go to see Mom.

He came with me to visit Paris and her baby and, surrounded by all that love, I wanted to cuddle into his side.

Only, that's not us. Not yet.

It's like we were pretending to be a real couple, and now that we are one, we're faking the make-believe.

What's stopping us from taking the leap? For all his

controlling tendencies, Baldo seems to have relinquished control in this case.

He's left me to lead on when and how we tell the family.

While a part of me understands why he did that, I still find it an unfair burden. If we're a genuine couple, shouldn't we tackle this hurdle together?

I know I asked him for patience, but he abandoned the topic all together.

And my fear of losing either him or my family is too real, so I don't act at all. Avoiding reality has always been my superpower.

"I'm nervous." I wiggle my shoulders as if I could shake off the feeling.

Baldo helps me out of the car in front of Rupert Montgomery's house. "It's going to be fine."

He snakes his fingers through mine, and we walk together to the large entrance.

We ring the bell.

"Have I told you how ravishing you look tonight?" Baldo wraps his arm around my waist, pulls me to him and kisses my neck.

"You're trying to distract me." I lean into his embrace.

"Is it working?" He grazes his teeth around the hem of my cleavage, and I sigh.

"Erm—" Rupert's butler clears his throat, and we jump apart.

Baldo snickers and leads me inside. We're ushered to a small, eclectic dining room. It's an airy room with light furnishings, and at such odds with the rest of the stuffy house.

Though the entry hall has changed somewhat as well. Modern art has replaced the heavy paintings.

Rupert has different tastes than his sister, and he didn't wait long to apply them here.

The man who greets us looks very different from the man I met two months ago. He is wearing a light blue shirt and brown slacks.

His skin is smoother, more radiant. There is an air of lightness around him. I guess this is the less grieving version of him.

Even his creepy smirk is gone, though as I look at him closely, his facial muscles don't move. Did he get Botox?

The evening flows with idle chitchat, mostly between Rupert and Baldo, focusing on business. And I'm happy I can just chew and count down the minutes till this ends.

Because Rupert might be more relaxed and warm than the last time, but he's still scrutinizing our every move.

Baldo doesn't miss any opportunity to touch me, to

Maxine Henri

praise me with respect and reverence, to kiss my knuckles. It's so effortless for him that I relax.

Why I'm even stressed is beyond me. In front of Rupert, we can be a proper couple. Not like with my family.

"I must say you two seem genuine," Rupert announces after the staff serves us dessert. "But I still have my hesitations. You're siblings, after all."

"Not blood related," I snap.

"Of course, of course, but still—"

"Frankly," Baldo interrupts, "I find it quite interesting that you're so eager to comply with your sister's wishes. It's not like she extended you much respect while she was alive."

I whip my head toward him. What is he talking about?

"Excuse me?" Rupert puts down his dessert fork. "Whatever are you implying?"

"You can't tell me you'd be okay if the inheritance fell to the hands of those despicable organizations, particularly to numbers sixteen to twenty-one on the list."

Rupert's face pales. And while I have no idea what they are talking about, I can see Baldo's words hit the intended target.

"Would you, Uncle Rupert?" Baldo urges.

Rupert clears his throat. "No."

"I see. So, in that case I'd suggest you stop questioning the integrity of the future mother of my children. Brook and I are married. End of story."

Future mother of my children.

I don't hear what is said afterward, because those words beat in my temples so loud I might faint.

Future mother of my children.

"So, this is what's going to happen, and believe me, there is more I can do to tarnish your name. Brook, if she chooses, will come up with an alternate list of organizations that can benefit from the inheritance, and deserve it. You will transfer the funds to them and stop pestering us."

Rupert drops his napkin on the table. "I think this dinner is over."

"Do we have an understanding?"

Baldo stands up and helps me to my feet.

Rupert adjusts his pocket square. "That would be against the terms of her will."

"Get creative then." Baldo smirks.

We leave the house.

"What is sixteen to twenty-one on the list?"

Baldo opens the car door for me, and I get in.

"Homophobic groups." He slides onto the seat beside me.

"Is Uncle Rupert gay? How did you know?"

"I have my sources, baby." He pulls me into his lap

Maxine Henri

and unbuttons my top, skimming his hand over the fabric of my bra.

I shiver and wrap my arms around his shoulders as he dips his head and kisses my neck. As usual, he finds the most sensitive spot that gets me all squirming and yearning for him.

Future mother of my children.

All the words he said tonight. I want to run to Mom and Dad and tell them everything, but as much as Baldo seems to be all-in with me, I'm still hesitant.

He trails his hand under the hem of my skirt and finds my underwear, and I push away all those thoughts for later.

* * *

PARIS
Little Micah smiled for the first time.

SYD
Sorry to tell you, but he is two weeks. It's farting.

LO
(laughing emoji)

PARIS
Come on, I need it to be a smile because I'm going crazy here.

I'll come over to keep you company.

PARIS

I love you.

"Wow, you look—" Baldo starts when Paris opens the door, but I elbow him and he lies, "radiant, sis."

Her hair is messy, her T-shirt is stained, and her breast is leaking.

She puts a finger to her lips. "Shh, he's just fallen asleep."

She tiptoes inside. Baldo looks at me, shrugging, and we follow.

Micah is sleeping in a bassinet by the sofa. Paris stares at him with adoration and then pleads with us.

"Finn went to get wipes. I forgot to put them in the delivery order. Could you watch him? I really need to shower. And get changed. He'll be down for at least half an hour. I'll be done in five."

She trips over her sentences like there's a prize for hushed speed talking.

My eyes dart between the sleeping baby, Baldo, and Paris, a bit of panic rising in me. I want to help, but like by cleaning her kitchen, cooking her a meal. I don't know what to do with a baby.

"Sure. You stink," Baldo teases.

Paris's lower lip trembles.

"Jesus, I was teasing you. Go take a shower. We'll watch the baby." He lunges into the seat beside the cot.

"Thank you." Paris dashes upstairs.

Okay, I guess we're going to babysit. Well, it's not like she's far away.

"Do you want anything to drink?" I whisper, walking to the kitchen corner of Paris's open concept day room that is the first floor of her townhouse.

As an interior designer, she remodeled the typical layout and opened up the space.

"Whiskey."

I whip around, wide-eyed. "We're babysitting."

He shrugs. "Exactly."

I roll my eyes, giggling. He seems to be completely unfazed by the fact we've been left alone with a newborn.

Getting two glasses of water, I walk back, but stop in my tracks.

Baldo picked up the baby, and he's sitting now, holding the tiny human in his large muscular arms.

His broad frame is a stark contrast to the delicate life cradled in his arms.

He holds Micah with such tenderness, protecting him in a safe embrace. His usually intense eyes are soft now.

He is whispering something to Micah while running his index finger up and down his teensy spine.

Tears prickle behind my eyes as a warm feeling

spreads through my chest. God, he's hot. And so completely in the moment of pure love.

The sight of this man—so imposing, yet so caring—fills me with an overwhelming sense of gratitude.

"Wow, look at that, you're a baby whisperer," Paris says behind me.

Baldo looks up and our eyes lock. His full of adoration, and I'm hoping he can find the awe in my gaze.

Because right in this moment, I know with irrevocable certainty that I love this man.

"Where is my whiskey?" he rasps.

I snort.

"You're holding him as long as he sleeps," Paris decides. "And if it's more than forty minutes, you're staying here."

"Not a chance." He chuckles.

"I'll pay you," she pleads, and I don't think she's kidding.

Finn returns and we drink coffee. It might be Paris's hundredth cup today. Not that she's finished any of them, guessing by the haphazardly scattered cups with cold, dark liquid all around the room.

Baldo joins us, holding the baby effortlessly like he's done it a million times. And I grin dreamily.

Future mother of my children.

After seeing him today, I'm sold on the concept.

"Since you're here, can you help me put together the stroller?" Finn asks.

"Why don't you get someone to do this shit for you?" Baldo hands the baby to Paris.

Finn shrugs. "My parents were distant and MIA, mostly. I want to be as involved as possible."

"Sure, but it's not like Micah knows at this stage. Get help, and get some sleep," Baldo says.

"Sleep is overrated." Finn chuckles and they retreat upstairs, where I assume the stroller is.

"Do you want to hold him?" Paris doesn't wait for an answer and pushes the baby into my arms.

He smells like innocence. So fragile, but surprisingly solid. The rhythm of his breathing and his warm weight fill me with peace.

"So, Lo told me the two of you are banging?" Paris says as we take seats in the living room.

Micah stirs in my arms but settles immediately. "Jesus, don't be crass in front of your son."

"Oh, come on, my days are spent with a newborn, diapers, breasts out of my bra... give me something juicy."

"We're together." I don't look at her, focusing on the tiny heartbeat against my chest. Hopefully, my thundering pulse won't wake him up.

"Well, that's unexpected and weird."

"For fuck's sake, Paris, we're not blood related."

"I know, but we grew up together. It would take a bit of getting used to that my sister and my brother... Is it serious?"

I sigh. "I think it would be, but we haven't told Mom and Dad yet, so we're kind of hanging in limbo."

"What are you talking about? The depth of your commitment has nothing to do with the outside world."

"Yeah, but it's a hurdle."

"If you make it one. Look, Finn and I faced all sorts of bullshit from his family, but we learned the hard way we can't let that define our relationship."

"Yes, but I'm glad I'm back with all of you. I don't want to lose that."

"Who says it's one or the other? I mean, we'll forever tease you about it, but that doesn't mean we're not happy for you."

"I don't think Dad would agree with that."

"I think you need to give him more credit. Did you know Lo fake dated Dom to appease Dad?"

"Really? Now I can see how he even got the chance to tame her. But that's exactly the problem. We're all doing things to make sure Dad continues to have a happy life, for as long as possible."

"Yes, but that might be our own way to deal with..." She sighs. "Being confronted with his mortality. I think at the end of the day, Dad just really wants to see us happy."

I bury my face in the bald head of the sleeping baby.

Baldo makes me happy. And as much as I want to believe Paris, I wonder if that's enough for Dad to accept us.

He refused to do that once before, after all.

Chapter 37

Baldo

We've been in New York for a month, and we're still hanging in some sort of suspended state. Growing closer every day, our relationship has found its own rhythm. I'm happy. Trying not to think about the fact that it's only for the time being.

At least the inheritance issue has been resolved. Rupert has released the funds to Brook, and she's disbursed some of it to different charitable organizations already.

I promoted some of my most reliable managers in Europe and Asia, and along with Chloe—who is still complaining about the distance—we've found ways to manage the business even with me here.

And still, the planner in me, the controlling bastard

that I am, has been restless. Brook asked for patience, but fuck it's hard.

She spends as much time with her dad as possible, but she hasn't talked to him about us yet.

And so while my life feels like a smooth ride beside the woman I used to think I had lost forever, it's only a question of time before things crumble.

Because we need to talk to our parents.

We don't attend events, because I don't want to pretend to be her brother for the fear of having our picture taken and Micah finding out.

I don't want to miss family dinners.

Or avoid my mother.

All the while, my patience is running thin.

The elevator door opens into a large foyer of the Madison Club where my brother, Gio, is a member.

I've been avoiding a meeting with all my brothers, though I'm not sure why. Well, one reason is that I blame them all for making my relationship with Brook so difficult. So taboo.

"Here he is." Gio stands as the hostess leads me to his table.

Fuck, but it's good to see them.

"Sorry I'm late." I take a seat after we shake hands and give each other a half-embrace.

Massi, Gio and Andrea are staring at me.

"What?"

"When was the last time the four of us got together?" Massi asks.

I shrug.

"Please, spare us the sordid journey down memory lane. We're here now." Andrea opens his menu.

He's always been the troublemaker, having issues with substance abuse and the lifestyle his fame as an artist threw at him.

But he's also partied in Europe enough for us to get together more than I have with my two older brothers.

We order lunch and talk shit, mostly about business.

"So, Lo told us you and Brook..." Gio leans back, smirking.

And here we go. "I guess everyone knows now."

"It's weird." Massi taps his lips with the napkin.

"Not for us." I drum my fingers on my thigh.

"Don't get all offended." Gio chuckles. "If you can manage her, go for it."

"What do you mean, manage her?"

"Look, I haven't spent much time with her, but she's been partying and wasting her trust fund in Europe doing God knows what—"

"Stop right there, Gio. Brook has a very successful career, and the fact that none of you knows about it says more about you than about her. She's a strong, creative person, who isn't full of herself and enjoys life.

"And if any of you think you're better than her, enjoy your high horse. None of you have any right to judge because none of you, including her sisters, haven't given a shit about what she's been through. Or what she's achieved in life."

I push my plate away, appetite gone.

"Nice speech, asshole." Andrea leans back, stretching his long limbs to the side of him, a playful smirk on his face. "You really care about her."

"So should you. We're family, after all, as you keep reminding me." I yank the napkin from my lap and drop it on my unfinished meal.

"Sorry, I guess you're right." Gio raises his arms in surrender. "But it's not like she stuck around or tried to share."

"Or maybe it's not like you cared enough about her for her to want to share."

All three of them stare at me.

"Are you in love with her?" Massi asks.

That renders me speechless. "What does it take to get a drink here?" I snap.

Gio chuckles. "You're in love with her. Now I didn't see that coming."

"Looks like we've missed a lot when it comes to the two of you," Massi says.

"Okay, so what now? You're going to propose?" Gio asks.

"We're already married, dickhead."

Andrea laughs. "That's right, cart before the horse and all that. What I don't understand is why you're still pretending."

You and me, bro, you and me. "She's not ready to talk to Micah."

"As weird as it would be for him, I'm sure he'd get over the sibling thing. It's not like you're blood related." Gio gestures to a server and orders three whiskeys, since Andrea doesn't drink.

"I'm not so sure about that, but in any case, it's Brook who needs to tell him and she's been stalling." I run my fingers through my hair.

"Did you tell her you love her?" Massi asks.

"Kind of a moot point since he hasn't admitted it to himself yet." Fucking Andrea cackles.

I glare at him, which only makes him laugh harder.

"Okay," Massi says, "I can't believe we're spending our lunch talking about relationships like some chicks, but here are my two cents. By all means, give her time, but it took me seventeen years to sort my shit out with Gina, and I lost precious time with my son because of that. And these two learned it the hard way too. Being scared of love is in our blood, but you need to grow some balls."

"Hey, I told Ivy I loved her immediately." Andrea spreads his hands, palms up, in protest.

"Yeah, and spooked her." Gio rolls his eyes. "As much as I hate to admit it, Massi is right. If she's stalling, she might need reassurance that she's not jeopardizing her relationship with Micah. That you're in it for real."

I busy myself with the new club for the next two days. Mostly because I'm a fucking coward. She might need some reassurance, but what about me?

Am I ready to bare my soul, only to be put in second place? And it's not like I can even hold a grudge. It's her father, after all.

The man who was a father to me growing up. A man I used to respect, who brought up four amazing women, and in the process held his own with the four of us. Not trying to take our papa's place, but to fill the void as much as possible.

The man who helped Mom through the rough time when she was left alone with four boys. It was thanks to Micah that she started smiling again.

I don't have many memories from those early years because I was so young, but I know Micah has been the best thing that could have happened to Mom.

He taught me how to ride a bike, swim, shoot a gun. He drove me to school, built airplanes with me. Was there when I got hurt. Cheered me from the sidelines when I played football in elementary school.

He loves Brook, and he's fighting a life-threatening disease. Who am I to challenge him?

And yet he's the reason I didn't get a chance to be with her when she needed me the most. And I want to be the man who can forgive him, but the sad truth is, I can't.

Doesn't Brook deserve better from me?

"Mr. Cassinetti." Pietro, the concierge, grimaces, or smiles, I guess, when he sees me. "I hope you're having a good day."

"Thank you. It's been busy. Is my wife home?"

"Yes, yes, she is. About that..." His eyes dart around, avoiding me.

What the fuck is happening?

"We asked Mrs. Cassinetti on several occasions to keep her music down, but—"

"Well, my wife likes loud music."

I leave him standing behind me and get to our elevator.

Not very neighborly of me, but loud music means Brook is dancing. And a dancing Brook is working through problems.

Hopefully she'll dance herself into a solution that saves us both from this limbo.

Sure enough, I hear the beat while still in the elevator. When I step out of it, she is swaying and gliding in front of the wall of windows.

She pushed the sofa to the side to make more room. I get closer and lean against the wall, enjoying the performance.

The bass pulsates through the air. The city lights cast a soft glow over Central Park, but it's Brook who illuminates the room, her silhouette a vivid contrast against the sprawling darkness outside.

She moves with a raw, uninhibited energy, her body synced perfectly with the rhythm of the loud music that fills the penthouse. Each movement is fluid.

I'm mesmerized, rooted to the spot. The world narrows down to this singular, captivating scene.

She embodies freedom in this moment, a spirit untamed by the concerns that weigh us down. A part of me envies that abandon, the ability to just let go and be consumed by the sheer joy of the moment.

She spins, arms outstretched, and suddenly, I'm hit by a wave of emotion so intense it nearly knocks the breath from me.

In that moment, her steps falter as she locks eyes with me. And I realize there is no joy etched on her face. She's been crying.

The sight propels me forward, all the hair standing on my nape. "What's wrong, baby?"

"I officially lost the TV series." She wraps her arms around my waist. "I can't believe fucking Dylan stole this from me."

"Goddammit." I hold her close. I have half a mind to get my jet ready and fly to London to beat the shit out of that bastard. "You should have let me deal with it."

She pushes away, her eyes blazing with angry energy. "Oh really, are you going to fix all my problems? And I'll just sit around and look pretty?"

"Fuck, Brook, that's not what I meant. I know that you're more than capable of taking care of yourself..."

"Yeah, is that why you kept watching me for years and interfering every time I got into trouble?"

"Whoa, whoa, let's step back here. I understand you're upset. You lost a project that was important to you."

"But I wouldn't have if I let you deal with it. Right?" she challenges.

Any other day, I'd let her use me as her punching bag. But under the spell of our idle, unresolved relationship, I'm not a willing participant tonight.

"You know what? Fuck it." I spin around and march to our bedroom.

I get to the bathroom, practically rip off my tie and get undressed.

Fuck Dylan and the lost production. This explosion is a consequence of my expectations, and her inaction.

Of my whining for attention, and her only giving it part-time. Fuck. What's wrong with me?

Stepping into the shower, I let the hot water melt some of the tension from my shoulders. Part of me is expecting Brook to join me, but another part is still reeling from the unexpected fight.

Perhaps it's better she stays away until we cool down.

I put a towel around my hips and walk out to the bedroom, but Brook isn't there. I don't find her in the living room or in the kitchen.

A cone of light gives me her location. What is she doing in the guest room? We have never used any of them. Okay, maybe once we fucked there against the window during our primal play.

I tap my knuckles on the smooth wood and turn the knob. "Brook."

It's locked. She fucking locked herself in. I barely stop myself from kicking the door off its hinges. Instead, I knock again. "Brook."

"I'm going to sleep here tonight. I need some space."

I lower my head against the door, my worst nightmares coming to fruition.

She's retreating already. And after I solved her inheritance problem, she has no reason to stay.

Fan-fucking-tastic.

Chapter 38

Baldo

The smell of bacon wafts to me and I groan. My head is spinning after I almost emptied the entire bottle of whiskey last night.

I didn't so much want to get drunk as I hoped it would help me sleep. Succumb to the darkness and escape reality.

I glance at the digital clock on the nightstand. Tough shit. I slept for two hours, and now I'm nursing a hangover of catastrophic magnitude.

The tantalizing aroma draws me out of bed. I find the sizzling bacon and Brook in the kitchen.

She makes a face when she sees me, scrunching it like she was in pain. "I'd say good morning, but you don't look like it's one for you."

So we're going to pretend last night didn't happen.

Fuck. I grab a bottle of water from the fridge and down it.

I lower my forehead against the cold stainless steel door, and almost jump when she puts her warm hand on my back. Instead, I tense.

Her small palm covers only a tiny space between my shoulder blades, and yet it sends tingles through my whole body. My cock stirs. I guess the fucker doesn't have a hangover.

"I found the bottle, so I thought you might need a good, greasy breakfast." Brook plants a gentle kiss on my back and returns to the stove.

"Are we going to talk—"

"Eat first. Sit down."

"Someone is bossy this morning."

She looks at me over her shoulder, her face a vision. "I have an excellent teacher."

And now my cock is at full mast. Great.

I climb onto the stool, and she pushes a plate in front of me. "Do you want butter on your toast?"

I nod, and she smears two slices of crunchy bread and hands them to me. "It looks delicious."

"And it will help your stomach. Do you need an aspirin?"

"For fuck's sake, can you stop, Brook? Let's not—"

"Okay, okay." She raises her arms in surrender. "But please eat while I tell you I'm sorry. I was really disappointed about the TV series, and so upset with Dylan. And with myself for having such a parasite in my life for so long. And I know you meant well.

"But I need you to let me fight my own battles and fail. I know it's your nature to make things better for me, but what I need from you is to support me even when I fail. I'm sorry I overreacted. But with everything else that's going on… I just needed some space."

With everything else that's going on. That's the core of our issue.

"But locking yourself away instead of talking? We can disagree, we can make mistakes, but we can't just bail out."

Her shoulders sag, and she has that tortured expression that makes me want to wage war on the whole world.

The problem is that the only war left to fight is in our own backyard.

"I'm sorry, Baldo. I promise I won't shun you."

"Well, at least I got a nutritious breakfast out of it."

"And it's breakfast with entertainment." She saunters over to stand between my legs.

"Entertainment?"

She smirks and drops to her knees, pulling the waistband of my briefs down.

"Brook?"

"Be a good boy." She wraps her lips around my cock.

*   *   *

I make her come in the shower, my little nymph, and then wash her hair, which is my new fetish.

I help her out of the shower and dry her before wrapping a towel around her. Grabbing another one, I hook it around my hips.

"The family lunch is today," she says tentatively while she combs her hair.

"I know."

Mom called me several times. I only listened to one of her voice mails, and I can imagine the rest of them. I'm not invited so much as I'm expected.

"Are you...?"

"I'll drive you there."

Am I now? Shit.

She stops the movement and watches me in the mirror, her eyes shining. "You are coming?"

She sounds so excited that my chest squeezes. But I'm not playing siblings with her there, so her excitement is premature.

"I'll see."

Her face falls at my noncommittal answer.

Because I'm a bastard, I walk away. I don't know why my tongue runs without consulting my brain.

I find a pair of brown slacks and a navy button-down and get dressed.

The elephant in the room has destroyed the morning's bliss. It's the story of our lives. Fuck.

We get ready and leave together like we're truly sharing the destination. And while we are, we also aren't.

"Why don't you produce the series yourself?" I ask her as we weave through the sleepy Sunday traffic in my new Volvo.

"Me?"

"That's what I said."

"I can't do that."

"Why?"

She stays silent, staring at me. Or I think she is, because my focus is on the road.

"I have no experience."

"You can hire people with experience. You were going to produce it, anyway."

"It's risky."

"As are all important things. And they're also the most rewarding."

She stares through the window for a while, and I can't help putting my hand on her thigh. To keep connected, still hoping for us.

"You think I could do it?"

"Of course. Brook, you're incredibly creative, and based on the amount of books you've put out in the last few years, you're hardworking and disciplined. And with your vivid imagination, I'm pretty sure you have a vision for that series that is a recipe for success, because who else can bring your hero to life if not you?"

"I don't even know where to start."

I can offer her help through a small production company I own, but I don't think she'd appreciate it. "You will figure it out, baby."

I chance a look in her direction, and she is smiling at me in that genuine way that punches me in the gut every single time.

We arrive at the Riverdale house, and I park beside several other cars in the paved front yard.

"Everybody is here." Brook sighs.

"Yep." I get out of the car.

We might have mended something between us this morning, but we're still dancing carefully around the key issue.

"Why don't you go in, and I'll take the Maserati for a spin." It's been sitting in Mom's garage since I drove it before our sham honeymoon.

I can't watch her struggle with this, so I'd rather run. Fucking coward. But it's better than being her brother.

Or seeing Micah. I haven't seen him since he sent me away, and now, understanding his deception, I can't imagine facing him.

"Are you sure?" She frowns, but it sounds like a plea.

"I hate the big get-togethers." I kiss the crown of her head. "Enjoy time with your dad, and I'll pick you up later."

Before she can say anything, I usher her inside and grab the car keys from the cabinet in the entry hall. Luckily, we don't run into anyone.

Chatter and laughter from the house pierce me with an arrow of longing. I dash out like the house is on fire.

I don't know what hurts more. That I'm missing out on time with my mom and siblings. Or that Brook stands there hesitating, but doesn't stop me.

I rev the engine and slowly weave through the cars belonging to my siblings, gravely aware that I'm the one driving away while they are staying.

I'm not far when my phone rings. I nearly let it go to voice mail, but it's Chloe, and work has always been my best distraction.

"Why are you working on a Sunday?"

She laughs. "Have you lost your mind? Nights and weekends are our busiest time."

I chuckle. "What's up, Chloe?"

"I made the offer on the club in Nice, and I'm happy to report we'll be opening a new location in two weeks."

"So fast? Can we swing it? With all the cash needed for our Manhattan club?"

"Yes, the property is in perfect condition, and it requires only minor touches to turn it into our brand. I have reallocated funds from the most profitable clubs in France to cover the first three months, but I'm confident we will turn profit sooner than that."

"Great job, Chloe."

"I know," she says gleefully.

"Thank you."

"How is married life treating you? Have you kissed your bride yet?" she teases.

I grab the steering wheel in a white-knuckled grip, but I don't answer. It's none of her business, after all.

"Baldo? Don't tell me you haven't kissed her yet? I mean, your stupid no kissing rule made sense for hookups, but you care about this woman. Your club was evacuated because of your caveman routine, so I know you care about her. Are you going to fuck it up?"

I *am* fucking it up. Not just a coward. A fucking idiot too.

"Chloe, I have to go." I swing into the left lane and U-turn between two sensible family SUVs.

I want to floor the gas pedal, but I'm still in the midst of Riverdale, unable to speed up.

The ten minutes it takes me to return feels like ten years, but I finally make it back. I rush to the house and follow the voices.

Everyone is gathered in the kitchen, and on the patio outside. Dinner hasn't been served yet.

"Baldo," Mom gasps, bouncing baby Micah in her arms. "You came." She smiles, her face full of relief. Fuck, another woman I need to grovel to.

"Where is Brook?"

"I'm here," she says from the entrance to the sitting room. She is clutching the handles of Micah's wheelchair.

His expression is stoic. If my sudden appearance surprised him, he doesn't show it. I stare him down for a moment, letting him know that this time I won't leave.

Everyone around us stops and stares at me. I grab Brook's hand. "We'll be right back."

The house remains in complete silence as I drag Brook across the hall to the library.

I close the door behind us and spin her toward me. "I'm sorry."

"No, Baldo, I'm sorry. I-I... You need to know I'm not choosing them over you." She grabs my hands and squeezes to the point of cutting off circulation.

"Stop, baby. Stop it. You don't need to choose. Take as much time as you need. Even if it's forever. I'm not pressuring you anymore."

"Are you leaving?" Her eyes swim in confusion.

Fuck. I'm doing it all wrong.

"I'm not going to pressure you, and I'm not going anywhere. Not without you. You've been in my thoughts, my heart, an irreplaceable part of my soul for as long as I can remember. You're as essential to me as air. And I know the situation isn't ideal, but I don't want to dance around it. Take as much time as you need, and I'll gladly pretend to be your brother for as long as you want." I flinch. "Okay, not gladly."

She gasps, stifling a sob and chuckling at the same time. "Are you sure?"

"Yes, but that's not why I came here."

"Why did you come?"

"To do this."

Chapter 39

Brook

Baldo's lips crash against mine with an urgency and possession that steals my thoughts. His lips, demanding but soft on me, sprout tingles all over my body.

I part for him, and he takes all I'm giving, but, oh, does he give back. He tastes like everything essential and everything forbidden. Full of sin and redemption. Filled with promise and acceptance.

His lips erase all my doubts. They negate any choice. Because there is no choice. There is just him. It has always been him.

He isn't just kissing my lips, he's kissing my whole being, every single nerve ending, each crevice in my soul.

Like he's rebuilding me, the connection recalibrates every frequency in my body, changing the energies, creating pathways for more. For going deeper. For us.

In that kiss, our past and present collide, creating a promise of the future we've yearned for since our lips touched for the first time all those years ago.

I'm completely lost in the moment, my mind floating, my body tingling, my core clenching.

Baldo's hands are in my hair as he devours me with such devotion that I struggle to take it all.

When we finally break apart for air, I almost collapse, my knees giving out. But he's there, holding me.

"You kissed me." My voice is a breathy whisper.

"Stop talking," he growls, and fuses his mouth with mine again.

It's like he wants to kiss me for all the kisses he refused to give me before. For all the kisses we didn't get to have over the years.

And I'm still the only woman he's ever kissed. The thought strips me of any inhibition, and I claw at his skin, climbing him, kissing him back with fervor.

A satisfied guttural groan escapes him, and I sigh with delight.

We break it off, panting, vaguely aware of where we are.

We stare at each other like we're rediscovering who we are.

"You kissed me," I say again.

"I should have done it a long time ago."

My grin is so wide it might dislocate my jaw. "I love you, Baldo Cassinetti."

"Oh, yeah, I meant to say that." He shakes his head, dazed.

"Then say it." I giggle and wrap my arms around his neck.

He studies me for a moment. "I love you, Tokyo." He lowers his lips to mine, but this time it's a soft, reverent kiss. "It has always been you, baby."

"And you kissed me." I giggle again, giddy and drunk on lust and love and joy.

"I might need to do it many more times to improve."

"To improve?" I laugh.

"I might fuck like a pro, but I probably kiss like a teenager."

Only Baldo can be cocky and humble at the same time. "You kiss just like I need it."

He narrows his eyes, but his lips are quirking up. "So, no practicing then?"

"Oh, definitely more practicing." I kiss him. "But you don't kiss like a teenager. You kiss like a man. My man."

He utters another sound that is all man and sex and pure hotness and need, and kisses me again.

"You came back to kiss me." I pant, but the joy is just bursting through me, stretching my grin almost painfully.

"Yes." He lowers his forehead against mine and smooths my hair before he cups my face.

"You came back to kiss me." It's like I need to repeat it to ensure it's real. That I'm not just dreaming it.

"Yes." He chuckles.

"I'm the future mother of your children."

"I hope so."

I close my eyes and take a deep breath. "Let's go tell Mom and Dad."

* * *

All my life, I've hoped for acceptance from my family. Yet the whole time I was running away, not sharing with them, hiding different pieces of myself.

Today, the man my father pushed away from me, and who in the process lost his own connection with our family, took a leap and decided to show up.

For us.

For our love.

For me.

When he encouraged me to produce the TV series

earlier, I felt supported and respected in a way I haven't felt in years.

Spending the night locked away from him was so lonely. I'm used to being alone, but after sharing my life with Baldo these last few months, the loneliness was more profound.

Yes, I was mad at him for his meddling, but I was madder at myself for pushing him away. Not only last night, but every day since we returned to New York.

I decided to tell everyone today because I don't want to hide anymore.

I love him.

And I want everyone to know.

The decision looked less solid in the light of morning, but I didn't want the fear of losing my father to stop me.

What stopped me was Baldo's decision to take his Maserati for a ride.

But he came back, and he kissed me.

Giving me the last piece of him he had kept out of my reach.

Showing me his trust.

Gifting me his love.

And I'm not going to fail him.

Dad's eyes fall to where Baldo's hand wraps around mine the minute we enter the kitchen.

Massi's daughter, Ali, is crawling on the floor, and baby Micah is crying in the other room.

Syd, Lo, Gina and Gio's Mila are helping Mom at the island.

The rest of the group is outside.

Dad frowns, his eyes darting from me to our linked hands. And then he looks at Mom, who stands frozen, her lips set in a straight line.

"Mom, Dad, can we talk to you?"

Lo groans. "We're never going to eat."

"Shut up," Baldo snaps.

"Let them be, for fuck's sake," Sydney berates her at the same time. "Let's go outside and give them some privacy."

Gina scoops up her little girl and everyone scurries away.

Nausea swims through me, and I'm probably drawing blood as I dig my nails into Baldo's hand.

Without thinking, my other hand moves, bringing my thumb to my teeth, but I drop it and take a deep breath.

"Dad, Mom, I know this is something you had a hard time accepting ten years ago, but we're adults now, and I hope you can trust that it's not just some teenage rebellion."

I pause. My gaze flits around, but I square my shoulders and look my dad in the eyes.

"We're in love."

Baldo brings our connected hands to his lips and kisses my knuckles.

Dad's expression remains solemn. But at least it's not anger.

"Micah, I'm in love with your daughter. And I intend to spend the rest of my life with her."

"Him?" Dad utters, looking at me with a disbelief and disappointment that shocks me.

Until now, I couldn't quite imagine that he really sent Baldo away back then, but his expression is full of hurt and something fierce I don't recognize.

Baldo snorts. "What do you have against me, *Dad*?"

I flinch, and Mom steps closer. It almost looks like she is going to join Dad, who is holding the armrests of his wheelchair with a white-knuckled force, but then she stops.

She halts between her husband and her son, not choosing sides this time.

"I will never forget the state she came home in that night. She didn't want to tell us, but she was hurt and bleeding, and didn't speak for days or leave her room."

"And you didn't let me near her." Baldo tries and fails to rein in his voice.

He drops my hand and rakes both his hands through his hair, shaking his head.

"After what you did to her? I wouldn't risk you getting close again. You had the nerve to show your face here again two days later," Dad shouts.

Oh my God. He thought...

"So you conveniently assumed I hurt her? What the fuck?"

"And what else was I to think? You kept sneaking into her room with your raging teenage hormones."

Baldo shakes his head again and looks at his mom. "And you believed that too. You believed that I would ever hurt Brook. Any woman, for that matter? You fucking took his side."

"Don't you talk to you mother like that." Dad's voice slices through the air. "I will never forget the night my little girl came home, scared and hurt, and she asked if you were home. She was relieved that you weren't, and she retreated to her room. What did you do to her?"

"I can't believe you would both jump to that conclusion. That I'm the monster."

They continue screaming at each other, no longer making sense, just throwing insults.

The shouting only gets louder. I cover my ears.

Don't they realize I'm right here?

Don't they realize they are talking about the worst night of my life?

Don't they realize what a big misunderstanding it has been?

"Skittles," I shout, and everyone freezes.

Baldo turns to me, bewildered. But then his expression softens. "Fuck, Brook, I'm sorry. I didn't mean to lose it."

I sigh, because I don't know what to say. I wish he hadn't lost it either, but this is not only about me or us.

This is about him and his parents as well. And I don't think we can separate all those layers. But we can try to have a respectful conversation.

"Dad, you made the wrong assumption. Looking back, I can see how that happened, but that doesn't excuse your behavior. I don't want to talk about that night anymore. It's painful, and I think it's time to look forward, not backward.

"You told me not so long ago how Mommy regretted that she never reconciled with Roberta. How family was the most important thing for her. You told me that time with people who matter is up there as the most important thing. Baldo matters to me, and if you can't accept that, we'll have to leave."

"Nobody is leaving," Mom thunders. "We're going to throw the steaks on the grill and enjoy each other's company. And if the two of you need to sit on opposite sides of the table, so be it. This family is large enough to create a buffer between you."

Holy shit, I almost forgot how formidable Mom is. How nobody ever contradicts her.

She raises her eyebrows, glaring Dad down. He sighs and nods. Then she turns to Baldo.

His jaw ticks as he taps his fingers on his thigh. He looks at me and his expression softens. "What can I help with?"

And just like that, the loud clan of the Cassinetti-Lowe family resumes the commotion and starts the late dinner.

And I get to spend time with the two most important men in my life. Even though they glower at each other.

Chapter 40

Brook

CELESTE

I can't believe I'll never be your maid of honor.

SAAR

Hey, why would you assume you'd be her maid of honor?

It's good I'm already married, so I don't have to choose between the two of you.

CELESTE

It's kind of sad you didn't have a real wedding.

SAAR

You're hopeless. Romance is dead.

Saying that makes you hopeless.

SAAR

LOL

> I'm leaving in two days. For two months (crying emoji)

>> (sad face emoji). With both of you gone, I'll be all jealous. When are you returning to France, Cel?

CELESTE
> Taking my time, ignoring the reality.

SAAR
> Are you sure you can't stay?

CELESTE
> I wish. My visa is tied to my dancing. I've been blacklisted in this town and without a standing engagement, I can't renew my visa.

SAAR
> You can get married (wink emoji)

>> I highly recommend a marriage of convenience. Worked out really well for me.

CELESTE
> (eye-roll emoji)

SAAR
> What about my brother?

>> He's married to my sister.

SAAR
> (eye-roll emoji) Not Finn, Cal.

"**B**rook, Celeste, this is my brother Caleb." Saar wiggles her shoulders and snakes her arm through that of a handsome man in an immaculate suit.

He looks like a lighter, more relaxed version of my brother-in-law, Finn.

"Ladies." He gives us a boyish grin.

"Merde." Celeste sighs beside me, and I'm pretty sure this is the first time I've seen her blushing.

She turns to lock the door of the dance studio, dropping the keys in the process, and I stifle a chuckle.

"Cal, would you mind if Celeste joins us for dinner?" Saar asks.

"What about me?" I ignore her obvious matchmaking efforts.

"You have plans tonight, sweetheart." The velvety baritone makes me whip around.

My husband leans against the black Escalade, one ankle over the other.

He's wearing a black button-down and black slacks, and I swear I could see him a thousand times and he will still take my breath away. Every. Single. Time.

"Do I now?" I practically float to him, drunk on the warm feelings he stirs in me.

He kisses me. Not a peck on the lips. He dives into

a wanton display of affection. The man has been trying to catch up on years of not kissing. I'm not going to curb his enthusiasm.

"Oh, for fuck's sake, get a room," Saar groans.

"Are you ready to leave?" he whispers.

I nod and hug my friends.

"This is a pleasant surprise." I slide into Baldo's lap as soon as we get into the back seat, and he engages the partition to give us privacy.

He kisses me again, his tongue swirling, seeking access. "I missed you."

"You saw me this morning," I mumble against his mouth.

"Yeah, fucking too long ago." He traces his hand up my thigh. "I think we need to go shopping soon."

"Whatever for?" I shiver at his touch, and at the memory of shopping the day of our wedding.

It's like a lifetime has passed since then. Like we're different people and yet we're the same.

"Yeah, I hate your pants."

"What's wrong with my pants?"

"The lack of access to your pussy."

I laugh. "You're a deviant."

"And you love it."

I grin. "Where are we going?"

"On a date."

In the absence of easy access to my underwear,

Baldo settles for sliding his hands under my shirt and finding my nipple.

I moan. "A date?"

"Yes, I realized we've never had one. Ever."

He's not wrong. When we were younger, we could only sneak around.

And since we got married, we haven't done much of the normal couple stuff. "We went to Mimi's in Lisbon."

"So we wouldn't die from hunger. That's not a date."

"Dinner is a perfectly respectable date."

"I would argue the point, but since I'm taking you out on one, I'm going to do this instead."

He captures my lips, and we kiss like teenagers the whole way to the restaurant.

* * *

"How do you even know about this place?" I take a bite of a huge burrito, the salsa dripping onto the wrapper.

Just like in Lisbon, when Baldo took me to a small, homey family restaurant, we are at a hole in the wall with tiny tables, and the best Mexican food.

"You mentioned you loved Mexican." He shrugs. "And this place came highly recommended on

TripAdvisor?" I arch my eyebrow, the flavor of the rice and beans exploding on my tongue.

"Actually, Massi is a silent partner here. He told me about it."

"What? I thought Massi was fully dedicated to Casa Cassi."

"He is, but apparently he invests in other places that show promise."

"Well, if all the places are this good, no wonder he is filthy rich."

Baldo throws his head back and laughs. "I'm richer than him."

Now I laugh. "Of course you are, darling," I mock.

He looks at me unimpressed, and that's when I notice it. "Why aren't you eating?"

"I hate Mexican."

"Why did we come here, then?"

"I told you, only the best for my wife."

"So you'll go hungry?"

His eyes darken, and he runs his hand up my thigh under the table. "I'll feast on you later."

God, can we go home right now? Goosebumps tingle my skin just from his promise.

"But you needed me well fed first?" I grin, the innuendo light but charged.

"Exactly."

"Are you trying to butter me up?"

His features still, and he looks away for a moment. Shit. So this isn't just a romantic gesture. He's trying to appease me as foreplay, but not in the sexual way.

"Talk to me, Baldo."

He sighs and removes his hand from my thigh. I mourn the loss immediately. Again, not only in the physical way.

"Ask me where I was before the fire in Lisbon."

I blink. What? "Why?"

"Because I don't want any secrets between us."

I sigh. "Then just tell me." I drop the burrito, because he said before I wouldn't like the answer.

He puffs out a long sigh through his lips.

"I went to see Art Mathison."

Not what I expected. I frown. "His company is on all those surveillance reports."

"Yes."

I snort, but it's more to cover my discomfort. Why can't he just say the thing? "Who are you trailing now? I'm right here. Do I need to be jealous?"

"I don't mind if you're jealous, it shows you care." He shrugs and picks up his iced tea.

"Who are you watching, Baldo?"

"Not watching. I was trying to find someone."

"Who?"

"The man who assaulted you."

That scenario is so outlandish in my mind that my

first reaction is a chuckle. But it sounds more like a wail.

His words form into comprehension and splash me with a cold shower of apprehension.

Oxygen doesn't reach my lungs.

My mind throws me back into that night.

The snake tattoo. The acid breath. The pain. The tears.

My right hand shakes violently.

I grab it with the other one.

"Is that even possible?"

"I wasn't sure. So many years have passed, and there weren't many clues to follow. But if there was anyone who could find him, it's Art."

I take a sip of water, but my mouth remains dry.

"And?"

"I found him. Well, Art did."

"Thank you."

I don't know why I say that, because I never wanted him to do this. I don't want to dig into that part of my past anymore.

And it's not like I'm going to press charges now, after all this time. A better person would. A better person would consider all the other victims. But I'm not that person.

I packed up and left the country. To survive. To heal.

"Don't thank me. As much as I would like to admit this is a misplaced attempt at chivalry, to avenge you, that's only a small part of my motivation. I'm doing this for myself."

"Then why are you telling me?"

"So you know that he's no longer a threat."

I laugh. "It's not like with him gone all the violence on the streets is removed. Besides, it's not like he'll be arrested."

"He could be."

I shake my head. This is the worst date ever. "I don't care."

"Brook, I have a file, a rock solid file that would give the DA enough to put him away for the rest of his life. Not for what he did to you, but that doesn't matter. I'll use all my influence to make that happen."

I had struggled with my decision to let the monster go unpunished, but I had to let it go because there wasn't much I could have done once I re-emerged from the fog of my trauma.

But Baldo is not seeing what truly matters here.

"Do you think you'd feel better after?" I ask. "Do you think destroying him would give us the years back? Would erase the hurt? Because after years of therapy, I can tell you the only way you can put this behind you is to forgive."

He shakes his head. "Did you forgive him?"

"Oh, Baldo." I take his hand in mine. "To forgive yourself. I forgave myself for all the guilt I had associated with that dreadful night. And you need to do the same, and if putting the monster behind bars is a part of that journey for you, then do what you need to do."

He stares at me, a war brewing behind his eyes as he taps his fingers on the table.

"I don't deserve you," he croaks.

I sigh. "You certainly have a lot of room to improve your dating game. Food ten out of ten, conversation barely one."

"I don't know how to deal with all this anger and guilt." His voice breaks, and the vulnerability of his admission hits me right in the chest.

"It takes time. And therapy. But you're not alone, baby. I'm right here, so please talk to me next time. Don't go rogue, paying Art Mathison and waging your own war. We're a couple now—let's share the burden."

He sighs, leans in and cups my nape, pulling me into a bruising kiss. "I don't deserve you."

"You can keep saying that, but you're stuck with me." I smile. "Now, change the subject and tell me something nice, so I can finish the best burrito in town."

He chuckles and pecks me on my forehead. "I went to see Mom."

"You went home by yourself?" I halt the bite on the way to my mouth, the rice falling out.

"Yes."

"This doesn't sound like a conversation that would improve my appetite. Let's not have dates anymore."

He chuckles humorlessly. "I'll get better at this, I promise."

Sighing, I take a bite. "So, you saw Dad?"

"Yes."

I drop the burrito again. Who cares. We can come here another time. I stare at him, curiosity and dread clawing at my insides.

"He apologized to me."

"He did?"

Baldo nods. "Maybe Mom forced him, but I accepted his apology."

A pent-up sigh escapes me from somewhere deep inside. "So, you forgave him?"

"Oh, baby, I wish it was that easy, but I'm trying. I don't think I'm ready to cast forgiveness in every direction," he says, alluding to our earlier conversation. "But with your dad, I'll make the effort."

And that's all I can ask for. We can't just switch our guilt, anger, forgiveness or acceptance on and off as convention demands, or others expect. There is no right way to cope with any of this.

But the fact that my beautiful man is slowly opening up is hope enough for me. For him. For us.

"I love you," I say, and the words have so much meaning for me that I find it hard to breathe.

He takes my hand and kisses my knuckles, and then frowns. "I wish I didn't give you this ring."

I pull my hand from him, cradling it to my chest. "Our ruby. But it means so much—"

"Exactly, and I gave it to you for a sham of a wedding. I think we need a re-do."

"Are you proposing to me, Baldo Cassinetti?"

"God, no. Not right now, baby. I'll do a better job of it. Like you deserve, darling wife."

Epilogue

Baldo

Six weeks later

"Baldo," Brook cries out.

She arches her back, goosebumps peppering her silky skin. God, she's so responsive. My cock is painfully hard, but I'm not turning this into a quick fuck.

Holding the ice cube between my teeth, I trace her torso inch by inch. She tenses, straining against the soft ropes on her wrists and ankles.

Tied to our bed, she's blindfolded, and her face is flushed after the two orgasms I teased out of her already.

A film of sweat covers her body, but the ice cube

contrasts the hot sensation, driving her crazy by the way she is thrashing. Trying to escape my touch while seeking it at the same time.

"Just feel, baby, let me take care of you." I circle her nipple with the fast-melting cube.

"Please," she whimpers. "I'm feeling frustration, mostly." But a moan eats her snarl when I drop the cube between her folds. She pants. "Please, please, oh God."

"I'll continue until your only vocabulary is my name."

"But—" This time my lips swallow her protest.

How I stayed away from kissing her for so long is beyond me. But the idea of Brook being the only woman I've ever kissed, and the only woman I will ever kiss, makes me swell with love, and unhealthy pride.

She was mine then.

She's mine now.

And she'll be mine forever.

"Would you like to come, wife?" I caress my cheeks against her, ready to blow just from the scent of her. The feel of her. The sound of her.

"Yes, yes," she says greedily, thrashing again.

"Shh, baby. Stop it before you hurt yourself." I run my hand up her arm to check that the restraint isn't digging too deep.

She whimpers, but stills.

Epilogue

"Good girl. And now tell me if you want to come all over my fingers, my face, or my cock."

She swallows. "For fuck's sake, Baldo, fuck me."

"Tsk, tsk, tsk." I spank her pussy.

She gasps and bucks. "On your cock. I want to come on your cock."

I capture her lips, quickly untie her legs, yank them over my shoulders and bury myself deep inside her.

"Fuck," we cry out in unison.

I pull out and slide right back in. My eyes drop to the vision of the woman beneath me. And suddenly it's not enough.

As much as my dick weeps in protest, I leave the heat of her. Brook groans and kicks with her leg, surely trying to hit me.

I make a quick work of her hand ties and pull away her blindfold. She blinks a few times while I lower myself back to her entrance.

This time I watch her as I plunge in, our eyes locked. I move with love, with all the adoration I feel for this woman.

With awe.

With reverence.

With commitment.

Grateful that my years-long obsession is now more. Mine.

Epilogue

***

Opening night starts with a line two blocks long in front of my new and first American club.

Celebrities and media fill the VIP area. The dance floor is teeming with moving bodies, the liquor flows.

"Congratulations, boss. What a fucking success." Chloe fist punches my biceps playfully.

"It's teamwork. If you didn't step in with Europe and Asia, it wouldn't have happened."

"Does that mean you're staying here permanently?"

"We agreed to travel back and forth, spending months in Lisbon and parts of the year here."

"It makes sense, especially with the Miami location on the horizon."

"Busy times, Chloe."

"So much fun." She claps her hands. "So where is Brook?"

I asked my wife to come later, when I won't be too busy putting out all the fires of the night like this, but my eyes have been scanning for her for the past hour. "She should be here any minute."

"Oh, there she is."

Brook and her friends step down the stairs leading to the main room, and I swear the music stops for a moment as everyone looks their way.

Epilogue

The three of them are certainly showstoppers, but my eyes remain on my wife, who's wearing a white dress à la Marilyn Monroe. My jaw tenses.

As if we're somehow connected, she spots me immediately among the hundreds of people. It helps that I'm at the mezzanine, looking down.

She smiles and says something to her friends before she makes her way to me.

She only needs to walk up a flight of stairs, but with people roaming around, she progresses slowly. But not for a second does she break our eye contact.

My cock loves that dress.

Me not so much.

"What are you wearing?" I growl when she reaches me.

She rolls her eyes and laughs. "Your face..." She looks at my crotch. "And your dick say you love the dress." She cups my nape and pulls me to her. Her breath hot by my ear, she whispers, "Every time someone admires me tonight, just remember you're the only man in the room who knows I'm not wearing panties, and the only man who takes this dress off later."

"Can't be soon enough," I grumble, and she laughs, unfazed by my caveman spiel.

"Congratulations, love. The place is spectacular,

Epilogue

which I already knew, but it's fucking packed." She tugs me down for a kiss.

"It is fucking packed."

"I'm proud of you."

God, this woman. "I love you."

"Will you dance with me?"

"Maybe later. Do you want to come and schmooze the VIPs with me?"

"Sure. Lead the way."

"Before we go, I've got something for you." I take her hand and lead her to one of the bars, where I retrieve a little box I've hidden there.

"What is it?"

I pull out a delicate golden cuff bracelet I got on my way to the club today. After our vigorous session of sex this morning, I discovered rope marks on her right wrist. She laughed it off, but I couldn't shake it.

I clasp it around her wrist. "I hope you used the lotion I left for you."

"After you applied it like a hundred times? Yes, I did." She rolls her eyes, and then admires the bracelet. "I love it. Thank you."

I kiss her, and we spend another four hours schmoozing, drinking, and even some dancing. I don't think I've ever danced in my own club. Or any club, for that matter.

Epilogue

Handing Brook a drink, I lean in to kiss her neck. "Where are your friends?"

"I'm here" Saar appears by our side.

"Hey." Brook hugs her, both women wiggling to the music. "Where is Celeste?"

Saar nods at the bar, where Celeste is in an animated conversation with a familiar dude.

"Is that your brother?" Brook sounds excited.

"Yeah, the dinner before I went to Europe was a bust, but I thought I'd nudge them a bit before she really leaves."

"They look like they are arguing."

"I know, but Cal has been on this strange mission to correct as many of our father's mistakes as possible, and he thinks helping Celeste after Dad fucked her over might be good for both of them."

"What did your father do to her?" I frown, lost in the conversation.

Brook turns to me. "Saar's father wanted to hurt Paris, and Celeste was one of the casualties of their feud. I'll explain later, but she can't get a job in the city and is about to lose her visa."

"Not sure she wants your brother's help," I say as Celeste throws her drink into his face and walks away.

"Oh, what happened, I missed it." Saar cranes her neck.

Brook squeezes my hand but looks sideways at her

Epilogue

friend. "Are you okay? You've been distracted all night."

Saar purses her lips into a straight line. "Some work issues, but nothing to worry about. I'll be okay." She turns to me. "Great job, Baldo, congratulations. I almost regret I didn't agree to get involved."

"You still can." Corm's voice comes from behind me.

Saar's nostrils flare. "On second thought, I'm glad I stayed away. I better go find Celeste."

"She really hates me," Corm mutters and follows her.

"This night was eventful without all this. I'm calling an emergency breakfast meeting for tomorrow." Brook chuckles.

"Do you want to go and check on Celeste?"

"No need, she's dancing already. I'll get the scoop tomorrow, but I'll check on them both before we leave."

I lean in and kiss her. Yeah, I'm never going to grow tired of that. She tastes like everything I've ever desired and more.

"I was thinking we could leave now."

"Are you sure?"

"Why do you think I flew Chloe over?"

She gasps. "You're a tyrant," she admonishes, but bites her lips, her eyes shining with heat. "I think you want to get rid of this dress."

Epilogue

* * *

We arrive home tired, but elated by the success of the night. We haven't moved from the suite I rented upon our return from Lisbon.

We wanted to look for our own place. But once we decided to live between New York and Lisbon, and with all my additional travel, we agreed we'll find a house when we have a family.

Which might happen sooner than later, as we are dedicating so much time to our bedroom activities.

I walk to the bar in the corner. "Do you want a drink?"

"Sure. Mix me one. I'll be right back."

I mix a gin and tonic for Brook and pour myself an inch of whiskey. She returns before I sit down.

"I got something for you." She hands me a black box.

"Thank you." I open the box and find a sleek black bottle with gold text. I frown. "You got me a bottle of lube?"

She bites her lower lip. "Us."

"Baby, I love the gift, but we have a drawer full of them. Including the flavored ones."

"They are edible? I didn't know that?"

I smirk. "It's because you're busy taking my dick when we use them."

Epilogue

She rolls her eyes. "Anyway, do you remember what you asked me after the fire in Lisbon, when we were in bed?"

"Baby, since you've made me into your sex slave, all the action is a blur."

She groans. "You're such an ass—"

I yank her to me, kissing her senseless. "I love the gift. What did I ask you after the fire?"

She bites her lip. "Permission."

I frown, and then it dawns on me. She said she'd give me access to her ass when our marriage was real.

I smile, my dick stirring at the idea, and there is an asshole in me that wants to throw her over my shoulder and act on her offer immediately.

What she's offering has a bigger meaning. The trust.

"Are you sure?"

She chuckles nervously. "God, no, but if I'm the only woman you ever kissed..."

"I'm the only man who got you to climax."

She kisses me. "That's true, and I plan for you to be the only man for every new adventure for the rest of our lives."

"For better or worse. In sickness and health." I grin.

"For richer... and richer." She chuckles.

"To love and cherish."

"Till death do us part."

Epilogue

Thank you for reading Baldo and Brook's story. Get a sneak peek of their future life in this bonus scene at www.maxinehenri.com/vow or scan the code below.

What's next? While I work to expand the world of the billionaires you love so much, *read Gina and Massi's second chance romance Reckless Fate. As one reader described it,* "**this one is a gem! It has tropes and drama for days. So many emotions. Next level writing! Lovely ending.**"

Author's Note

Thank you for reading Brook and Baldo's story. I hope you enjoyed it as much as I loved writing it. With these two, I felt like I was just recording the story. It played so vividly in my mind.

Did you love hanging out with the family? These two estranged family members brought the siblings and parents together in this last book of the Reckless Billionaires.

I didn't want to finish writing it because it meant saying goodbye to the Cassinetti/Lowe clan and I wasn't ready for it. I guess that's always the case, I'm in love with the characters I'm writing and I can't let go.

But here we are and I'm letting them go…to you, dear reader. And I hope I fulfilled my mission to provide you with entertainment and ultimate escape.

Author's Note

I've lived this series for the past two years and there are so many people who have supported me on the journey.

Mr. Henri and my two sons, thank you for believing in me.

Editor Jess, your guidance, ideas and, at times, annoying logical observations made this book and all the others so much better.

Dan, thank you for spotting all the hidden mistakes. Grace, thank you for keeping my readers' group alive. Jaycee, the covers are beautiful.

One of the most generous writers out there is TL Swan (go read her books if you haven't yet) and I'm so grateful for all her wisdom and humor. Tee, you inspire me.

Craig Martell, Melanie Harlow and Sky Warren, thank you! You're incredibly successful and still find the time to share your knowledge and experience.

All the influencers on Instagram and TikTok, and advance readers, I appreciate you, your time, and support more than I can express.

Dear reader, thank you! I have the best gig in the world and you make it happen every day.

It's the end of an era (or a series) and I feel a bit lost. But no worries, the new one is already brewing in my head. I promise to bring the characters you know and love back, so you can enjoy them more (or just selfishly because I miss them).

Love,
Maxine

Also by Maxine Henri

Reckless Billionaires Series

Reckless Fate (Massi and Gina's Second Chance Romance)

Reckless Desire (Sydney and Hunter's Single Dad Romance)

Reckless Dare (Lo and Dom's Fake Relationship Romance)

Reckless Deal (Gio and Mila's Grumpy/Sunshine Bosshole Romance)

Reckless Hunger (Andrea and Ivy's Age Gap Romance)

Reckless Bond (Paris and Finn's Accidental Pregnancy Romance)

Reckless Vow (Brook and Baldo's Marriage of Convenience Romance)

Untamed Billionaires Series

Fall in love with the morally grey heroes obsessed with their women

Chosen by The Billionaire (Art and Violet's Enemies to Lovers Romance)

Chased by the Billionaire (Ness and Rocco's Age

gap/Innocent Heroine Romance)

Stolen by the Billionaire (Phillip and Lena's Forbidden Love Romance)

Tempted by Charlie (A Fake Relationship Novella)

If you loved this book, please spread the word and leave a review here. One sentence is enough to help other readers and make me very happy.

About the Author

Maxine Henri is a contemporary romance author who infuses her stories with steamy passion and complex characters. When she's not crafting stories that will have you swooning, she can usually be found sipping on a cup of black tea while reading a good book. Or traveling to new destinations.

Maxine believes that stories matter. They facilitate emotional journeys, inspire and entertain. And when it comes to books and fiction, stories are a great escape and probably the most beneficial addiction on this planet.

Her billionaire romances are the perfect escape, offering a taste of luxury and adventure. Maxine introduces heroes who may have a dark past, but are always balanced by a lighter side. And her leading ladies? They're strong, independent women who may be a little broken, but always find their way in life.

You can connect with her on any of these platforms:

facebook.com/maxinehenriromance
instagram.com/maxinehenriromance
bookbub.com/profile/maxine-henri
amazon.com/author/maxinehenri

Made in the USA
Columbia, SC
02 June 2024